The Comedian from Hellfire

The Comedian from Hellfire

a Stu Fletcher, PI mystery novel

Jeff Ridenour

This book is a work of fiction. Names, characters, places, and incidents are the product of the author's imagination or are used fictitiously. Any resemblance to actual events, locales, or persons, living or dead, is coincidental.

Publisher: Karlsbad Middleford Press **KMP**
North Charleston, South Carolina

ISBN-13: 9781974398768
ISBN-10: 1974398765

Other novels
by
the author

A Bad Game for Amateurs
The Art Procurer
Aged in Charcoal

to the memory of

Ross Macdonald
and
his Lew Archer novels

Acknowledgements

I hereby thank my wife Ronda Lynn and my good friend Richard Parker, philosophy professor emeritus at Cal State Chico, for their keen editing eyes. I alone am due demerits for any remaining errors.

The most difficult character in comedy is that of the fool,
and he must be no simpleton that plays that part.

-- MIGUEL DE CERVANTES

I

June, 1967

I was wrapping up a case in Bakersfield when Murky Murtrans tracked me down there and asked me to drop by his ranch on my return to Santa Maria. His birth certificate reads Clyde Jacob Browning, but Murky Murtrans is the stage name he chose when he began performing as a one-man vaudeville comedian act back in 1923 in the Catskills. Anyone these days who calls him Clyde or Mr. Browning gets a cold shoulder. Make that two cold shoulders.

From New York Murky made a highly successful transition to Hollywood, where he parlayed roles as a character actor -- in both movies and TV, as a funny man and as a serious actor -- into millions of conservatively invested dollars, some of which bought him a ranch that included a couple hundred acres of vineyards in the low hills east of Santa Maria, near the Sisquoc River. One of his neighbors is Fess Parker, who played Davy Crockett in the eponymous Disney series during the 1950's.

Along with reaping millions of dollars from acting and endorsements, Murky acquired four wives along the way. His first wife, Ethel, died of ovarian cancer in 1931, after ten years of happy marriage. His biographer is the one who makes the happy marriage claim. I've never heard Murky himself own up to that contention.

His fourth wife, Cynthia, died two weeks ago from a blow to the back of her head, administered with a pool cue in the billiard room at their ranch, sometime in the final hour of Murky's retirement party, attended by sixteen of Murky's friends, relatives, and staff. That made for seventeen suspects -- including Murky, whose relationship with Cynthia of late, by Murky's own admission, had been, to use Murky's unfortunate term, "choppy".

The Santa Julietta Sheriff's Department was in charge of the murder investigation, but Murky asked me to conduct a parallel inquiry, given that Murky's relationship with the long-time sheriff, Sam Cuddleston, had been for years, again in Murky's own phrase, "damned ugly".

The shortest, but not the quickest, route from Bakersfield to Murky's ranch included California Highway Route 166, also known as the Cuyama Highway, which crosses a low, inland mountain range known as the Cuyamas. Pronounced *koo-AHH-mayz*.

I had traveled that road only once before in my lifetime, back when I was six years old. My father, bless his good intentions, thought he would be doing my mother and me a kindness by shortening the end of our trip from seeing relatives in Indiana to visiting my Uncle Jack in Santa Maria by taking Highway 166. The day had been hot and the road is as twisted as a cornered rattler. Halfway across the Cuyamas I began to feel dizzy. Then I felt sick to my stomach. Next thing we knew I had vomited all over the back seat of the car.

"You came across the Cuyamas? I wasn't in that big of a hurry to see you, Fletcher," was Murky's greeting when I finally arrived, shaken but with my stomach's contents still where they belonged.

Murky offered me what he was already drinking, a double Wild Turkey, neat, which is the Southern way of ordering a drink straight -- no ice, no lemon, just liquor. I settled for a Budweiser. He chased his cat off the sofa and sat there himself, gesturing for me to sit in his own overstuffed leather chair.

"So who are the sheriff's prime candidates for killing Cynthia?" was my first question.

"Betty Sue and, of course, me," he said.

Betty Sue was Murky's third wife. She is, or had been, an actress, if you could call her that. More like a costume filler, an extra with no speaking parts. When a scene called for a crowded elevator or a crowded room, she was part of the crowd. One of the unspoken side benefits for those *with* speaking parts was getting to screw those without any scripted lines, having dressing room quickies between takes. Maybe those counted as a benefit also for at least a few cast extras. After all, it landed Betty Sue a husband for a few years.

"Tell me why you and Betty Sue head up Cuddleston's list," I said.

"Well, it's kind of a long story," Murky said, falling into a rural Alabama accent he had successfully buried decades earlier -- except when whiskey teased it out of its grave.

"Keep it short, please. I know how long your long stories can be."

"All right. By midnight at my retirement party I was two or three whiskeys down the pike, as you surely can guess."

I said, "How about three or four doubles."

He laughed. "Yep. I reckon you know me better than I do."

Everyone knew Murky's capacity for fine Kentucky bourbon. Sadly, Murky, though he knew his limit, rarely chose to stay within it.

"Go on," I said.

"You see, Betty Sue was kind of flirting with me over behind the piano and, of course, I felt fully obliged to reciprocate her amorous attentions."

"Fully obliged. Of course."

"Then, right in the middle of Betty Sue's planting a big ol' French kiss on me, in walks Cynthia and spots Betty Sue doin' --. Well, doin' what she was doin'. So Cynthia walks right over, gives Betty Sue a smack on her face, then says to me, 'Just who do you think you are married to, currently-wise?'"

Currently-wise. That was Cynthia all right. A woman without a high school diploma talking as she mis-imagined someone with a Ph.D. might talk.

"And then?"

Murky shrugged. "She stalked off and parked herself in the billiards room, with the lights off, to sulk."

"Did you follow her and offer an apology?" I said.

"Nope. It was then I sort of realized how shit-faced I was, 'cause suddenly it was all I could manage not to trip over the damned piano player."

"I hope you didn't spill any of your expensive bourbon on the piano player's tuxedo."

"Now you're making fun of me, Fletcher."

"I am and I apologize. What happened next?"

"The next thing I remember was I stood outside and watched a pair of guys in uniforms pushing Cynthia away on a gurney toward the back of an ambulance and they weren't pushing very fast."

"And Betty Sue? What did she do after Cynthia slapped her?"

"Damned if I know. You'll have to ask her."

I most certainly intended to do just that.

II

Murky Murtrans grew up in rural Alabama.

"The pissant burg I came from was so remote from the rest of the world that we didn't even have so much as a single nigger in my county the last time I was there, which was twenty years ago."

Making it 1947.

On a map the town he came from is called Hellfire. It lies in Burris County, eight miles from the Mississippi state line, on County Road 816. From Murky's descriptions of the place it's a little roach of a town, with a one-room Baptist church and clusters of single-wide trailers raised up on cinder blocks. And out at the front of each trailer park stands a forty-foot-high flag pole flying a Confederate flag as big as five bed sheets.

A sawmill making stringer pallets sustains the town. Other businesses include a gas station, an auto-repair garage, and a tiny post office. A flower shop caters to maintaining flowers on the nearby cemetery. But for groceries and pharmaceuticals town folk are obliged to drive fifteen miles east to Buck & Maggie's Food & Essentials Store in Jettlesville.

The town derives its name from nearby Hellfire Lake, which locals claim often displays flashes of fire, especially in the summer. One explanation of the phenomenon is that the lake is a popular place for lighting bugs to show off their yellowish glows. A second account is that there are pockets of methane beneath the lake which sometimes give off bubbles of gas that ignite when reaching the surface. A third account, popular with the local Baptist preacher, is that the lake is a sister to the lake in the Book of Revelations and gives the world an insight into what the fires of Hell itself will be like.

Murky's preferred story, derived perhaps from personal experience, is that the brief blue flames seen on the far, dark, swampy edges of the lake result from high school boys floating naked on their bellies on inner tubes, carrying books of matches, smoking cigarettes, and lighting each others' farts.

As for Murky's lineage he claims he never knew either of his grandfathers. Both men died during the Spanish-American War, although neither died heroically. His father's father, Zeb Browning, died of a ruptured spleen, acquired from excessive rough-housing with a fellow soldier during Army basic training in Spartansburg, South Carolina. His mother's father, Clem Gallagher, drowned when he was knocked off a dock by a crane while loading food supplies onto a Navy destroyer at Newport News, Virginia. His death occurred just eleven weeks after joining the US Navy.

He allows that he had two wise grandmothers, Nora O'Day Browning, and Sarah Gallagher, the latter known better as Sade or Sadie. Sadly, both died of the Spanish flu in 1918, when Murky was twenty years old. He says he learned to appreciate humor from Granny Sade, who was the funniest person he has ever known. "Non-stop hilarious," was how he described her. "With humor that was as full of sin as a rusty nail. Deadly if you walked straight into it unawares." Apparently, too, she owned a series of talking parrots, each named after a pirate captain and, concomitantly, taught to swear like a seasoned sailor.

Grammy Nora, he claims, was an uncommonly quiet woman, but capable of pithy observations and fierce criticisms when she did speak. Her sharpest jabs, Murky told me, had been aimed at Hellfire's Baptist pastor, a man locals called Fearful Ted, known for terrorizing the town's youngsters with stories of wicked children being spit-roasted alive in the Devil's fires for all eternity.

Murky says he was one of six siblings, but he was the only one to have survived beyond the age of two. Thad drowned in the well at age one and a half, Little Pete died of tuberculosis, Peggy and Joseph died of pneumonia, and Merle succumbed to meningitis.

"I didn't have a crippled little sister to watch over like you often see in the movies. Peggy was dead before I was born."

Murky told me, "Town folks later assured me 'God had shed His grace on me.' When I asked them why He hadn't spread His grace around, been more generous with it, and have given some to my little brothers and sister, I was admonished not to question God's ways. When I asked, "Why not?" they all crossed their index fingers to make the sign of the cross, and they'd flash their teeth and hiss at me to protect themselves from my surefire malevolent curiosity."

Murky fell solemn when he spoke of his parents, Ida and Griffin Browning.

"Pa was an auctioneer and, to make a little extra, he played the fiddle for local barn dances. Ma was...well, she was just Ma. A good cook and full of common sense. That shoulda been her epitaph. Pa had a temper and liked his moonshine. After they both were dead, their next door neighbor, a sweet man named Eli Monroe, told me that Ma and Pa fought like cats 'n' dogs all the time when I wasn't around. But then, he said, they'd cool on down, give each other a hug, and finally they'd dance around the kitchen together as if they were attending an emperor's ball."

I doubted that Hellfire's remoteness had anything to do with the absence of colored people. More likely poverty and unabashed hatred by whites drove Negroes north in search of jobs and perhaps at least a spoonful of respect. World War Two provided them war-armaments jobs in places such as Indianapolis, Fort Wayne, Cleveland, Toledo, Flint, and especially Detroit.

Many employers were willing to hire coloreds because they paid them a lower wage than they paid whites doing the same work. But better half a loaf in Michigan, Ohio, or Indiana than no loaf at all in Alabama. Even the openly racist, Nazi-sympathizing Henry Ford hired people with dark skin. For all his pro-Hitler remarks, Ford produced thousands of airplanes, tanks, and bombs destined to hammer the Germans and the Japanese. And many of those weapons were made by men and women of color.

In high school Murky had been the class clown. His first show-business break came when he won an amateur auditioning competition in Nashville. The Grand Ole Opry invited Murky to do a three-minute stand-up comedy routine in between headline performers. He claims he fed the audience a rapid-fire stream of anecdotes just enough off-color to make folks snicker, but not blue enough to cause the Bible-thumpers among them to object. Just to scowl, no doubt.

"By the time my three minutes was up I had the old biddies in the front rows cacklin' so hard their dentures fell out," he liked to tell anyone who would listen.

It so happened that a New York talent agent was sitting in the audience and after the show he signed Cee Jay Browning to a three-week contract performing in the Catskills for one week each at Grossinger's, Kutshers, and the Concord, three of the headline resorts of what was known as the "Borscht Belt", because of those resorts' popularity with Jewish vacationers from New York City and elsewhere along the East Coast. And thus Clyde Jacob Browning turned himself into Murky Murtrans. How and why he chose that name remains unknown -- except to him.

Also, because nearly all Catskill comedians in the 1920's were themselves Jewish -- think of Milton Berle, Sid Caesar, and Alan King as prime examples -- Murky somehow managed to convince the New York agent in his Nashville audience that, on Ellis Island an officious immigration officer had looked at Murky's arrival papers and decided that Chaim Yakov Braunstein required Americanizing into Clyde Jacob Browning.

I suppose Murky will go to his grave still laughing about that sly feat he pulled off, fooling the talent agent, although how the agent mistook the Murk's rough-and-tumble Alabama-ese for a Russian Yiddish accent beats me.

No doubt it was some of the jokes Murky says he included in his three-minute routine that convinced the agent Murky was a Jewish émigré. The first was:

IRS calling on the telephone: "Is this Rabbi Rabinowitz?"
Rabbi Rabinowitz: "Yes, this the rabbi."
IRS: "Do you have a man named Samuel Cohen in your congregation?"
Rabbi: "Yes, I do."
IRS: "Did Samuel donate $10,000 last year to help build a new addition to your synagogue?"
Rabbi: "No, but he will this year."

The next three jokes, and ones which surely made the Bible-thumpers wince, were:

Question: What does a Jewish man mean by the phrase "Schmuck Luck"?
Answer: When his wife tells him she's pregnant two months after he's had a vasectomy.
Q: What is the difference between Catholic wives and Jewish wives?
A: Catholic wives have real orgasms and fake jewelry.
Q: Why do Jewish men have to be circumcised?
A. Jewish women won't touch anything unless it's 20% off.

Boom! The agent was sold. Murky found out later the agent was a married Jew from Alpharetta, Georgia -- a mere 169 miles from Murky's hometown of Hellfire. *Oi vey,* y'all.

Betty Sue grew up in Louisiana and moved out West from Baton Rouge at the urging of her older brother, Arlen, who was already in Hollywood when he wrote home to Betty Sue, extolling in vivid terms the virtues of the motion picture industry and of living in proximity to it. Arlen had moved to Hollywood wanting to become a gigolo to Hollywood starlets. Handsome as he was, that idea did not pan out for him, Murky had told me. The town was full of handsome, young studs -- which I already knew -- not all of them scruffily dressed and penniless, nor afflicted with a Cajun drawl. So instead of bedding actresses, Arlen found himself humping broom sticks and mop handles as a night janitor for a maintenance firm, cleaning movie sets belonging to Columbia Pictures and RKO.

I confess that I do not even begin to comprehend the caste system that sorts young Southern white women into higher or lower social standing, ranging from president of a Tulane University sorority down to ugly white trash in the slums of New Orleans. As the daughter of a dirt-poor mom and a moonshine-swilling dad, who worked respectively as a waitress and a fry cook in a greasy spoon diner three blocks off Bourbon Street, Betty Sue ranked close to the bottom of that arcane scale.

However, after arriving in Hollywood, Betty Sue made out better than her brother. *Made out* in more than one meaning of the phrase. Attractive and shapely, Betty quickly found herself on many a casting couch, humping her way into numerous small movie roles, occasionally even a role with one or two speaking lines, usually short lines, such as "Oh, my goodness" or "Hmm. That's interesting." One such role placed her in several scenes with Murky. One full-term pregnancy later she was Mrs. Murky Murtrans.

Unfortunately, the child was stillborn. Murky was crushed and initially blamed Betty Sue, he said, for not giving him a decent return on his investment in her. Later he blamed the God he didn't believe in -- for not living up to His omni-benevolence characterization.

While I was reflecting back on Murky's history -- at least as he had told it to me over past visits -- I had lost track of what Murky had been saying.

"Ready for another beer, Fletcher?" Murky said as he drained his bourbon.

We had moved into the billiard room, where Cynthia had died. Before I could answer, a deputy sheriff came bursting in on us from a side door.

"Did you ever hear of knocking first, Boy?" Murky said.

"Your whole house is a crime scene, Mr. Browning. I don't need to knock."

Calling Murky Mr. Browning set off fireworks.

"Crime scene or not, Buddy, you need to show some proper respect and abide by common courtesy. Understand?"

The cop ignored him, pulled out a tape measure, and began measuring from where all the cues were racked to the chalk outline where, I presumed, Cynthia's body was found lying on the billiard room floor. How that maneuver was going to advance the sheriff's investigation I had no idea.

Murky walked over and stepped on the deputy's tape measure.

"I asked you a question, Sonny. I expect you to conduct yourself in a civilized manner and give me a proper answer in a respectful tone."

The young cop stood, took a step toward Murky, leaned forward so the two men's faces were inches apart, and said, "I could arrest you, Mister, for interfering with a police investigation."

Murky turned to me.

"Fletcher, I haven't heard such a hilarious, deadpan one-liner since W.C. Fields died."

Turning to the deputy, Murky said, "Son, have you ever considered becoming a stage comedian?"

The deputy stepped away, unable to comprehend how hard he had just been put down and not sure how to respond. Murky didn't give him time to reply.

"Well, Boy? You sure as hell ain't gonna be able to afford a ranch like mine here on a deputy sheriff's salary. In fact, next time Sheriff Cuddly and me sit down together over a glass of milk, I intend to raise the issue with him over whether or not you still warrant drawing a salary. From what I see of you so far, taxpayers are gonna be worrying if their hard-earned money isn't bein' wasted on a pencil prick like you. And when taxpayers worry about the efficiency of his budget, Cuddly starts sweatin' bullets. Big bullets."

Again, the deputy had no response. He folded his tape measure up and hastily departed.

I said, "You, Cuddly, and a glass of milk? You told me your relationship with the sheriff is, and I quote, 'damned ugly', unquote."

Murky laughed.

"Cuddly and I go way back. Yeah, there have been some harsh words between us. Long before he got himself elected sheriff, I once threw a punch at him. I missed, of course. We were both drunk as Irish fiddlers."

III

Murky and I sat in his living room for the next two hours going over aspects of his wife's murder. He had even made a list of all umpteen party guests and had placed a red star next to each guest he suspected capable of killing Cynthia, meaning having a motive for doing so. Most of the names were starred.

We were interrupted when Murky looked out the window and saw two more deputies combing through his shrubbery.

"Damned cops! If I owned a Rottweiler I'd turn it loose on those two."

As a former cop myself I said nothing, but Murky must have read my thoughts.

"Don't get me wrong. I don't hate cops. I just hate anybody pokin' and pryin' around my property."

I said, "Later I may need to poke and pry."

"You have my blessing, but them two don't."

"Thank you."

"There is *one* cop I hate and it's not Sam Cuddleston or any of his people."

Then Murky told me about the sickening episode that angered him mightily.

"I'd gone up to Fresno to pick up my niece, Peggy Ann, at the start of Christmas break last year. She's Cynthia's sister's daughter and she's a junior at Fresno State. Peggy Ann's mother, Nancy, had been ill and we had her staying out in one of our guest cottages."

Murky paused to pour himself another bourbon.

"Anyway, my truck broke down on the way back here. On Highway 41, halfway between Lemoore and Kettleman City. Luckily, or so I thought, a California Highway Patrol officer came along and offered to take us into Kettleman, where he knew there was a towing service. I gladly accepted his offer."

Murky took a sip of bourbon.

"As we were riding along, Peggy Ann in the front and me in back, I saw that the cop had a shotgun sitting bolt upright, locked in position, between the driver's and front passenger's seats. I casually said, 'That sure is a sturdy weapon to have on your side when you're backed into a corner.'"

Murky paused, remembering, and his look darkened.

"The cop looks at me in his rear view mirror and say's, 'Yep. This here is my nigger-gitter.'"

Murky said, "I failed to reprimand him for such a crass remark in front of Peggy Ann, but now I wish I had, although things would still have turned out ugly."

"What else happened?" I said. Surely what he had just told me wasn't enough to place the cop at the top of Murky's Most Hated list.

"When we reached the outskirts to Kettleman City -- which, as you know, is nothing but a few gas stations and fast food places -- the cop pulls way off the road, next to a small grove of trees."

Again he paused, perhaps wondering if he should continue.

"I thank him for the ride and started to get out, but the cop says to me, 'You stay where you are. She's the one who is going to thank me,' and he ordered Peggy Ann out of the car."

I said, "You don't have to say any more, Murky."

"Like hell I don't."

"Okay."

"I told Peggy Ann to stay put, but she said, 'It's okay, Uncle Murky. No telling what he'll do if I don't go.'" Then the cop says, 'She's right, you know, Big Uncle,' and he locked me in the back of the patrol car.

So Peggy Ann went with him behind some trees. When she came back she still had some of the cop's semen dribbling off her chin. I wanted to kill the guy, but Peggy Ann said to me, 'At least he didn't make me put his shotgun barrel in my mouth. Let's just start walking away as fast as we can, Uncle Murky, and hope he doesn't shoot us in the back with his precious nigger-gitter.'"

I didn't know what to say, so I said nothing. I just shook my head in disappointment. I learned from my six-year stint on the City of Burbank police force that more than a few cops are as heinous as criminals. That is why I quit. I couldn't look some of my fellow officers in the eye anymore, knowing the activities they engaged in, both on duty and off.

Murky refilled his tumbler, thankfully this time with soda water.

"Now don't get me wrong, Fletcher. I ain't no nigger-hugger. But I do believe them people ought to be treated fairly. I ain't sure you can legislate fairness, though that tall Texan in the White House is givin' it a go. Anyway, that cop was just lookin' for an excuse to shoot some colored boys."

Them people. Right. Murky clearly failed to grasp that words can treat people unjustly, too. But I was not about to educate him on the subject.

"Of course neither Peggy Ann nor I said anything about the incident to Cynthia or Nancy. But the next day I wrote a letter to CHP headquarters in Sacramento to complain about that cop and suggest he be fired. I had written down his name and badge number. I ain't heard nuthin' back yet at all. Don't suppose I will."

I decided to steer Murky back on track, discussing possible murder suspects.

"You see from my list, Fletcher, that Lois and her boys did not attend my gathering. Lowell is off in Australia, chasin' deadly species of jellyfish. Lewis is with the U.S. State Department, stationed in Sweden. So I didn't expect *them*. But Lois didn't show up either. She only lives in Santa Monica, but I reckon she still holds a bagful of grudges against me, even after all these years."

Lois was Murky's second wife. That marriage had lasted six years.

"I see a Jesse Browning on your list, Murk. Who's he?"

"That's Ethel's boy. Well, me and Ethel's. That's Little CJ. Clyde Jacob Browning, Junior. You know a bit about him already from past conversations we've had. He don't care to be called Little CJ anymore. Nowadays he insists folks call him Jesse. Jess for short. Reverend Jess, for that matter. He's a preacher man now, damn his hide. Or rather, damn his soul. I was surprised to see Jess show up. I reckon he came as a courtesy to Cynthia. My relationship with Jess is one of: I'll ignore you and let's you ignore me. That's why he no longer abides bein' called Little CJ. Especially after a row we had when I first learned he had been ordained. I ain't got a religious bone in my body and Jess's becomin' a preacher man drove my ox straight into the ditch. I went into a rage and told him then he was gonna be doin' nothin' but shillin' Santa Claus-for-grownups stories to folks who can't tell a strawberry from a lemon. Holy Christ Almighty! He's not just any kind of preacher, but he's a hellfire and damnation Bible-thumper."

Murky paused to catch his breath. Then sat down and continued.

"You'd never know he's that kind of man away from his pulpit. He's pretty civilized otherwise. He's even building a nice, new church up in San Luis Obispo. Hell, I don't even know what brand of Bible-banger he is. Some flavor of Baptist maybe. Or possibly a Pentecostal. An Evangelical this or that. Them people all look and smell alike to me. I can't stand being around any of 'em for five minutes. Imagine, Fletcher, spending five whole fuckin' eternities listenin' to their inanities."

Them people again.

Murky then remembered something.

"Jess did once show a violent streak, but it was more comical than dangerous. I even worked the incident into my stage routine a time or two. He was just a kid and Ethel had grounded him for some minor, silly-ass reason. She confined him to the house and our big porch."

He paused to chuckle.

"It was summertime and it was hot. Flies buzzing everywhere outside. Well, Jess fetched himself a swatter and spent all afternoon battin' down flies. Wham, wham, wham!

Then, every so often he'd sweep dead flies into a pile, scoop 'em up with a dustpan, dig a small hole at the edge of the porch, and give them flies a mass burial. He'd even mutter some kind of prayer over them."

I said, "Sounds pretty harmless to me." *As flies to wanton boys....*

"It was. Except you should have seen the look on his face and see how hard he hammered them flies. It was almost as though he was imagining every one of those flies to be Ethel."

Just a kid being a kid, I thought. But I could see how the tale would make an audience laugh.

I said, "Have you given any thought to the possibility that the person killing Cynthia was using her as a means to get at you?"

"Hell, yes, I have. Half or more of the people on that list would take pleasure in takin' a pool cue to me. Or, better yet, a baseball bat. And not just to knee-cap me, but to bash my head in."

Half or more? I could see I had my work cut out for me.

"What was Cynthia's relationship with Jesse?" I said.

"Nuthin' naughty, if that's what you're thinking. On Sunday mornings for the past three or four months Cynthia drove herself up to San Luis to attend services in Jesse's church. She's the one who told me that from his pulpit Jess rains down fire and brimstone. She said she went there just to hedge her bets. On the slim chance there is an afterlife, she wanted a comfy one. Lobster tails, dry martinis, a cabana next to the swimming pool."

As I scanned his list Murky pulled his chair over next to me.

"Fletcher, let me tell you a story that may give you reason to think I did not kill my wife."

"Okay. I'm listening."

"When I was in junior high school back in Hellfire my first love was a girl named Effie Jamison. I kissed her on her lips one day just before the beginning of Mrs. Pruitt's English class. I hoped to light a fire under her or else have her slap me hard. Well, she spent the entire class period -- we were readin' some bunch of dumb Shakespeare sonnets or other -- grinning from ear to ear."

"Score one for Murky," I said.

"The very next day she showed up for school with a big ol' red welt on her right cheek. So I asked her how she came by it and she said Shandy Katz had slapped her. Now Shandy was the class bully. Mean as he was ugly. So after school I chased Shandy down and sucker punched him right in his gut. Doubled him over and watched him puke on the playground merry-go-round. Soon enough he chased after me and asked me why I had done such a mean thing to him. So I told him."

"Shit, CJ. Effie, she dared me to slap her and you know me. I don't back down from dares."

"Boys don't hit girls, Shandy. Ever or never. You understand?"

"I tell you, CJ, she dared me. She even stuck her chin right out toward me and said, 'Go on. Or are you a coward?' So I slapped her."

"Next thing Shandy knew, he was doubled over, pukin' again. Then the next day Effie walked right up to me -- in front of the whole class -- and planted the longest, wettest goddamned kiss on me I've ever had. And the whole class applauded. Well, not counting Mrs. Pruitt. She just gave me her usual scowl."

Okay. So *boys don't hit girls* was the rule at Hellfire Junior High. But in the world beyond Hellfire plenty of men hit plenty of women -- without being dared to do so. Murky's story may or may not sway a jury, provided any judge would permit him to tell it.

Anyway, I recognized a few other names on Murky's list, but his constant patter had worn me down. I needed some air. I felt slightly queasy about the case already and it wasn't because I had driven through the Cuyamas earlier in the day.

IV

I used Murky's telephone to call Amanda Reynolds to see if she'd be available later that afternoon or early evening. Amanda is a criminal defense attorney with an office in Santa Julietta. She hires me regularly to perform investigative work for her and a few days earlier she had told me she had just taken on a new case that required my services.

The drive from Murky's ranch to Santa Julietta is some sixty miles, requiring more than an hour over the slow, two-lane road. I had driven eight miles, nearing the turnoff to tiny town of Sisquoc, when a sheriff's car came racing up behind me, its red lights flashing. I was sure I hadn't been speeding, so I had no idea what the deputy wanted of me. Then, as the officer emerged from his patrol car, I saw it was the same deputy that Murky had berated while I stood and listened. I pulled my driver's license from my wallet.

After the deputy examined it -- more closely than was necessary -- he said, "Do you know how fast you were going just now, Mr. Fletcher?"

I said, "I do. Forty-eight miles per hour, two miles under the speed limit."

"Sorry, sir, but I clocked you going sixty-two miles an hour."

"Perhaps you did. When was the last time you had your radar gun officially calibrated?"

"Just last month."

"Excellent. Then you should feel confident letting me copy down the gun's serial number so my attorney can ask the court to verify your claim," I said.

"I'm not required to do that, Mr. Fletcher."

"Sure you are. You know the rules."

"I repeat. I am not obliged to hand over my radar gun to you."

"No, no. Of course, you don't have to give it to me. But what you must do is hold it so that I can copy down the serial number."

"I'm not even required to do that, sir."

While quibbling with him, I noted the name on his name tag: Colby Gray.

"Refusal is a guaranteed way to get my ticket dismissed. And for you to piss off the judge. So I suggest you cooperate."

"You'll be the one to piss off the judge. He'll hold you in contempt so fast you won't know what hit you."

"I doubt that."

"Why not?"

"He'll admire my chutzpah."

"Your what?"

"Chutzpah."

"What's that?"

"Brass balls."

He laughed.

"You've got plenty of brass all right. Balls? I doubt it," he said, smirking, pleased with himself for imaging himself being clever.

"See you in court, Cowboy."

He handed me the ticket. After he returned to his car I noted that he had put the date of my court appearance to be on May 9th. This was June 9th already.

V

Amanda Reynolds was still hunched over her huge desk when I tapped on her door, heard her command to enter, and stepped into her tidy office. The stack of files rising from one corner of her desk reminded me of any one of several office buildings in downtown Los Angeles.

"You're late, Fletcher. Lucky for you I had a huge lunch."

"Lady Luck has been in my pocket all day today."

I told her about not getting sick crossing the Cuyamas, about picking up a new client in Murky Murtrans, and about taking on a sheriff's deputy over a speeding ticket.

"I wouldn't count your winnings yet with either Murtrans or the cop. Both Murky and Cuddleston's boys have a way of coming back to bite people in the ass."

"Sufficient unto the day are the winnings therein."

"Just don't spend them too soon.," she said.

'I won't. Helping Murky is going to be a can of worms. A very large can."

Amanda said, "I read about his wife's murder."

'Yeah. A dozen or so suspects at Murky's retirement party, including Murky. That's not counting the staff."

"I'm sure you'll turn up something Cuddleston doesn't."

"So what's cookin' here?" I said.

"A new client to defend."

"Yummy."

Amanda gave me a don't-be-so-sure look.

"Not so tasty?"

"Our client is charged with rape on the UCSJ campus. Not just a run-of-the-mill frat rat, but a Big Man On Campus. Richard Sylvester Claymore the Third."

"As in heir to the Condor Wineries franchise?" I said.

"The very same."

I paused before saying, "Not to disparage your talents, but why did Papa Claymore pick you to get his son off?"

"Fair question. First, it was Grandpa Claymore -- the Condor himself -- who chose me, I'm told. Much to Papa's dismay. The Condor wanted someone local."

I said, "Most locals are twits."

"Agreed. That's why Papa wanted a big name from The City. But Grandpa had heard of me and liked what he heard."

I said, "Wow! You do stand out, if the Condor has heard of you."

"I do."

"Why is baby Richard attending UCSJ? I would have thought Harvard, Duke, or some other snazzy place back East."

"Ricky wanted to stay local."

"Stanford and Cal count as local. And snazzy."

"Ricky had poor grades, Fletcher. Ricky is not the sharpest tool in anyone's shed. Papa had to bend some rules and some arms to get him into UCSJ."

I laughed.

"What's so funny?" Amanda said.

"I'm just trying to picture my dad trying to coax the admissions committee to accept me at Stanford."

"Long Beach State did all right by you. And you them."

"Sure. But all they handed me was a diploma. Not a golden key to corporate boardrooms and executive potties."

"Then I suppose you'll just have to continue to piss behind dumpsters in dark alleys."

I gave Amanda a sad look and a nod.

"I don't have to ask how the kid got a draft exemption. No flat feet, no scoliosis. Probably no brain damage either, although you said he had low grades."

Amanda said, "Every male his age in every college in the country has a temporary draft exemption. Didn't you have one at Long Beach State?"

"I started college after I came home from Korea."

"Oh."

I didn't resent guys like Ricky Claymore getting a student draft deferment. More power to them. At least that way they postponed the time when they'd come back home from Southeast Asia in body bags. I was lucky I hadn't done the same. I felt I'd paid my dues, but many of my fellow platoon members at the Battle of Osan paid a far higher price than I did.

We were the first four hundred American troops to arrive in Korea, twenty-year-olds and younger, given eight weeks' training, then sent to face what seemed like the entire North Korean Army. And later the Chinese. We fought like hell, but we were overrun time and again by battalions backed by Russian tanks, until we were finally forced to retreat in grand disorder -- at least those few of us who were still among the living. We were told afterwards how brave we had been in our executing much-needed delaying tactics, until fresh UN troops arrived to replace us. Well, if being scared shitless and fighting for your life counts as showing bravery, then so be it.

At the time I thought that, by retreating, we few survivors would be branded cowards. Instead, our commanding general praised us for holding the line for so long. I had no idea how long *for so long* constituted. All I could remember immediately afterward was picturing wave after wave of enemy infantry coming at me. Time collapsed into the moment. Pick a target and fire. Then quickly choose another, and another, then another, all the while hoping my weapon wouldn't jam.

I suppressed the thought of today's college boys being turned into cannon fodder in the name of saving one large batch of Asians from being trampled by another large batch of them. Since 1950 I have imagined more than once that I had been killed in Korea and my body sent home. If my California gravestone read: *He Helped Save South Korea,* I fervently prayed that someone would come along in the dark of night and spray paint beneath my epitaph. *Big Fucking Deal* or else. *He Did No Such Thing.*

Finally I asked Amanda, "What's my assignment?"

She took out a clean legal pad and began to write.

"There are two approaches to this defense and I'm not sure which path to take. Partly that will depend on what you come up with. Down one path we'll focus on the victim, a shy, attractive freshman coed named Wendy Simmons. We'll need background on her, of course. We'll need to discredit her in multiple ways, if possible. Primarily, we'll want to know about her sexual activity or lack of. Is she a virgin? Or was she before the alleged rape? If she's sexually active, how active. Slightly? Somewhat? Or is she a total slut? I also want to know what she was wearing at the time of the alleged incident. Was it provocative? Was she, in the usual phrase, asking for it?"

I said, "And I'm the one who gets to ask her close friends and spiteful enemies about this matter."

Amanda gave me a smile that told me I was in for some rocky roads ahead.

"I'll pay you double on this case, Fletcher. And, believe me, you'll earn it."

I assumed that meant, in part, that the Claymore elders had coughed up an enormous retainer for Amanda's legal services and would continue to pay large sums in order to keep their Little Ricky from going to prison.

The original Richard Sylvester Claymore had married Carla Antonia Casstellone in 1925, after graduating with a degree in hydrological engineering from UC-Davis. Carla Antonia was a member of one of the families belonging to the Italian-Swiss Colony cooperative at Albi, a small town just northwest of Fresno.

With money from his own inheritance upon on the early death of his father and with money granted him by Antonia's father, Richard the First bought hundreds of acres of prime, arable land between Atascadero and Cambria, south of Hearst Castle, and turned that land into vineyards of superior quality to those at the Italian Swiss Colony and named the several production centers turning out wine Condor Wineries. He chose Condor because his own mother grew up in Chile amid prime vineyards in the foothills of the Andes, where soaring condors were symbols of success.

"And the second path?" I said.

"Prove somehow that Wendy Simmons misidentified her rapist, if it was rape. We need to show that Ricky wasn't at the party or, if he was, he was busy toying with some other eligible bimbo at the time when Wendy claims she was being taken against her will. Alternatively, suggest or prove that Ricky can't get it up. Or that he's a queer. Whatever it takes."

Whatever it takes. Right. Some days I wish I had become a barber. The issues I would be obliged to confront would surely be less weighty. The pay would likely end up the being about the same. More importantly, I could go home at night and sleep soundly. Plus have Sundays and Mondays off.

"Which path do I start down first?" I finally said.

"Check out Wendy's background first, please. If she proves to be a slut, Ricky's squalid character will surely weigh a lot less with a jury," Amanda said.

"Ricky is squalid?"

"Squalid is more befitting his upscale station in life than slimy."

"And you have to defend this guy. Make him look good. Ugh!" I said.

"No, I do not have to defend him. I choose to defend him. And I do not have to make him look good if you come up with information that makes Wendy Simmons look bad."

"Lucky me. When do you want me to start?"

"How impatient is Murky Murtrans?"

"I'm the one who will require patience. I already told you that the suspect list has more names on it that the Santa Maria telephone book."

"Is Murky paying you? Or is this a *pro bono?*"

"Surely you jest. My history with Murky falls somewhere between being a stranger and being a nodding acquaintance," I said, exaggerating considerably. "No freebie from me for Murky. He's already given me a three thousand dollar retainer."

"Well then, given that you and I are bosom buddies, I obviously take precedence," Amanda said, peering over her reading glasses to see my reaction.

"Bosom buddies, are we? On what date did that begin?" I said.

"On our second date. When we shared a chateaubriand for two by candlelight at Maxwell's."

"In my dreams."

Amanda smiled a wicked smile.

"And only in your dreams. Start working on who killed Cynthia Murtrans. Wendy Simmons and three of her girlfriends -- ladies you will need to interview cautiously -- are off on a summer holiday in Italy."

"Summer holiday? Italy?"

"Your hearing is ever so keen, Fletcher. Yes. Therapy, no doubt, will be her explanation. The calming effects of art and food in Florence and Venice."

"May I begin my interviews with them there?" I said, smirking.

"On your dime? Sure."

"I don't have that many dimes."

"No interviewing Wendy by the way," Amanda said solemnly.

"Oh, come on." In a mocking voice I said, "Miss Simmons, are you truly as slutty as all your girlfriends claim you are?"

"Wow! That's perfect, Fletcher. Just the right inflection. I've changed my mind. Go for it. The girls will be back in Santa Julietta Monday night."

VI

Hollywood lacks the public glitter of a celebrity-rich town such as Las Vegas. Aside from glamour stars publicly quarreling with their glamorous spouses, played out on the pages of weekly scandal-mongering newspapers, nearly all of Hollywood's serious metaphorical fireworks occur behind the quiet facades of movie lots. There, agents representing actors, actresses, and screenplay writers battle with movie moguls, whose minions consist of a phalanx of accountants.

The weapons of war are mathematical formulae, written in a language mostly consisting of the terms *net* and *gross,* against which are applied *points* and *percentages.* So when Michael Caine's agent negotiates with Paramount Pictures for Caine to star in *Alfie,* and when Elizabeth Taylor's agent negotiates with Warner Brothers for her to head the cast of *Who's Afraid of Virginia Wolff?*, the war prize consists of how many pennies each side gets every time a movie-goer plunks down his $1.25 at one of hundreds of box offices across the country.

However, as we all know, the casts of very few movies consist exclusively of star-grade actors and actresses. On the credit screen of the movie where she had had those scenes with Murky, Betty Sue Murtrans rated as a third banana, meaning she was listed merely as "With", while top bananas were listed as "Starring" and second bananas listed as "Also Starring". The movie was a Western titled *Cimmeron After Sundown,* wherein a well-known star in stock cowboy movies, Robbie Rohmers, played The Dalhart Kid, wearing a white Stetson and riding a golden Palomino named Zephyr.

Betty Sue was not cast as The Kid's initial love life, but rather as the girl who hoped to capture his heart. Standing between Betty Sue, playing a Plain Jane named Mary Jo Travers, stood a busty, foul-mouthed, long-haired blonde always shown wearing black mesh stockings and off-the-shoulder dresses. Her name was Caper LaRue, a New Orleans dancer hall girl who had inherited a sprawling Kansas cattle ranch from a fallen uncle, a victim of a no-holds-barred range war among cattle owners eager to wear the crown of the King of Kansas. Caper, as ruthless as any of the male cattle barons, hired the Kid to protect her interests -- and expand them, if possible.

How could a fast-draw artist like the Kid not fall for the young, rich, gorgeous woman called Caper? Mary Jo was the daughter of another fallen ranch owner, an ally of Caper's uncle. She wore her hair tied back, made her own simple dresses, rode a horse awkwardly, and was afraid of guns. Through the first two reels the Kid never gave Mary Jo a second look.

Now, twenty years after the 1947 release of *Cimmeron After Dark,* as I stepped into the office of Betty Sue Murtrans's current agent, a woman by the name of Karla Wojenski, I looked around and saw not even a photo of Betty Sue in her prime, let alone a promotional poster of the film. Granted, Ms. Wojenski's work space was small, located on the second floor of a low-rent office building near the intersection of Davis and Jackson Heights. But I had educated myself ahead of time to the fact that Karla Wojenski's clientele list was short and limited to women only, although I suspected that included a transvestite or three. But no overt males were among those she represented in the cutthroat business of getting actresses auditions for roles in screenplays of big-screen films, television series and one-offs, spots in commercials, and voiceovers for either cartoons or daytime soap opera ads.

"Sorry. You're not my type," the woman I assumed was Karla said, as she emerged from a curtain-as-door.

"I know. I'm looking for one of your clients. Betty Sue Murtrans."

Karla gestured for me to take a seat on a well-worn love seat across from her photo-strewn desk.

"Elizabeth is currently incommunicado," she said in a low, faux-Betty-Davis voice, as she took a seat across from me.

"Communicado is a city in Mexico, is it?"

"Most amusing, Señor. Uh... I didn't get your name," she said, arching an eyebrow.

"Fletcher. Stu Fletcher."

A smile. "Sorry. We're still not bonding."

"Clever."

"Normally, I'd make you tie me up and tongue-lash the answer out of me. But, to repeat, you're not my type."

I pulled out my wallet and withdrew a fifty. "Let's try a more conventional way of loosening your tongue."

She out-waited me. So I slowly fetched out a second fifty. Quick as a magician she snatched both bills from my fingers.

"Try La Jolla. And here's a hint. It's not in Mexico."

"Still, La Jolla is a big place. UCSD, Scripps Institute, the Red Rooster."

"You know about the Red Rooster, do you?" she said.

"Never slept there, but yes."

"I almost like you."

"Betty Sue?"

"You have a plane to catch, Mr. Stu Fletcher, not shaken, not stirred?"

"I do, and I may have to tie you to the back of it. Then watch you wiggle and squeal as we take off."

"Ooooo! You do make a mean treat. I mean threat."

I waited.

"Okay. The Golden Palm Tree Hotel, on Belair Drive, a block from the beach. I'm sure you can tease Betty Sue's room number from the desk clerk."

After leaving Karla Wojenski's office I didn't head for La Jolla. Instead, I drove to a more upscale section of Hollywood, where Murky's agent,

Jock Silverado, maintained his offices. Known in his former life as Jacob Silverman, Jock conducted his business from the top floor of a seven-story building, the offices of which all faced west. And, although you were unable to see the ocean from behind Jock's posh desk, clients felt as if Jock himself ought to be able to view the tides come and go from his majestic chair, perhaps even command them.

"Fletcher, eh? Yes, I've heard Murky speak favorably of you. Pressing business in Bakersfield kept you from attending Cynthia's murder, you say? Come now. No business in Bakersfield qualifies as pressing business. The cleaning, pressing, and alterations business, maybe. But not *pressing* business in any other sense."

"*Urgent* then," I amended.

"That's better," he said, grinning and finally gesturing me for me to be seated. "I almost like you already."

Almost like. I was beginning to think every agent in Hollywood bought his fortune cookies from the same local bakery. But I didn't say so.

Jock was fifty-nine years old and going bald. His deep tan spoke of hours spent on golf courses hustling his clients' acting virtues to film studio Big Cigars, which meant the clubs were private, exclusive, and the kind Groucho Marx once remarked he wouldn't care to join if they were willing to have him for a member. Jock Silverado obviously didn't share such a reservation.

There is money to be made, I learned, from representing "Also Starring, "Featuring", and even "With" level actors, providing the agent maintains a sizeable stable of such unmemorable-to-the-public film players. And Jock did. An agent's percentage of Nothing is always easy to calculate, no matter the cut -- and without pencil and paper. But ten percent or fifteen percent of Something takes some figuring. And it adds up, no matter how nameless the characters are who cash the royalty and residual checks.

How many movie-goers recognize the names Royal Dano and Robert J. Wilke? Yet both have appeared in many dozens of feature Westerns and those same movie attendees would recognize each man's face, pegging each merely as a Bad Guy. Memorable, too, are Ward Bond, Ben Johnson, and Harry Carey, Jr., only they are each memorable as a good guy, nearly always additionally noted as one of John Wayne's sidekicks.

Each of those five guys has been paid over the years to play the role of a good guy or bad, and collecting a percentage of each of their checks was an agent representing him, meaning marketing him to the producers of Western films. Such marketing often occurred on country club tees and greens and Jock Silverado was one of those doing the selling. His product? Often it was Murky Murtrans.

"Too bad about Cynthia. She was a sweet lady," Jock began, as he lit up a medium-sized cigar, then banged his desktop ashtray on the edge of an unseen wastebasket to empty his previous cigar's mortal remains.

"I understand she didn't almost like you," I said.

"Aw, it was nothing. She thought I pushed Murky too hard, tried to sign him to too many film and television contracts. Holy cow! She, of all people, ought to know just how tough it is to land good roles. I've worked my ass off for Murky and she complains that I'm trying to kill him." He paused, then said, "Oh, wait! You think maybe I killed her because of her being a whiny bitch about my driving Murky to gather ye roses whilst the sun shines? Is that why you're here?"

"Is that why you think I'm here?" I said.

"Yeah. What other reason would there be?"

"You tell me, Jocko."

"Let me tell you something, Fletcher. In ancient Sumerian the words *talent agent* and *asshole* are both derivatives from a word that means *source of endless pain and grief.*"

I was attentive to the fact that he had dropped the Mister from Mr. Fletcher before I responded, "Who delivered that anecdote first? Henny Youngman, Sid Caesar, or Jack Benny?"

He laughed hard. "God, you are wicked. You'd make a perfect straight man."

"No thanks. I already have a shitty job."

He opened his arms, hands palms up. "See what I mean? You're great."

"What I really want is your opinion about who killed Cynthia Murtrans. If you want to place yourself high on the list, okay. That's up to you."

Jock said, finally in a serious tone, "It's not who killed Cynthia, but what. And the answer to that is: Age. By that I mean: Age kills everybody who ends up with no good acting parts left for themselves, and especially those who can't act worth a damn to begin with."

"Depression leads to suicide, yes. But Cynthia didn't kill herself," I said, pointing out the obvious.

He held up an index finger. "Ah, but maybe she hired someone to do the job she was too cowardly to perform herself."

"That's possible, I suppose. So then tell me who she hired?"

"You're the detective."

"What if it wasn't suicide by proxy?" I said.

"Then the point would be to hurt Murky and Cynthia was just an innocent tool to get at him."

"Then why not get right to the point and kill Murky?"

"Not dramatic enough, dear boy. Your suggestion there is in line with many a pedestrian screenplay throughout the ages, including today. Most scripts these days just fill the screen with killing and suppose what they portray represents both justice and satisfaction on the killers' parts, as well as giving the audience satisfaction. But no! Indirect revenge is far more interesting, makes for better drama. I mean: The very best revenge cannot come from killing the one you want to suffer. Bang! you're dead. Yes, but where's your suffering? Nowhere. You're gone. Dead. Kaput!"

"Go on," I said.

"Find someone who grasps the ancient Greeks, Shakespeare, or even, I hesitate to add, the Old Testament. The Torah, the Old Testament, not that bucketful of moral pabulum that starts with Matthew, Mark, Luke, and John."

I must have looked puzzled to him.

So he said, "In Othello, to pick a great example, Iago tries to get Desdemona poisoned in order to get at Othello."

I nodded and congratulated myself on barely staying awake through my Shakespeare's Tragedies class at Long Beach State. Who would have thought my recalling the plot of *Othello* would spare me embarrassment years later, allow me to understand what a suspect was telling me.

However, I reiterated my earlier point. "Do you really suppose she might have paid someone to bash her head in?"

"Maybe she left the method up to the killer," Jock said.

"And her point in setting up her own murder?"

"A combination of self-pity and to hurt my client."

"Dramatic. I'll give you that. But only if she lets the world know that's how it went down. A fat lady, wearing a helmet and holding a spear, singing about how poor Cynthia couldn't stand her diminished status in life, wanted to hurt her husband, and thus paid some tavern drunk the price of a tankard of ale to bash her head in."

"Holy crap, Fletcher. You could be a screenwriter, too."

"You mean opera composer," I said.

"Same difference, although there aren't too many screenwriters who can also scribble down the musical scores to the bullshit they crank out."

"But wait," I said. "Cynthia wanted Murky to retire. She was the one pleading with him to give up acting."

"Nonsense, dear fellow. She didn't really meat it. No, no. You fail to grasp the dynamics of that marriage. The harder Cynthia pleaded with Murky to do x, y, or z, the harder he resisted her pleas. Then eventually she would cease her urgings and lie down in the mud to pout, to wallow in her self-pity, and Murky could then go on about his business, unimpeded by Cynthia's sniveling."

"Give me some names, Jock. People with a motive to kill Murky's wife."

"Who killed Desdemona?" Jock said.

"Othello's closest advisor."

"Right."

"Who, in Murky's case, would be --?"

"Murky took advice from no one," Jock said.

"Yes, but who whispered in his ear a lot, successfully or not?" I said.

"You could start with me, I suppose." Jocko smirked.

"Precisely, which is why I'm here."

VII

"Most of my differences were with Murky," Jock said, sitting back in his chair and relaxing a bit. "I never saw that much of Cynthia. As you surely know by now, she was represented by Karla Wojenski."

"But when you did see Cynthia, what was it like?" I asked, supposing it wasn't all cake and ice cream.

"That bitch was hell on wheels. She didn't listen and when she opened her mouth you got a ten-minute monologue. No wonder she never had any speaking parts in the roles she stole from more worthy actresses. I'm sure directors figured she'd improvise and ad lib a reel's worth of non-stop blather."

"You just claimed that she stole roles. How and from whom?"

"How? Are you kidding? Young chicks auditioning for minor roles like the ones she tried out for mostly did their screen tests naked and on their knees. Hell, occasionally even big name young gals had to --." He paused. Then he said, "I'm sure you've heard the rumors about Judy Garland."

"A few."

"Of course, Frances Gumm couldn't act worth a shit. Sing? Eh, maybe. Anyway, Cynthia couldn't act or sing. But she must have given decent head to land as many roles as she tumbled into. Let me tell you something, Fletcher. Plenty of exceptionally qualified actresses left this town and walked back to Kansas solely because they either refused to drop to their knees, or didn't know what to do when they got there."

I had heard the rumors, but had forgotten Judy G's birth certificate read: Frances Ethel Gumm. I also strongly suspected that no lovely young thing who came to Jock Silverado seeking representation ever walked back to Kansas *empty-handed* -- so to speak. I also felt certain that Jacob Hillel Silverstein (aka Jocko Hillman Silverado) tutored many an aspiring young actress in the art of fellatio.

Yet another reason Jocko potentially had for killing Cynthia and for using Cynthia's murder as a warning to Murky lay in the rumor that Murky had been giving thought to changing his agent, dropping Jocko, despite Jocko's many years of devoted service to Murky.

I wanted to confirm or disconfirm that rumor before confronting Jocko with it. Currently I had no idea what reason Murky might have, if he had a reason, for wanting to work with a different agent. In Hollywood relations between some actors and their agents, so the rumors went, were less harmonious than those between actors and their spouses. And money itself was rarely at issue.

Jocko's phone rang and, after answering, he covered the mouthpiece and gestured for me to leave.

"It's been charming, Fletcher. Call me again sometime. But for now ta-ta."

I exited, closing the door loudly, then put my ear to the door to try to eavesdrop.

I heard, "Some jerk detective trying to figure out who killed Murky Murtrans's wife. What do you want?" But then I heard the clack of heels coming from around a corner of the nearby hallway, so I began to walk toward the sounds, pretending to be in a hurry.

The heel-clacker turned out to be a cute young redhead engaged in trying to chew gum and file her nails while walking a straight line. And, by golly, she was achieving a fairly decent job of doing all three as I passed her. I didn't look back until I reached an exit door, by which time she had vanished. I wanted desperately to go back to find out if she was a client of Jocko's, but I didn't.

The hour was too late for me to drive to La Jolla. LAX was nearer. So I headed there, until I realized that, by the time I figured out what plane Wendy Simmons and her girlfriends would be arriving on from Italy, they would be on a shuttle bound for Santa Julietta. .

I placed a phone call to find out when the last shuttle of the evening from LAX landed in SJA, then calculated I could arrive and meet that plane if I drove like the proverbial bat out of hell. So I did, and, while all the other bats from the LA caves were being stopped for speeding, I slipped into a parking space at SJA without being caught for driving "in excess of". Unfortunately, the airplane Wendy and her friends arrived on, had landed an hour and a half earlier, leaving me without anyone to interview.

Consequently, I found myself having dinner by myself in a roadside diner, eating chicken curry and drinking cheap white wine, while deciding my next move. By the time I reached my home, near downtown Santa Maria, I had settled on getting up early in the morning, interviewing Wendy on the lawn of her dorm, then contributing my car to the freeway sclerosis of Highway 101, as I headed south toward San Diego to pay a visit to Betty Sue Murtrans.

The bronze plaque near the front door of Ferguson Hall, the dormitory where Wendy Simmons had been assigned, told readers the dorm was named after Ivy G. Ferguson, a well-heeled donor to UCSJ. Of course, the plaque described Ivy more respectfully than "well-heeled", but that was the gist of the brief narrative. Had I been asked to describe Ivy's key talents, beyond generosity, I also would have hailed her as the patron saint of late sleepers. When I arrived at 7 a.m. not a coed was stirring, not even a Mousekateer.

Long ago, as in when I enrolled as a freshman at Long Beach State University, first classes each day began at the odd time of 7:40 a.m.. That meant I had an almost one-on-one relationship with my French 101 professor, a middle-aged crone as gnarly as the trunks of the five-foot junipers that clung to the cliffs of California's weathered coast. Madame Fornay would have been my private tutor, save for the pair of sophomore coeds whose overeager desire to shout "Viva La France" from the top of the Eiffel Tower, made them fertile buds in Frances Fornay's vineyard of tender white grapes.

Neither of the two young ladies was named Bebe, Fifi, or Gabrielle. But, in any case, we three constituted a petite vineyard, to be sure. But then most vineyards of genuinely French grapes also are small -- unlike most of the vineyards in Santa Julietta County and unlike nearly all classes at UCSJ.

The two coeds had begun to struggle when they realized that French verbs take a different form for both the singular and plural pronouns to which they attach, e.g., that "I suck", you (and only you) suck, "it sucks", "we suck", "you all suck" and "they all suck" each conjugates differently -- or *couples* differently, as Madame Fornay so slyly explained. I must add that even worldly-wise Frances chose the verb "to couple" as her example of the verb that conjugates, Kama Sutra-wise, rather than use "to suck". I daresay, in fact, that she also omitted pointing out that the declarative form of that verb pretty much translates "Go suck!".

Both girls dropped French 101 precisely at the moment when they found out that, additionally in French, adjectives do not always precede the nouns that they modify. Sometimes they do; more often they don't. Sometimes it's a mixed bag, so to speak. To wit: English -- *The big white banana ripens.* French -- *La grosse banana blanche mûrit."*

Years later, when I passed this anecdote along to Murky, he instantly hopped on it, so to speak, and responded quickly, "What she meant was that, in all Latin languages, adjectives take it in the rear from their nouns. At least, by God, that's how I'd teach students to remember that fact, if I were their French, Spanish, or Italian instructor. You got to connect such facts in their minds with real-world facts they're sure not to forget. Right?"

From Santa Julietta I drove to La Jolla in just under four hours, counting stopping for lunch in San Juan Capistrano. La Jolla hugs the north shore of San Diego and is home to the San Diego campus of the University of California. Part of that campus contains the world-famous Scripps Institute of Oceanography and other pieces of the university I knew only by name. As a kid living in San Diego -- or Sandy Eggo, as my classmates often deliberately misspelled it -- I rarely had occasion to venture into that part of town. The area is hilly for one, and for two, La Jolla is a long way from the naval base where my father was an instructor of pilots.

Even so, I had no difficulty finding the Golden Palm Tree Hotel, where Karla Wojenski told me I might find Betty Sue Murtrans. Finding out Betty Sue's room number required some imagination -- in the form of my Yellow Cab driver's hat.

"Cab for Ms. Murtrans," I told the balding man at the reception desk.

"I don't see any cab," he said, craning his neck to look over my shoulder toward the hotel's entry driveway.

"The lady requested we park inconspicuously. She's a move star apparently."

The clerk dialed a room number, but, before he could speak, I reached across the desk and suppressed the button to room 227.

"That's it," I said insultingly. "Go ahead. Broadcast her name so the whole hotel can hear you."

He looked around cautiously, surely taking note that he and I were only the two people within hearing distance. But he relented and removed his finger from the buzzer.

"You're not room service," the woman wearing a short, pink bathrobe and white shower cap said, giving me a pout when she opened the door. "Who are you?" she said, changing her tone to surly as she began to shut the door.

""Hello, Mizz Mutrans. I'm the man who may save you a trip back to Santa Julietta County, where the sheriff will want to talk to you about being a co-conspirator in the murder of Cynthia Murtrans."

She stepped back into the room and I followed her, closing the door behind me.

"It's *Missus* Murtrans, by the way."

"Sorry. That title does not automatically transfer back upon Cynthia's death," I said.

"Oh, yeah? For all you know, Murky and I got remarried yesterday."

"And you're spending your honeymoon here, by yourself, eating room service fare. Right."

"Who are you, anyway?"

I explained her ex-husband's renting my services to find out who killed his fourth wife.

"And you're here because you think I killed that rotten bitch?" she shouted.

I put a forefinger to my lips. "Shh! Your next-door neighbors may be listening."

She took a quick glance at the walls that formed the walls of each adjacent room, before turning her gaze back toward me to see if she could tell if I was serious or joking.

I whispered, "Aren't you familiar with the rule of not speaking ill of the dead?"

"Do I know you? Were you part of the cast of *She Fell to Her Death*?"

"No."

"I co-starred in that film, you know."

"The one who fell to her death?"

"No, no. I played Loretta's sister. The one the detective later found out pushed her out the window."

"So you've had practice."

"Being a co-star? Of course, I have. Many, many times."

"You played Norma Desmond in *Sunset Boulevard*, right? Opposite William Holden."

Betty Sue's face sagged before she said, "No such luck. Mr. Wilder was forced to choose Gloria Swanson over me. To his everlasting regret, I might add."

How can you regret your leading actress's getting an Oscar nomination for the role you put her in, I wondered. And, I recalled reading that, as the film's co-writer and director, Billy Wilder had first approached Mae West, Greto Garbo, and Mary Pickford to play the role of Norma Desmond, an elderly, washed-up, delusional actress who was incorrectly imagining she was about to make a comeback.

"Who sent you? How did you know where to find me?"

She stepped closer, whether to see if I would flinch or whether I would step toward her, I couldn't tell.

"Jocko sent me."

Her eyes brightened.

"What role is it? Who's directing?"

"I've already explained that. The role is: Who killed Cynthia Murtrans? The director is Samuel B. Cuddleston."

"You shit! Jocko didn't send you. What are you? A plainclothes cop?"

"Yeah. A plainclothes detective. What a sharp observer you are," I said, carefully avoiding saying I was a cop.

"Well, let me assure you. I didn't kill Cynthia." She looked toward the bedside table where a half-empty bottle of whiskey and a pair of tumblers resided. Room 227 was a suite and I took a quick glance toward the bedroom door.

"He's long gone," she said.

"Who is?"

"The guy you're wondering about. I think his name was Juan Pablo." She paused and giggled. "Probably still is, eh?"

I immediately thought of the movie that came out two years previously, *The Night of the Iguana,* the film built from Tennessee William's play by that name and starring Richard Burton, Eva Gardner, and Deborah Kerr. This Betty Sue was no Deborah Kerr, but that didn't mean that, like the woman Ava Gardner played, Betty Sue Murtrans couldn't enjoy the company of a Latino gigolo or two.

"So who do you think killed your successor?" I asked, as I made myself comfortable on her unmade bed.

"Coulda been anybody at Murky's party. Anybody at that gathering would have preferred to part her head with a hard blow to parting her pussy with a hard cock. A real cock or otherwise, you understand. Plenty of women wanted that creature dead."

"Who, for example? Besides you."

"Sandy Onigrin, for one."

"The publishing heiress?"

Sandra Lynn Onigren (nee Winthrop) headed up a tabloid empire that included four grocery-checkout-stand gossip publications specializing in innuendo, lies, and fantasies regarding who in Hollywood was cheating on whom.

"Why Sandy?"

Debbie generated a camera-ready smirk.

"It's not what you think, my plainclothes friend. She wants to buy Murky's ranch, but Cynthia told her the ranch will never end up with her name on the deed."

"Why not?"

"An ancient feud, going back to the dinosaurs. First, Cynthia resented the fact that, before Cynthia married Murky, Sandy generated too few stories about women chasing Murky. With lots of stories circulating that dozens of gorgeous young bimbos were in hot pursuit of her potential husband, Cynthia looked that much better for her being the one who landed The Murk. Instead, Sandy waited until after the marriage to spin those tales, thereby making her, Cynthia, look like maybe she was a bum fuck or something even worse."

"I see."

"Do you really, Mister Plainclothes Cop?"

"Did Murky know about any of that?"

"Of course, he did. And comedian extraordinaire that he is, he laughed his head off. Awarded Sandy a jillion style points."

"Was Murky willing to sell his ranch to Sandy?"

"Ask Murky."

"I will."

She laughed. "Don't trust the answer he gives you. You should know by now how close to his vest he plays his cards."

Until there is a full glass of bourbon between that vest and his five aces, I thought. And, on the subject of bourbon, Betty Sue just then took a long, lascivious stare at her half-empty bottle, although, I'm sure, her thought of the moment was that it was still half full.

"Care to join me in a drink?" she said. "Sorry, but the room only provides two glasses. I suppose you could drink from mine, but, I assure you, Juan Pablo doesn't have malaria, cholera, or any other tropical diseases."

"How do I know you don't?" I said.

She took my right hand and pressed it against her forehead, then forced it down onto her chest.

"The only tropical fever I have is the one Elvis sings about. The one about Captain Kidd and Pochahontas"

I decided to let her "Captain Kidd" error slide.

"Why don't you save your ardor for Juan Pablo when he returns?" I said.

"You're no fun."

What could I say to that accusation? Nothing convincing, short of .... Well, sometimes words fail, even from such a gifted poet as I credit myself with being. And I was in no mood to prove -- speechlessly -- that was indeed capable of "fun".

VIII

Avenida De Libre is an unregulated swarm of student apartments that had been aggressively developed by builders eager to take advantage of a demand for housing by students eager to get away from dormitory living, a life burdened with university curfews and sundry other bureaucratic restrictions. Because the area lacked zoning, developers did their best to cram as many living units as possible into less than two square miles. That left little room for parking spaces. What each apartment building lacked in parking spaces for its tenants, it made up for with a giant swimming pool in a central courtyard.

I was here because I had been told belatedly that, after her rape incident, Wendy and her best friend, Roxanna Galboni, had moved temporarily from their dormitory into a two-bedroom apartment in a sprawling complex named Ocean Views Deluxe. Roxana's parents were picking up the tab.

The pool gracing Wendy Simmon's apartment complex shimmered in the morning sun. No swimmers yet. I charitably assumed all the apartment dwellers had already decamped for classes on the nearby UCSJ campus, though a better explanation for the courtyard's quiet was that most of the building's occupants were still in bed.

I had called the previous evening and made an appointment to talk with Wendy. Amanda had relented and provided me with her class schedule, which showed that on this day she had no classes until after lunch.

On the phone she had made clear she would only talk to me with her roommate present, and that my interview with her must be conducted outdoors, in this case next to the pool, which suited me just fine. Wendy had added that she was agreeing to meet me only because her attorneys insisted she cooperate with Amanda Reynolds. Her annoyance undisguised, she told me her lawyers said that directive included Amanda's designated minions.

Minions? And she was only a first-quarter freshman.

She didn't come from an upper class background either. *Minion* is a word the privileged class knows well and teach to their children at an early age. But Wendy's background placed her in the middle of the middle class. Her father was a tax accountant for Los Angeles County Public Works and her mother was a surgical nurse at the Shriners' Hospital of Los Angeles. Wendy's parents and her two younger sisters, Hannah and Louise, lived in a modest house near Veterans' Park in Culver City, a few miles north of LA International Airport.

Wendy introduced her roommate as Roxanna Galboni, a long-time friend, schoolmate, and neighbor from Culver City. Wendy said Roxanna's parents had just moved to Santa Julietta to be near their daughter. Roxanna was a freckle-faced redhead who wore eyeglasses with dark red frames, lipstick a shade or two lighter than the frames, and ruby-red earrings. None of the reds -- hair, frames, lipstick, earrings -- went well with the other three, but her winning smile more than offset her weakness in facial artistry. She looked as huggable as a child's doll.

Wendy stood three or four inches taller than Roxanna and wore her blonde hair in a ponytail. No lipstick, no earrings, no glasses. Her blue eyes lacked the coldness that many pairs of blue eyes exude. Instead, her eyes, coupled with her toothy smile, gave off a friendly warmth I quickly decided I had misread.

"Daddy's lawyers told me I must cooperate with you. However, he insisted I should meet with you only in his presence and only in his office. I assured him that would not be necessary. But, as you see, I've asked Roxanna to bear witness to what is said."

"In no way do I wish to make you uncomfortable, Miss Simmons."

What I mistook for a toothy smile was, instead, a well-contained, civilized snarl.

"Your very existence makes me uncomfortable, Mr. Fletcher."

Hyperbole masquerading as understatement. And she was only seventeen years old.

I began with, "How well did you know Richard Claymore prior to the night you've accused him of raping you?"

Fully composed, she answered, "I first met him an hour before you know what."

"Tell me what happened during that hour."

"He had four drinks and wouldn't leave me alone."

"What were the four drinks?"

"Wine."

"How many drinks did you have during that hour?"

"One."

"How many before that hour?"

"None."

"What was your drink?"

"Same as his. Red wine."

"Did he get it for you?"

"Yes."

"What did the two of you talk about during that hour?"

"I don't remember."

"Try."

Roxanna said, ""What can that possibly matter?"

I turned to her. "Please, stay out of this. You're here strictly as an observer."

She snorted and bit her lip.

Wendy said, "Okay. I'll ask. What possible difference does it make what we talked about?"

"Trust me. It matters," I said, as evenly as I could.

"We never talked about sex, if that is what you're trying to get me to admit."

"I'm not," I said and waited.

"I suppose we had the same inane conversation everyone else was having. What's your major going to be? What non-major courses interest you? What dorm are you in? School stuff."

Inane. Another over-the-top word for a young woman just starting college. Her better- than-average vocabulary warned me not to under-estimate her.

"Until he raped you, were you comfortable with Richard?"

"Not especially."

"Yet you spent a full hour sharing yourself with him socially," I said.

"Sharing myself?" She came out of her seat. "That's a misleading way of describing what went on."

"Okay. In your own words."

"That monster spent almost the entire hour doing all the talking and all he talked about was himself."

"What did he say about himself?" I asked.

Glaring at me, she raised her voice. "All he talked about was himself and about how rich and grand his family was."

"Make you feel envious?"

"Made me want to puke."

"And yet, you spent a whole hour listening to him."

"He wouldn't leave me alone," she shouted.

"There was no escaping him?"

"The place was crowded. Packed with people."

"I would think that would make it easier to ditch him, if he was annoying to you."

"I tried. Believe me. I tried to get away."

"If the party was crowded, how did he manage to get you alone? Especially if you were trying to get away from him?"

"I don't remember.. Damn you! I don't remember."

Roxanna stood up.

"That's enough, Mr. Fletcher. Can't you see how much your badgering has upset her?

Wendy, let's go."

Wendy gave her roommate a pouty nod. Roxanna helped her stand and the two of them turned and walked away, leaving me to stare into the swimming pool.

IX

I caught up with Holly Sanderford just as she was exiting her room in Lourdain Hall.

When I introduced myself, she said, "I just got off the phone with Wendy. I know all about you."

"Then you know why I am here."

"I don't want to talk with you. Go away."

Holly was short, but wore her black hair long, making her appear taller than she was. Her eyes were the color of amber and went well with her bronze skin.

I said, "You don't have to talk with me now, but in that case we'll have you deposed."

She laughed.

"Deposed? I'm not the queen of anything."

I explained, "Deposed in the sense of having an attorney question you under oath. Your answers are written down by a court recorder and, when it's all over, you have to sign your name, a testament that you told only the truth."

"Okay. Let's talk, Mr. Private Investigator. But not in my room."

"Of course not. Let's walk to the Union Building and I'll buy you coffee."

"Coffee is bad for you. You may buy me a Dr. Pepper."

"Okay."

Seated in the Union with a bottle of Dr. P in her hand, Holly said, "Does it make you feel young again to be sitting with a hot eighteen-year-old?"

Young again?

"No. I still feel my age."

"Droopy, are you?' she said, smirking.

I refused to bite on that remark. Instead, I started my planned line of questions.

"Was the party in question your first party at UCSJ?"

Playing drama queen, she cocked her head and stared up at the ceiling for a moment, allowing me to suppose my question either misplaced or rude. Then looked at me.

"By 'the party' I assume you refer to the one where Wendy was raped by that monstrous creature."

"Yes. Allegedly raped."

"Yes. It was my first party on campus. I believe it was the first party for all of us girls."

"By 'all of us' to whom do you refer?" I said.

"Oh, listen to the man. *To whom.* An educated detective."

I repeated, "All of us."

"Let's see. There was Wendy, Poppy, Heather, Marcella, Portia, and me. Or is it 'Portia and I'?"

"You forgot Roxanna," I said.

Holly scowled. "Did not. Roxy wasn't invited."

"Why not?"

I got a look suggesting I was foolish.

"Why not? Because Roxy simply doesn't cut it. You've met her. If you were her age, is she the kind of girl you would want to --."

"Want to what?" I said.

"Hold hands with?" And broad smirk.

"Is that what you thought you were attending? A hand-holding party?"

"Of course, that's what we thought. Poor, naive us."

I quickly abandoned my prepared line and picked up on *naive*.

"Tell me. What was it that proved you all naive?"

"Oh, my! Shouldn't it be obvious by now? We had landed in a den of savages. Brutal, wicked beasts."

"All of them brutal?"

"Why, yes. As it turned out," she said. "Nothing but hungry animals."

"So did you help feed them."

"They required no help, Mr. Detective. They know how to eat." She giggled, then added, "Without utensils even."

"But only Wendy got raped, right?"

"You are indeed correct, my poor man," she said, stretching out her words and giving me a look of mock-pity.

"How far do you and Wendy go back?"

"Second grade. Mrs. Palmer's room. Alhambra Elementary. My family had just moved to California from New Jersey."

Holly had no trace of an East Coast accent left. She was an all-California girl now.

"How much time did *you* spend holding hands with Richard Claymore?"

She scowled and made a little shuddering motion with her shoulders.

"Please! He's not my type."

"By which you mean --?"

"He wants too much too fast."

"How did you find this out?" I said.

"A little birdie warned me about Ritchie C."

"Does your little birdie have a name?" I asked.

"Her name is ---. No! I'll call her Jasmine."

"Okay. And this Jasmine assured you Richard is someone capable of rape?"

"Oh, she assured me, all right."

"Did you share this insight with Wendy? With your other girlfriends?"

Holly bit her lip.

"Well?"

"I don't remember. Maybe did."

"And maybe you didn't?"

"I just told you. I don't remember."

Then I hit her with, "Did you have sex with anyone at the party that night?"

She exploded, as I expected she might.

"None of your fucking business, Mister. Jeezus!"

"That's okay. If you won't tell me, then under oath you can tell a courtroom full of strangers."

She tried to mask her senses of horror and revulsion, but they showed anyway.

"I didn't screw anybody that night," she finally said, making it sound as though it were a point of pride.

"Oral maybe?" I asked.

I took her silence to be a confession.

"Look, Miss Sanderford. If there is a trial -- and unless you, Wendy, and the rest of her friends who just returned from Italy come clean, there is certain to be one -- your entire lives, including your entire sex lives, will be front-page news for weeks in every newspaper in southern California."

A shrug from Holly, but behind it I detected terror.

I went on. "And don't think you young ladies can get together to fabricate a joint history of innocence, because Richard Claymore's attorneys will shred your concoction into itsy bitsy shards and do it in ways that will leave your mothers in tears."

For that I got an angry, defiant look.

"Okay. You've been given fair warning. What I've just said is not a threat, just a clear-eyed explanation of what is going to happen," I said, draining my coffee cup and standing up.

Holly stared off into the distance, likely picturing herself in a courtroom witness box. I left her in that mode and assumed she would quickly inform her girlfriends, including Wendy, of her tête-à-tête with me. Accordingly, I saw no immediate need to interview the other Italian-trip girls.

Wendy's attorneys would later remind the girls that the law protected loose girls, naughty girls, even wildly loose and naughty girls from allowing men to rape them. On the other hand, we all knew that juries are less inclined to believe women with casual morals when they claim they were raped. My job was to see if the mantel of *loose woman* fit Wendy Simmons.

The sign in Gothic print on the 4'x8' sheet of plywood read: *COMING SOON – a resurrected version of the Church of the Holy Redeemer Resurrection.* Behind the sign lay two acres of knee-high grass, heavily mixed with an assortment of thistles and other thorny weeds.

The pre-resurrected version of CJ Browning's church lay a mile and a half down Wentworth Road, behind a grove of peeling eucalyptus trees. The building looked more like an abandoned barn than a holy temple. Maybe because that was what it had been. The family dwelling to which the barn once belonged had, I was told, been lifted from its foundation and hauled into San Luis Obispo, where it now served as a storage annex for the county library.

With the help of many church volunteers, the weathered barn's broken timbers had been replaced and two coats of white paint had been hastily and sloppily applied, giving the barn a look suggesting it held its shape solely by the grace of prayer -- and maybe a bit of duct tape and bailing wire. The Jesus worshipped there was a redeemer of humble beginnings, not the Jesus of European oligarchs, whose well-financed cathedrals reached to the heavens. Even the steeple atop the barn was modest, a short, plastic affair delivered from a mail-order house in St. Louis, sold to the congregation by a fast-talking peddler who had dotted rural Americana with similar steeples, buyers granted a choice of short, medium, or tall ones.

The buyer of the steeple for CJ Browning's Church of the Holy Redeemer was Peggy Ann Lorgran, who told CJ a tall steeple cost more than she was willing to pay, particularly given that she was not even a believer, let alone a church member. Murky joked that Peggy Ann only bought a short steeple to shut CJ's wife up.

I introduced myself to one of the volunteers and asked for CJ Browning.

"Sorry, sir. Reverend Browning has gone into town to buy candles, putty, and glue at the hardware store. I'm his wife, Genesis. May I help you?"

"Not unless you were at Mr. Murtrans's retirement party, where Murky's wife was murdered."

"Oh, dear. Wasn't that just awful? So tragic! Not to mention untimely. Did you know that Mrs. Murtrans was going to be our church's biggest benefactor?"

I said I didn't know that.

"Oh, yes. She had pledged a quarter of a million dollars toward the birth of our new church."

Interesting.

"And what did Mr. Murtrans think about that?"

The look Mrs. Browning gave me told me all I needed to know about Murky's estimation of that idea.

"But Cynthia assured CJ and me that her husband would not attempt to interfere in any way with her generous pledge," Genesis Browning said.

I bet otherwise. In fact, I had no doubt that Murky spit fire and brimstone on the notion. Whether he murdered his wife in order to stop her was a matter I needed to look into. I'm sure Sam Cuddleston was delving in that direction. *Delving.* I thought about that word and pictured an underground coal-mining machine, it's giant screw boring into a vein of shiny black rock.

"May I make you a cup of ginger tea, Mr. Fletcher? Our church creed opposes caffeinated drink. So I'm afraid I'm unable to offer you coffee."

"Not even acorn coffee?" I said.

She looked embarrassed and I apologized.

"I was only joking. I'm fine."

"I know a bit about acorn coffee, Mr. Fletcher, and it's too expensive on our tight church budget."

"Maybe when you get your generous contribution from Cynthia Murtrans you can afford to keep some on hand."

I regretted the remark the instant it emerged from my mouth.

"Perhaps, but I doubt it. CJ has other expenditures in mind."

Her comment was followed by a downcast look. I suspected she had very little to say in how church money was allocated.

I said, "I understand that your husband was at Murky's retirement party, but I've yet to here any mention of whether you were present."

She gave me an enigmatic smile.

"Yes, I was there, but I left early. I had other pressing matters, as in migraine-level pain pressing against my temples. Mr. Murtrans understood my leaving and forgave me. He is well aware of my affliction."

"You know Murky then, I take it."

"Oh, indeed I do. He is a foul-mouthed heathen, and much too fond of drink and --."

"And?"

"And all the sins of the flesh."

"All, you say?"

Her eyes shifted away.

"I have not known him in the sense you imply, sir."

"What sense is that? I simply cared to know if you were acquainted with him?"

"Yes, but not biblically. I swear I'm not."

"No need to take any oaths, ma'am. I'm not accusing you of anything."

"Oh, I think you are. I confess that Mr. Murtrans possesses strange and wicked powers over women. But I have not succumbed to his entreaties."

Succumbed to his entreaties? Pulpit-babble.

"Okay. You went home with a severe headache. Right?"

A nod.

"When was the last time you saw Cynthia Murtrans, Mrs. Browning?"

She thought for a couple moments before saying, "I assume you mean besides at the party. It was the morning of the day before the party. She came here to discuss the details of her donation, because both our church planning committee and the city of San Luis Obispo's

Community Development Department were eager to move forward with plans for our new church."

"Were there any issues or problems?" I said.

"No. It was all pretty routine. Cynthia was pleased with CJ's vision and mostly came here to tell him she would be glad to speak to city officials, explaining her financial backing of our new church plans."

"Mostly. What else did she come here for?"

"To assure us that her husband had agreed not to interfere with what she was doing for us."

"Back to the party itself. When did you last see her there?"

"When she slapped Murky's previous wife. I was just on my way out the door when that happened."

"And you went straight to your car and drove home?"

"I did."

"Anybody see you leave? By that I mean outside the house?"

""Yes. I believe I saw Mrs. Murtrans' sister, Nancy, standing over by a tree talking to someone and smoking a cigarette."

"Who was the other someone?"

"I couldn't see."

"Was that person smoking?"

"Not that I could tell, but then I only gave them a quick glance. It was dark and I didn't want to stumble."

"Mrs. Browning, how would you describe the relationship between your husband and his father?"

That she was unable to suppress a grimace did not surprise me. Murky himself had admitted that he and his son had not been on the best of terms for many years and that he was certain a large part of Cynthia's development of a coziness with CJ stemmed from her realization that it gave her leverage on Murky, playing on Murky's never assuaged guilt over the way he treated CJ's mother, Ethel, before she died, and the life-long neglect he demonstrated toward CJ afterward.

"The Bible is full of verses explaining a father's responsibilities toward his children. Murky Murtrans has conformed to none of those exhortations. My husband has suffered greatly from fatherly neglect and has tried mightily to rise above it. But years upon years of either scorn or silence has driven CJ beyond the limits any child could bear. And in adulthood CJ has tried not to become mean-spirited toward Murky, tried to view his father as a sinner in dire need of forgiveness."

"The result of which has been?" I asked.

"My husband has practiced what he preaches. He has forgiven Murky. As have I."

I wondered.

"Do you have a favorite candidate for being Cynthia's murderer?" I said.

She did not have to pray or meditate on the subject.

"Mr. Murtrans himself."

"Why so?"

"Because I'm convinced he came to believe his marriage to Cynthia was a mistake."

"Why not simply divorce her then?"

"Too expensive. Have you forgotten that California is a community property state?"

I hadn't. But I assumed Murky could hire better lawyers, lawyers who were better at hiding his assets than lawyers Cynthia could hire would be at finding them. Still, I had to confess that Cynthia was loose with money, spending freely both on herself and on others. Too freely, in Murky's mind.

X

I waited another half hour for CJ Browning, but he failed to materialize. Meanwhile, Mrs. Browning failed in her efforts to convince me Murky thought his marrying Cynthia was a mistake. She knew Murky less well than I did and knew Cynthia scarcely at all. Her mistaken estimate was based entirely on conjecture, though I failed to tell her so. Maybe I should have, but didn't think doing so was worth the bother. Genesis Browning would remain fixated in her uncorroborated beliefs, be they beliefs about the nature of God or beliefs about the nature of Murky Murtrans.

I drove into San Luis Obispo, hoping to find CJ still at the hardware store, but was told by the counter clerk he had left ten minutes before I arrived. She said she knew who CJ was because she was a member of his congregation. Mrs. Browning had told me CJ drove a 1955 black Ford pickup. so I had watched for such a vehicle on my way into town. None had passed me going the other way. So I assumed CJ had other errands to run. The possibility was more charitable than thinking Genesis Browning had lied to me.

My drive home from San Luis to Santa Maria was interrupted by my spotting a car tailing me and it wasn't CJ Browning. The beige Chevy Impala was nearly indistinguishable from sand on the local beaches and was perhaps meant to be. An unmarked police car maybe? One of Sam Cuddleston's uniformed goons? I had a particular deputy in mind.

I exited east toward Nipomo and headed to one of my favorite haunts, Jocko's. No connection with Murky's agent, Jocko Siverado. Jocko's in Nipomo is a bar and grill, best known for having the best Santa Maria-style barbecue, sirloin tip grilled both in and over a coastal red oak fire, no sauce, just a dry rub of salt, pepper, and garlic -- with sides of pinquito beans and garlic bread.

I parked in Jocko's lot and grabbed my camera. As the beige Chevrolet passed by, I snapped a photo, then wrote down the license plate. The car continued on, but I watched as it turned around and parked a block away.

Inside Jocko's I bought a handful of quarters from the bartender, then used the public phone to dial up Sandra Waters, a friend at the California Department of Motor Vehicles in Sacramento. She answered on the first ring.

"How urgent is this one, Love?"

I said, "Yesterday will do."

"You know the going price of yesterdays," she said.

"A bottle of Louis Latour Chardonnay, 1965," I said.

"Two bottles, Dearie. The price has doubled since Ronnie the Ray Gun became governor last year."

"Has it been that long since I hit you up for a number?"

"Yes. And in the meantime I've had to pay for my top-drawer bottles."

"You keep your wine in drawers?" I asked.

"Hardly, Dear. You know I don't." Just then a man came through the front door and began looking around. "Call me back at this number." I read off the bartender's under-the-bar number, one he shared with me some months earlier, when he was pressured to do so by Amanda Reynolds, who apparently threatened to expose some indiscretion or other of his if he failed to do so.

"Before you hang up, you'd better give me the license number you want, Fletcher."

"Oh, right." And I read her the numbers from the Chevy's plate.

The man at the front door was not wearing a sheriff's uniform and I didn't recognize him, but I felt certain he was the driver of the beige Chevy that had been tailing me. He appeared to be in his mid-thirties and although his clothes were casual they were also expensive-looking. His black leather jacket was more befitting a motorcycle jockey -- riding a very pricey motorcycle. And, when he turned away from me, toward the bar, there was no Hell's Angels emblem on the back.

At the bar he sat and asked the bartender something that elicited a definitively negative headshake. And then a second one. Then the man spun on his barstool and scanned the room, making me edge back further into the shadows next to the public phone.

His face was clean-shaven and his black hair cut short. I concentrated, trying to remember if I had seen him before, finally deciding I hadn't. When he left I hoped he noticed my car was gone. As I came in, I had slipped the keys and a twenty-dollar bill to a young woman named Kelly Lee and asked her to drive my car around for ten minutes, away from Jocko's, then park it in the grocery store lot two blocks further away from the freeway than Jocko's.

The man in black headed toward me, so I ducked into the women's powder room, startling a pair of ladies, both middle-aged red-heads, looking intently into the broad mirror and fine-tuning their lipstick. I put an index finger to my lips and gestured toward the door with the thumb of my other hand. They both grinned and nodded before returning to their facial upgrades.

The ladies finally left and then outside the bathroom door I heard one of them say, "Are you looking for someone?"

I pulled my .38 from the back of my waistband when I heard a male voice say, "Did you see a man come this way?" He then accurately described me, right down to the color of my socks.

The lady replied, "Why, yes. I'm sure he was the one I saw go out the back door. He seemed in a hurry. Are you a policeman?"

I didn't hear him answer, but did hear a door slam shut. Then the taller of the two redheads opened the bathroom door, stuck her head in, and said, "Your man in black went out the back door and headed toward the front of the building. Are you in some kind of trouble?"

"Not that I know of, but that man has been following me since I left San Luis."

"Well, good luck losing him."

"Thanks."

I had wanted to wait another five minutes, but a tipsy blonde came into the women's room, saw me, and scowled mightily.

"Sorry. I took a wrong turn," I said.

"Probably the story of your life, Mister."

Perhaps she wasn't as drunk as I supposed she was.

I waited near the phone for five minutes before approaching the bartender, a cheerful, graying man by the name of Hugh.

"Do you know that man who was asking about me?" I said.

"I know who he is. I can't say that I know him. His name is Giovanni Alba and goes by Gio. He works for Richard Claymore. The old man, that is. El Condor himself. What he does for the Condor I don't know. Some sort of flunky."

"Thanks," I said and I slipped Hugh a twenty. "Mind if I use your back door?"

"Just close it behind you, so as not to piss off the health inspector."

I nodded and left. Peering into the parking lot I saw Kelly Lee walking back toward Jocko's. When she neared the front door, I stepped into view and said, "Thanks, Kelly. I appreciate your help." I walked over and handed her an additional ten spot. "You look thirsty."

"Gonna join me?"" she said as she took my money.

"Not this time. I need to find out if I really lost that guy."

"I saw him driving out of town as I reached Thompson Avenue."

As I walked to my car I mulled over and over again why Richard Claymore the First would have me followed. I was on his side, working for his grandson's interest. Or was I?

XI

Shifting my attention back to who killed Cynthia Murtrans, I headed toward Murky's ranch, stopping home in Santa Maria just long enough to check my mail. Two utility bills and three fliers, one for a half-priced pizza, one for ten percent off on a transmission overhaul, and one urging me to subscribe to a set of ten magazines for the price of five. Mail only the US Postal Service could love -- as revenue generators. I tried to calculate how many bulk-mail half-cent postage stamps it took to pay my postman's annual salary, but the effort gave me a headache. I stopped for gas and bought a bottle of RC Cola to help line my stomach before Murky handed me a tumbler of whisky without any ice.

Seeing CJ's truck parked in front of Murky's house surprised me. I could hear Murky's doorbell ringing when I pressed the buzzer, but no one answered the door. So I walked to the back of the house, where loud voices from inside greeted me clearly, but I couldn't see anyone through the rear house windows. So I let myself in through the back door, then stood in the back hallway and listened to the hostilities.

"Cynthia was the best wife you ever had, Old Man," CJ said.

"Better than your mother?" Murky replied.

"I really don't know because I hardly got to know her before she died. And afterwards the only version I ever heard was from you, and that consisted of a laundry list of her faults and little else."

"I regret ever marrying that woman. And sometimes I think your very existence is the best argument in favor of abortion that I can think of," Murky said.

"Your generosity toward me is boundless. Thank you so much."

Murky sneered. "Generosity? That's all you soulless preachers think of, how you measure people's characters. By how much money they're willing to pour into your collection plates. That's what Cynthia was to you. A slot machine whose arm you pulled after feeding her nickel after nickel of false flattery and phony charm.

"Well, I'm not going to honor her pledge to you to help build a new barn to the glory of that holy huckster who so loved the world that anyone could dwell forever in his golden paradise, could buy an acre lot in heaven, for the right price. Why, a sinner can even buy forgiveness on an installment plan, checks made payable to the preacher man whose barn he sits in weekly to sing psalms and pay homage to the huckster man -- in both words and cash."

CJ's comeback was, "California is a community property state, you old fool. You may be a Scrooge McDuck, but half of that golden stash of yours belongs to her. And she promised me a quarter of a million dollars. I have that in writing and I'll take you to court over it. I swear I will."

"Toilet paper, Boy. That's what her pledge is now. With her dead, that pledge means nothing. It's now worth nothing. Zip, zero, nada, CJ."

"We'll see about that."

I could hear Murky pouring himself another drink. Then he added, "You're forgetting a codicil to my late wife's pledge, aren't you, Son. You haven't fulfilled that part of the legal framework to your getting any money from Cynthia, have you?"

Silence from CJ.

"Well, Boy? Have you divorced that pathetic creature of a wife you're leashed to? Have you taken her to court yet? Of course, not. Cynthia knew you couldn't cut the rope, meaning she knew that money was forever safe from falling into your hands. And that devil woman's."

In a soft voice CJ said, "Cynthia cancelled that demand, Pop. She decided to give me the quarter of a million without my having to get a divorce."

"Bullshit! Where's the paper that says that?"

"She was simply going to tear up the codicil. I swear she was. I have witnesses even."

"Witnesses? Who? That greedy wife of yours? She'd say anything to get her hands on that money."

"Other members of the church as well."

"All with a prejudice, a vested interest. Liars all. My lawyers will carve their words, souls, and characters up into tiny shards, expose them for the venal charlatans they are. Devout Christians they call themselves. My attorneys will reduce you all to blubbering little shits, have you all down on your knees confessing to being heartless swindlers, hustling in the name of a holy fraud."

"We have God on our side, you rotten heathen, you immoral bag of wind."

"If that's your best shot at me, get your sorry ass out of here," Murky shouted.

Seconds later I heard a door slam. No doubt CJ would be puzzled to see another car in the driveway, but I wasn't even sure he could connect the dots and recognize the car as mine. I made throat-clearing noises and presented myself to Murky.

"You hear any or all of that, Fletcher?"

I nodded.

"Anything I miss?" I asked.

"What was the first you heard?"

"CJ was telling you Cynthia was the best wife you ever had."

"Well, the ostensible reason my kid showed up was to see if he might be allowed to be the one to officiate at Cynthia's funeral."

"Will there be a funeral?" I said.

"Hell, no. No funeral, no memorial service, and certainly no damned celebration of life. None of that crap."

I said, "I've heard Cynthia promised CJ a sizeable chunk of money toward building his new church."

"She did. But I'm canceling that. Let him sue. He's not gonna get one red cent from me, even if he goes ahead and divorces that holy-roller hag he's tied to."

"When did you find out about Cynthia's pledge?" I said.

Murky poured me two fingers of Jim Beam without my having to ask. He handed me the tumbler and said, "The day before my retirement party."

Also the day before Cynthia's murder.

"Who told you?" I said.

He gave me a strange look before saying, "Cynthia's sister, Nancy, told me. Nancy came to me saying she knew Cynthia didn't intend to tell me and also knew I'd be pissed as hell when I did find out. So Nancy said she thought it best to tell me, rather than have me overhear the news accidentally. That way, she said, she could talk it over with me and be a lightning rod for the rage she knew I'd feel."

"Is that the way it worked out?"

"Not exactly."

"Meaning?"

"I went into a rage and stormed off."

"What happened next?" I said.

"Damned good thing Cynthia wasn't home. Or I'd have --."

"Have what?"

"Nothing."

"What did you do, Murky?"

"I drove into Nipomo and took my anger out on billiard balls for three hours."

"You have a billiard table here," I reminded him.

"Yeah, but it's harder to get drunk swillin' three hours' worth of cheap beer than it is downing three bottles of expensive whiskey."

"When did you finally confront your wife?"

"That's just it. I never did. Instead, the morning of my party I drove into Santa Julietta and put a preemptive stop-payment on any large check Cynthia tried to write to CJ or to his church committee."

"And when you returned home on the day of your party you didn't confront Cynthia about her pledge to CJ?"

"Nope. I wanted to see her face when she found out the bank wouldn't cash her damned check. Wanted to laugh at her when *she* confronted *me*."

"And did she find out about what you did that day?" I said.

Murky shook his head.

I said, "Did anyone else find out? Did you tell Nancy maybe?"

"Nancy's the last person I'd tell. She'd go blabbing to Cynthia so fast the house would shake from the whirlwind. I wanted Cynthia to write the check and hand it to CJ, who would then try to deposit it in his church's account. Kaboom! The bank would tell CJ the check was no good and the sparks would begin to fly."

"What about Cynthia's requirement that CJ divorce Genesis?" I said.

"What about it?"

"That could take months."

Murky laughed.

He said, "All CJ would have to do initially is to jump over a stick three times and shout 'Genesis, I divorce three' three times -- while he was jumpin'. As soon as he did that I'm sure Cynthia would reach for her check book."

"What are the chances Nancy told Cynthia that she had spoken with you?"

"Ask Nancy. Better yet ask Peggy Ann, because Nancy will as likely lie to you as tell you what she really did. Nancy may be our in-house spy, but her daughter does a damned good job of spying on the spy."

"Is Peggy Ann trustworthy? Will she tell me the truth?" I asked.

"Dunno. Sometimes she lies just to cause a commotion. Peggy Ann has learned to stir pots by watching her mother."

"But you're fond of her, right? Would she tell me the truth if you asked her to?" I said.

"I may be fond of her, but she lies to me, too. And sticks to her lies through thick and thin."

Murky poured himself another drink.

"Come with me, Fletcher."

He led me to an alcove off a short, dead-end hallway, spilling a bit of his drink along the way. Once there, he showed me a hidden spy hole about the size of an index card. The hole was masked by a piece of wood paneling that matched the surround wall.

"Go ahead. Take a good look," he said.

Peering through his peephole, I looked into his private office and immediately wondered why he would have any need to spy on himself. But then I realized he might, on occasion, allow others to use the office. Finally, I turned and gave Murky a puzzled look.

He answered my bafflement by saying, "The night of my party I went looking for Jocko and couldn't find him. Walked from one end of the house to the other, checked outside. Couldn't find him. Exasperated, I decided to check out my office, figuring maybe he had so hot a deal going that couldn't wait and was on the phone to Hollywood."

Murky drained his glass.

"The door to my office was locked, which is the way I always leave it. But there are a couple other people besides me who know where I hide the key."

He rattled the ice in his glass, rattled it hard.

"Anyway, I came here and checked my peephole. Well, it turned out that good ol' Jocko had a hot deal going all right and it clearly couldn't wait. There was Jocko, sittin' in my chair and on her knees in front of him, naked as a jaybird, was Peggy Ann, givin' him a blowjob."

By now Murky was rattling the ice so hard that he spilled the cubes on the floor.

XII

I left Murky to drink more bourbon alone. I went to find Nancy to see what her stories were. If any of what I had heard so far since arriving at the ranch again was true -- and I had my doubts about some of it -- I would have plausible reasons to suspect both Murky and Genesis Browning of killing Cynthia.

Then, as I headed for the guest cottage where Nancy was staying, I heard a commotion out in front of Murky's sprawling main house. A woman's screeching and cursing in Spanish dominated the hubbub. When I reached the parking area I saw two sheriff's deputies wrestling with a man and a woman.

One deputy pinned the man to the ground, although barely. The man kicked wildly and flailed his arms. His nose bled, with blood oozing down onto his thick gray mustache. The other deputy stood behind a short, dark-haired woman, his arms wrapped around her, pinning her arms to her sides as she spat loud, abusive, colorful epithets. My limited gringo Spanish led me to understand she said, "Let me go or I will turn your children into goats that will chew your grandchildren's heads off." Or something close to that.

When the woman saw me she lowered her voice and directed her anger toward me, while simultaneously beseeching me -- in English -- to help her.

"Please, Señor, to fetch Master Murky to help my husband and myself escape these sons of the devil. And if you don't, I will call up the ghosts of the dead to twist your bones into the shapes of ...."

Before she finished her curse, the deputy wrestled her to the ground. Then, from behind me, I heard Murky's voice.

"Juanita! What the hell are you and Alberto doing here? Damn it! I warned you two not to come back to my ranch. Ever!"

The deputy let the woman get off the ground, though he continued to hold her by one wrist. The woman wrenched her wrist free and said to Murky, "I come back for the rest of my belongings. These men, the policemen, do not let me take what is mine."

"And take a whole lot more as well," Murky said.

"Only what is mine, Señor Murky. Have you not trusted Alberto and me for all these many years we have worked for you?"

"A trust I now know was misplaced, eh? You and your husband stole us blind."

"That is a lie!" Juanita said. "We never once steal from you."

"Not according to Cynthia," Murky said. "A new pair of small diamond earrings vanished right after you cleaned her room last week. That's why she fired you, you ungrateful bitch. Petty larceny she was willing to tolerate, even though I warned her that eventually you'd take something valuable."

"I stole no earrings! That is a lie!"

The deputy holding Alberto said, "You want us to go and search their place, Mr. Murtrans?"

Murky said, "Yeah. You do that."

The deputy restraining Juanita added, "Meanwhile, we can pop both of them in jail overnight on suspicion."

"Add suspicion of murder to the charges, Deputy," Murky said.

"I was just going to suggest that, Mr. Murtrans," the second deputy said.

"With all the hullabaloo going on at my party it would have been easy enough for one or both of these two to sneak back here and wait until they saw Cynthia alone in the billiard room."

I sighed and quietly added two more suspects to my list. I knew from my own experience just how much anger could well up immediately after the feeling of being terminated unjustly, although I had no way of knowing yet whether Juanita was guilty or innocent of stealing Cynthia's diamond earrings.

What seems to me to be a hundred years ago now I was fired from the Burbank PD. An internal investigation into an undercover investigation of an armored car heist, where one of our own was a suspect, ended up by getting two of our undercover cops killed. The police suspect ended up getting cleared. But a kangaroo court made up of three fellow detectives I'd pissed off in my early years on the force, including one who had been promoted to captain just before the bank-heist incident, decided I had been guilty of negligence in getting the two undercover cops killed.

At the time, I was divorced and dating a newspaper columnist working for the *LA Times*. The charge against me was that I leaked, via pillow talk, the names of the two undercover cops and that my lover had then leaked the names to the investigative reporter who was covering the bank heist.

No such leaks ever occurred. But how does one prove an absence of such pillow talk? I was convicted on the basis of suspicions alone. No one holds Internal Investigations enquiries to court-room standards of evidence.

After watching the deputies take Alberto and Juanita Salazar off toward 48-hour detention I again went in search of Nancy Lorgran, Cynthia's sister. At the large, stylish log guest house I knocked and the voice of Peggy Ann, Nancy's daughter, beckoned me inside.

I had met Peggy Ann on several other occasions, all at the ranch. She was fond of riding horses and came to the ranch often to spend a day following one of the trails that led from the ranch up into the forested foothills. Occasionally, Murky said, he accompanied Peggy Ann up to a picnic site next to a small lake cuddled under a granite cliff. This, despite the fact that Murky allowed that not only was he a poor horseman, but that he possessed more than a slight fear of horses, a fear his horses easily detected.

"Mom's not here, but you're welcome to wait. She might come back soon," Peggy Ann said, as I stepped across the threshold.

Might. I decided to wait anyway.

"You're that detective Uncle Murk hired to figure out who whacked Cynthia over the head, aren'tcha. Mister Fletcher, right?"

"You may skip the 'Mister'. Most people just call me Fletcher."

"Sweets me, Fletcher. Have seat."

She was wearing a two-piece gold outfit with red trim. Her bare midriff was tan and when she sat down on the love seat across from me her upper garment shifted slightly, revealing an absence of a tan line where there ought to have been one.

"Do you think I'm gorgeous, Fletcher?"

I held her gaze while I decided how to react.

"Well? Don't act like I've got to beat a compliment out of you."

"That won't be necessary. Yes, you are very attractive."

"So who do you think is better? My mother or me?"

"Do you mean to ask: Who is more attractive?"

"Now you're pretending to be naive. Stop it!"

"Excuse me?"

"Oh, come on. You've met my mother and you've seen me around. So I'm sure you've wondered who is better in the boudoir."

"May we change the subject?" I said, irritated.

"No, we may not. You're a detective, meaning you've got to be full of endless curiosity and I bet that includes sizing up me and my mother. Wondering what we'd be like as bedroom playmates. So who'd you rather have for a hot time on a cold night, Mister Detective Fletcher?"

"Suppose I say neither and leave it at that?"

"Oh no. No way. No coppin' out."

"Okay then. Let's just say I prefer to keep the comparison to myself. Detectives are allowed --. No, they're obliged at times to keep secrets. The answer to your question is one I'm obliged to keep secret."

"Why?" She gave me a faux-pout.

"Because I'm in the middle of a murder investigation and the answer may prove vital to the solution."

"Oh, bullshit. You're just trying to wiggle out of giving me an answer."

I nodded. "That, too."

"Murky's not shy. He says I'm definitely better than my mother."

"And what did Cynthia have to say about that?" I could have added Jocko Silverado to my question, but decided not to.

"What? Do you think I killed dear old Cynthia because she found out I was screwing Murky? Forget it, Mister. Cyn didn't give a rat's ass who was riding Murky's li'l ol' rod. Jeezus, Fletcher. Wake up and smell the corpses."

"Meaning?"

"Meaning Lois Murtran's half-sister, Paulette, died ten years ago. Find out who murdered Paulette and you'll surely find Cynthia's killer."

I knew that Lois had been Murky's second wife and that her maiden name was Walker. But I was unaware she had a half-sister or that the woman had been murdered. Maybe I had some heavy new research to do. Or maybe Peggy Ann was making up a story. But even if the latter, I had to do the former in order to prove it. Mercifully, Nancy walked in just then.

XIII

"Well, well. Looks who's come sniffing around my daughter. It's Fletcher, isn't it?"

Nancy was wearing a pink and white bikini that failed to flatter her. *Mutton dressed as lamb* I believe the British call the look when older women try too hard to dress like their daughters. Or granddaughters. Nancy's bleach-blonde hair didn't match Peggy Ann's golden blonde hair, but her golden tan -- complete with an absence of tan lines -- matched her daughter's look. Or tried to.

"If you care to refer to my coming here to ask you both a few questions as sniffing, that's all right. Hound dogs sniff when they are on the trail of escapees," I said.

"Who has escaped, pray tell?" Nancy said, sashaying slowly over to a chair and flopping down in it, throwing one bare leg over a chair arm.

"Cynthia's murderer."

"Don't look here, for chrissakes. We didn't kill anyone."

"Perhaps you have some idea who did," I said.

"Trying looking harder at my brother-in-law."

"Tell me why he is your prime suspect?"

Nancy smiled and pointed a finger at her daughter.

"Sniffing, Fletcher. Peggy Ann is not an escapee from anywhere and Murky is not a detective. But Murky has spent a lot of time recently sniffing around my daughter. Hasn't he, Darling? And his wife was none too pleased with his behavior."

"Go on," I said.

Jeff Ridenour

"I do believe my sister finally confronted her husband regarding his none-too-secretive amorous advances toward Peggy Ann. The most recent altercation, I am told, was positively volatile, fireworks worthy of a Fourth of July finale."

"Your daughter has suggested in rather plain terms that both you and she were humping Murky. What did Cynthia have to say about that?" I asked.

Mother shot daughter a nasty look.

"Did Cynthia confront you about your adulterous behavior with her husband?" I said.

Nancy to Peggy Ann. "What lies have you been telling this man?"

"Just the truth, Mother. Tab A in slot B; Tab A in slots C and D. Slot A howls because Slot A is no longer connecting with Tab A. Cynthia screamed at both me and my mother, Mister Detective. Mummy brazenly denied having sex with Murky; I did not."

"Did not deny it, or did not have sex with Murky?" I said.

Peggy Ann gave me a dreamy look. Then languidly said, "Must I remind you that you are the detective in this stage drama? Put on your deer stalker and pull out your magnifying glass, Sherlock."

I looked at Nancy and said, "Did your daughter confess to killing Cynthia? Did you confess to Peggy Ann?"

Nancy said, "If I had killed my sister, I would not have bashed her over the head with a silly pool stick. "

"How would you have gone about it?" I said.

"I'd have poisoned her G&T so I could watch her fall on the floor and foam at the mouth, watch her die slowly, stand over so she would know that I was the one who did her in. I most certainly would not have skulked about, waiting for her to enter an unlit billiard room so I could sneak up on her and pull a Lizzy Borden."

Peggy Ann said, "Mother, Lizzy Borden gave her mother lots of whacks, using an axe."

"I know that, Darling. Don't be so literal-minded."

Peggy Ann laughed. "Literal-minded? Ha! Ha! Ha! This, coming from a woman who never reads anything. Not even comic books. Why, Mister Fletcher, my mother doesn't even know her A, B, C's. When she was playing all those fourth-rate parts in tenth-rate TV soap operas, she drove the poor script assistants bonkers. They had to read her lines to her on all the pre-taping read-throughs, then mime her lines to her on re-takes whenever she flubbed a scene, because she couldn't read her part in the screenplay. She's what is called functionally illiterate."

"I am not."

"You are! And Cynthia used to tease you about it repeatedly," Peggy Ann said, giggling. Turning to me, Peggy Ann said, "Mother and Cynthia grew up poor in Nebraska. When they were teenagers their own mother, Grandma Sharon, ran away from Grandpa Henry, and came to live with Sharon's sister, Elsie, in Fullerton. Both girls went to work full time and Mom never finished school beyond the ninth grade."

Nancy said, "So there! Have you shamed me enough? Or do you want to tell him what ugly jobs I held, right up until I got knocked up by your father?"

"I'm sure you'd tell it so much better, Mummie," Peggy Ann said, putting her hands together in a faux-pleading gesture.

"At least I was never a whore, like you, Daughter."

"Oh, come on, Mother. You screwed every hand-me-down, back-lot grip and best boy Cynthia got tired of screwing as she moved up the movie-set food chain until she tumbled onto the mattress of the great Murky Murtrans, the one, the only 'Comedian from Hellfire'."

Nancy, indignant, said, "If it weren't for my sister, you still wouldn't have a pot or a window."

"Nor would you, Mother."

"I'm not especially proud of my life, but I'm thankful that my sister stood by me all these years, most of them lean --for both of us."

I admired how deftly Nancy had deflected her daughter's attack.

"Tell me, Mrs. Lorgran, how was Paulette Walker murdered?" I said, catching Nancy, but not Peggy Ann, by surprise.

"Paulette? What does she have to do with anything?"

"Just tell me how she died," I said.

"As I recall, she was hit over her head, just like Cynthia."

"With a pool cue?"

"No, with a baseball bat. But Jeezus. That was ages ago, down in La Mirada."

"Where did the bat come from?"

"It was hanging on the wall at the entryway to her apartment, a gift to her foster son, Garrett, from the whole Dodgers team. Lots of signatures on the bat. Garrett was four years old when he developed a brain tumor. He died on the operating table, but not before an LA news channel featured him one night. Tear-jerker story of the night, or some such. The day after the newscast two Dodgers players visited Garrett at the hospital and presented him with the bat. A day after that he was dead."

"The police never caught Paulette's murderer?" I said.

"I don't think they tried very hard. Paulette was a married to a mulatto. And for cops a half nigger equals a whole nigger; a half white equals no white at all. And a white police force figures it was a case of niggers bashing niggers in some Niggertown brawl where poor, all-white Paulette got caught in the middle. Maybe she was even trying to break up a fight, but the cops figured that was no business of theirs."

Half-sister, foster son, mulatto? I wondered why she didn't toss in an old wooden Indian, a brass-balled monkey, and a Dodo bird while she was spinning her yarn. But I decided I had to press on. I remembered from my Burbank days how reluctant every white member of our department feared going into any place Nancy Lorgran categorized as a *Niggertown*.

"They determined that a black man killed her?" I said.

"They didn't determine anything. They just assumed."

"What do you think?" I said.

"That happened years and years ago. My thoughts on who killed Paulette have all run down my leg and slithered away into the sewer."

I said to Nancy, "Your daughter thinks Murky might have killed her."

Peggy Ann said, "No 'might have' about it."

"No way," Nancy said. "Murky was doing a live comedy routine in Pasadena at the time the cops figured Paulette was hammered. I know. I was there watching him."

Peggy Ann said, "Yes, but he could have killed her earlier, then have taken off for Pasadena. Maybe the cops were wrong about the time of death."

I suddenly liked Peggy Ann. Well, no. I mean I disliked her less. She was right. Police methods for determining time of death were not as accurate as they are now. Close usually, but not always a horseshoe ringer. Frankly, the methodology today isn't all that much better.

Nancy sighed. "Come on. How can anyone kill another person in cold blood then turn around and tell jokes for an hour? No! Murky couldn't do that."

Yet, the look in her eyes told me that maybe, just maybe, he could.

"By the way," Nancy said, "When do you think Cynthia's body will be released?"

"Ask the cops," I said.

She shrugged.

"Doesn't matter, does it? Murky doesn't plan to hold so much as a memorial service, let alone a funeral. Not even a simple funeral, damn him. He claims he doesn't believe in any of that 'crap', to use his term. What a heartless bastard."

XIV

"Tell me more about Paulette's murder anyway," I said. "It's what now? A ten-year-old cold case?"

Peggy Ann seemed to know much more about the details than Nancy. So she provided me with the background.

"Paulette was divorced when she met Sammy Archer, who directs all-black films at the Herman V. Sellers Studios down in Compton. The coloreds, you may know, have their own version of Oscars night. The BAMA awards they call them. Stands for Black Academy of Movie Awards. And instead of handing out Oscars, they give out BSA awards, Black Sheep Awards."

Nancy piped in. "It's truly an ugly thing to behold."

I wondered where she had seen one, but I didn't want to interrupt Peggy Ann, who spoke as though she had first-hand knowledge of BAMA night.

"Sammy already owned a couple of Black Sheep, so he could get away with taking a white woman to BAMA night without catching too much shit. Or so he thought, at least. Anyway, he ended up taking Paulette, although rumor had it she was his fifth choice, because the first four women he asked turned him down."

Still, why Paulette, I wondered. She apparently was a third- or fourth-tier level actress. On the other hand, she was white, which is all that counted for this man to achieve shock value among the attendees.

"How did Paulette know this director?"

Nancy spoke again.

"Good question. One no one seems to know the answer to -- even to this day."

Peggy Ann continued.

"Meanwhile, it turns out that good ol' Uncle Murky was screwing Paulette." Looking at her mother, she added, "We all know how The Murk loves to screw his wives' sisters, don't we, Mother?"

I expected Nancy to give Peggy Ann a withering glare, but she didn't. So I saved Nancy further embarrassment but urging Peggy Ann to continue with the story of Paulette's murder.

I said to both of them, "The investigation into Paulette's murder failed even to turn up any suspects?"

Nancy said, "Sammy's wife was a suspect, but she had a rock-solid alibi for the time frame the coroner estimated Paulette was killed. She was partying with friends down in Long Beach."

Peggy Ann added, "The cops interviewed several colored boys who were at the BAMA awards and who had openly expressed to Sammy their displeasure with his having brought a white gal to the ceremony, but that came to nothing."

Nancy tossed out a stereotype. "Probably because those coloreds all look alike."

"They do not, Mother."

"Oh, that's right. Some of them have bigger cocks than others, don't they? You'd know far more about that than I do, Dear."

"Oh, come, Mother. I've heard all about how sensitive your gag reflex is when it comes to going down on young, black studs. Why, I bet you've been invited to the BAMA's."

"I'm sure we're boring Mr. Fletcher." Looking at me, "Aren't we, Mr. Detective?"

I wouldn't have called it boredom, but I did think I had heard quite enough on the subject of colored men.

"Murky was never questioned?" I said.

Both women shook their heads. I made a mental note to contact La Mirada PD to see what more I could learn about the murder of Paulette

Walker. I didn't have any contacts there from my previously having been a detective with Burbank PD, but I had a friend, Al Declavic, still on the Downey police force who might know someone in La Mirada's homicide division. Downey was practically next door to La Mirada.

As I left the two women a sheriff's car pulled up to the front of the main house. Two deputies climbed out, one of them the asshole who had stopped me and tried to intimidate me. I watched them knock, watched Murky open the door, then saw Murky hold out his wrists for the jerk deputy to clasp handcuffs on him.

"What is this all about?" I said as I approached them.

The deputy I didn't recognize turned and said, "Mr. Murtrans is being arrested for the murder of his wife."

"On what evidence?" I said.

Before the jerk cop could stop him, the other one said, "A neighboring rancher told us that Mrs. Murtrans told him that two days before her murder that she was in fear of her life and that this man here threatened to kill her."

I couldn't help but laugh. "Of course. and two nights later she was a cheerful hostess at Mr. Murtrans's retirement party. That showed she had a whole lot of fear of the guest of honor, right?"

The deputy shrugged and replied, "I'm not the prosecuting attorney."

The other deputy added, "Maybe he threatened to kill her if she didn't play hostess."

I said, "And with more than a dozen guests present she would not have bothered to mention such a threat to any of them, eh?"

In a loud, exasperated voice, Murky yelled to me, "Fletcher, that rancher's name is Ben Rondle. He and Cynthia have been plotting for months to sell off my vineyards to that thieving bastard. I wouldn't have it and told them both so. Whatever I may have said to Cynthia, I was just trying to rattle her, to get her to back off."

The non-jerk deputy said to me, "That's what they all say, isn't it, Mr. Fletcher? Suddenly they never mean what they said."

"There's more to our arresting him than just what that rancher heard," the jerk deputy said. "Mr. Murtrans's agent and niece have both come forward to say they each saw him enter the billiard room shortly after his wife walked into that room. They also told the sheriff that they saw him emerge less than five minutes later, looking around cautiously to see if anyone was watching. Then he hurried away."

Murky shouted, "That's all bullshit. They're both liars! Liars, liars, liars, I say. Neither one of them was anywhere near the billiard room."

Come along, Mr. Murtrans," jerk deputy said. "You can tell your story to a jury."

Murky again. "Get me that hot-shit lady lawyer of yours, Fletcher. I don't care what she costs. Just line her up to cover my ass. And assure her I'm innocent as a newborn babe."

As a newborn babe? We all knew better than that. But then hyperbole was a standard technique in professional comedy routines. Murky, after all, was a master comedian. Only the stage he was on now -- facing a murder indictment -- was not known for its humor.

As for Peggy Ann and Jocko Silverado, Murky had told me they were busy having oral sex in his office at the time Cynthia was clubbed to death, while he was also engaged in playing the voyeur.

After watching the deputies gracelessly force Murky into the backseat of one of their cruisers, I turned back to search for Peggy Ann and her mother. But they were gone, according to the maid, an elderly woman named Mirasol, who had arrived to perform the daily cleaning in the guest house where Nancy was staying.

"The ladies, they leave in a hurry, Señor. They stir dust, as the cowboys say on TV."

I pictured Peggy Ann and Nancy wearing black hats and riding away on gray horses."

But I was not Roy Rogers, Gene Autry, or the Lone Ranger, about to give chase on Trigger, Champion, or Silver. I had a more ambiguous task to pursue.

XV

I sat in Amanda Reynolds's office, watching her fill out the necessary paperwork to make her Murky Murtrans's attorney of record. All Murky had to do, when Amanda and I visited Murk in the county jail, was sign on the lines where the sticky blue arrows pointed.

"Do you intend to work with me on his case, Fletcher, or will you continue to act as your own agent?" Amanda said, as she continued to scribble and flip pages.

"Do you have a preference?" I said.

"Well, of course, I do. Your remaining independent will save me all kinds of money."

"Liar! Either way, my expenses will all come out of Murky's pocket."

"But will I charge Mr. Murtrans more for your time than you will?" she said.

"Maybe you will, but then you'll skim a percentage and I'll end up getting less. So I guess I choose to remain my own man."

"Understood. In which case, you're dismissed. I'll see Mr. Murtrans by myself."

"Wait! How can you fire me when I haven't signed on?"

"I meant: Get out of here. Go your own way. Be gone. That kind of *dismissed*."

"Ah!" I tipped my non-existent hat and started to leave.

"Don't forget you're still working for me on the Claymore case."

"So I am, in which case, I'd better be on my way."

"Wait, Stu. Regarding Murtrans's defense, for your first move I want you to question the neighboring rancher, the one Sheriff Cuddleston's people claim heard Mr. Murtrans threaten to kill his wife."

"I thought we just agreed I was going to remain independent," I said.

"Right. And your next step -- as an independent investigator -- should be to check out that rancher."

"Yes, Ma'am."

I then remembered being followed by the man who turned out to work for The Condor and explained the incident to Amanda.

Her reaction was to drop her pen and bite her lip before saying, "That makes no sense. Are you sure?"

"I am."

"I'll ask the old man what that is all about when I see him. He's coming in tomorrow morning to discuss again the possibility of getting bail reduced for the client."

I loved how she could speak of a person she was defending as though her client was a as faceless and nameless as a brown paper bag.

"Yes, Mrs. Murtrans came to me to discuss the possibility of my purchasing her and her husband's two hundred and forty acres of Pinot Noir and Chardonnay vines. I failed to realize at the time that she had not so much as discussed such a sale with her husband."

Samuel Rondle looked like what I imagined a wine sophisticate should look like. His white hair, Van Dyke goatee, and horn-rimmed glasses made him look like Colonel Sanders minus the fried-chicken entrepreneur's white hat and white suit. Instead he dressed himself in the style of a Spanish grandee, somewhat befitting his current station in life as an owner of central California acreage. I say *somewhat* befitting because the Rondle Ranch consisted of a mere one thousand acres, miniscule by the standards of eighteenth century grandees.

He invited me into his hilltop manse, which sat back from Foxen Canyon Road over a quarter of a mile. The long driveway up the hill was lined with majestic oaks that reminded me of the Spanish oaks lining the entryways to antebellum mansions I had seen in the Deep South.

Without asking me if I wanted a glass of wine, he opened a bottle of red Rhone and decanted it carefully, then poured us each a half glass.

"A three-year-old from my own vines," he said as he handed a bulbous glass to me.

I twirled the wine slowly before bringing the glass to my nose. Scents of blackberries and wildflowers filled my nostrils.

"Very pleasant," I allowed.

"Imbibe, sir. The taste will please you as well."

I didn't sip so much as wet my lips at first and the sensation was indeed delightful. I was no connoisseur, but I knew what I liked and Mr. Rondle had produced a wine very much to my liking.

He gestured for me to take a seat in one of two overstuffed leather chairs and I did without spilling my wine as I sat. I had already explained my role to him when I phoned to make my appointment with him. So he understood the nature of the line of questions I was about to propose to him and even anticipated some of them.

"Mrs. Murtrans gave two reasons for wanting to sell their vineyard acreage. First, she said neither she nor her husband possessed adequate knowledge of oenology to produce a worthwhile crop. Nor did either of them have the will -- the gumption, you might say -- to indulge in an education on the subject.

"She did say that they had hired an expert to manage their vines and the harvest, but that he had proved to be a hopeless alcoholic and they fired him after two months. It turned out, too, that the man had misrepresented himself on his resume. He was a gardener with no experience overseeing vineyards. And now she said both she and Mr, Murtrans lacked any inclination to hire another manager. But I have since learned one or the other of them did hire a new man to oversee their grapes. Why she lied to me, I do not know."

He then sat back and stared into his wine glass, as if he were waiting for a vision to emerge from the shallow depths of the remaining Rhone. Finally, I interrupted his reverie and asked, "What was Mrs. Murtrans second reason for wanting to sell the vineyard portion of their estate?"

"Oh, yes. I'm sorry. I get lost in thought. My mind wanders. Her added reason for wanting to sell is that she had a project for which she needed a large sum of cash, and the sale of their vines was going to provide the necessary financing of it."

"Did she say what her project was?" I said.

"To help build a new church for her step-son, she said. I gather that the step-son is a local minister who currently peddles his Jesus tales out of a rather shabby house of God, a place too small and unworthy of God's respect. I do not know whose assessment that is, hers or the minister's."

He paused and gave me a wink, then went on.

"The hope, she said, was to lure, entice... whatever... more lost souls into the fold than the present establishment could hold on Sunday mornings. I dare say I've driven past the place a time or two and had to agree with her that, for a edifice with such a grand purpose, it lacks a certain desirability, if you know what I mean."

"Yes. I've seen it. Been inside even. It does lack appeal to anyone contemplating becoming a new member of the congregation. Did Mrs. Murtrans mention how her husband felt about selling the land to you?"

"She said she had yet to discuss it with him. And then she hastily added that she intended to, but was afraid he might not only balk, but explode at the notion of her coming to see me behind his back. Then -- without my bidding her, I assure you -- she erupted into a lengthy monologue about how terrified she was of her husband all of the time and how he recently had even threatened to kill her."

He drained his glass and quickly refilled it, offering me another splash as well, seeing that I had only barely drunk from my glass. When I declined, he sat back down and continued.

"I have never met Mr. Murtrans. So, obviously, I did not directly overhear him threaten his wife. Rather, I had to take her word that he told her he would kill her under this or that circumstance. But I recognize genuine fear when I see it. You see, Mr. Fletcher, I was a frontline physician in Italy during the Second World War. And the most difficult wounds I confronted there were not those involving torn flesh and gushing blood. Rather ...." He paused to tap the side of his head. "Mental trauma. Soldiers are so horrified by what they had witnessed in combat that their minds ceased to function normally. And in many, many cases those broken minds have never healed."

"If Cynthia Murtrans was that traumatized, Dr. Rondle, how was she able to function as a perfect hostess on the night she was murdered? That, I believe, was only a day or so after seeing you for the last time."

"Part of the mind's methodology in coping with severe trauma, we have learned slowly over the years, is to engage in habitual routines, repetitive gestures and activities. For example, a textbook case written up by a well-known New York psychiatrist tells of a patient, a man who returned from the Korean War with what was then called shell shock. Upon discharge, he went to his mother's home in Tennessee and spent ten hours a day, every day, for the rest of his short life, playing the piano, playing Mozart concertos he had learned as a teenager. Beyond that activity, he was scarcely functional. And he died five years later, at the age of thirty-four. His death certificate read: Death by natural causes."

I said, "And you think Cynthia Murtrans was that severely traumatized, in shock due to threats made by her husband?"

"It's possible. But in no way was her mind rattled as badly as the young Korean War veteran. I'm merely suggesting that, on a far smaller scale, her mind was frozen in a similar way that, while scared shitless -- if you'll allow me to use a common and highly descriptive vulgarism -- she could carry on in many of her normal ways."

I said, "*Scared shitless* more aptly applies to soldiers in death-threatening situations. And a *frozen* mind? You don't mean that literally, of course. But how dysfunctional would she be?"

"I am not a psychiatrist, Mr. Fletcher. I was a surgeon. But as a war-front surgeon dealing with minds ripped apart, as well as bodies, I can assure you she was, as another saying goes, 'not herself'."

"Yet she came to you with the idea of selling part of her and her husband's ranch. That involves complexities of thought, surely, not commensurate with someone whose mind is frozen, even in a meta-phorical sense."

"I would categorize her fear as suppressed, repressed. As I say, I am far from familiar with all of Dr. Freud's analytical descriptive tools."

"But whether suppressed fear, repressed fear, or whatever, you recognized it in her?"

"Yes."

"And she explicitly claimed that her husband made threats against her life?"

"Yes again."

"And on this basis Murky Murtrans has been indicted for murder."

Dr. Rondle objected.

"I have not read the indictment. I am unaware of what the totality of evidence amassed against him is. All I know is what I heard Cynthia Murtrans tell me, and that is what I passed along to the sheriff's department."

Along with a surgeon's amateur psychiatric analysis of a woman's state of mind. Harumph. Once on the witness stand, Benjamin Rondle will find his testimony facing Amanda Reynold's sharp scalpel. If there is a trial. My hope was to find Cynthia's murderer before Murky and Amanda found themselves sitting side by side at the defense's table.

XVI

On my drive back to Santa Maria I kept a sharp lookout for both sheriff's cruisers and mystery followers, but didn't see any trace of either. Once home, I treated myself to a cold beer and a hot shower before calling my modest answering service. Messages are few and I kept telling myself I could probably save the expense without losing any business were I to cancel my usage of the service. But the thought of my being responsible for sending several middle-aged and elderly women wobbling toward the unemployment line brought me up short.

Years ago I had signed up with *Maeve Archer's Calls Missed* answering service "for very small businesses". I met Maeve just once -- when I signed up -- but never met any of the other women whose voices greeted me whenever I phoned in for messages. Yet, many a time, when I had been on a case and stressed from lack of sleep or lack of success in finding a missing teen or a murderer, I would sometimes call in for messages I knew would not be there solely for the purpose of hearing a friendly, soothing voice reassure me that my life was not the failure it seemed to be. For Maeve's telephone ladies were more than message takers and message givers. They were all voices of encouragement, voices that massaged the tensions from my taut nerves, erased my headaches faster than a handful of aspirins.

"You have one message, Mr. Fletcher. It came in two hours ago from a man who identified himself only as Hugh. He said he is a bartender at Jocko's in Nipomo. His message to you is that he has a piece of updated information for you that you will surely find very useful and that you may stop by Jocko's this evening between the hours of 4 p.m. and midnight."

"Thank you, Helen. I appreciate it. Always good to hear your lovely voice."

"You are most welcome, Mr. Fletcher. I hope to speak with you again soon. Good day."

Updated information from Hugh. Of course, he would want me to stop by in person. One is unable to reward information properly via telephone, although I suppose I could use Western Union to wire him a cash tip the way California Hispanics use Western Union to send a portion of their earnings to relatives still living south of the border. The distance from Santa Maria to Nipomo, however, is all of eight miles -- and with no border issues in between.

By the time I arrived at Jocko's Steak House, the restaurant was beginning to fill with dinner customers and the bar was already full, all the barstools taken by men, most of them wearing plaid shirts and cowboy boots. Behind the long bar Hugh was so busy he looked as if his work would go more smoothly were he to clamp on a pair of roller skates.

I waited patiently at the end of the bar reserved for waiters and waitresses ordering drinks for restaurant patrons. It didn't take long for Hugh to notice me and to gesture he'd be with me as quickly as he could manage.

A minute later Hugh placed a Budweiser down in front of me.

"Thanks for coming so quickly, Mr. Fletcher. My news is that the dude who was following you the other day, Giovanni Alba, doesn't work for El Condor anymore. The old man fired him a few weeks ago. He now is working for a man named Paolo Galboni. Ever heard of him?"

"Yes. He's an upstart wine competitor of El Condor."

"Right," Hugh said. "But I've been unable to find out why he was having Giovanni follow you."

I lied and said, "That's okay, Hugh. I'll see if I can uncover what Mr. Galboni is up to."

Of course, I pretty much already knew. I then slid a twenty-dollar bill onto the counter and started to leave, but the man on the barstool next to where I stood grabbed me by my shirt sleeve.

"Hey, Mister. A bottle of beer don't cost no stinkin' twenty bucks, even includin' the bartender's tip."

I said, "That's okay. I'm feeling generous tonight. My horse paid twenty-five to one at Santa Anita this afternoon."

"Holy crap! You got any tips for me on tomorrow's races?" he said, eyes wide.

"As a matter of fact I do. Take Shit-for-Brains to win in the fourth race."

"Hey! You sure? I didn't know an owner was allowed to name his horse that."

"Then take Break-the-Rules to place in the sixth."

"You sure?"

"Positive. My money's on him to win," I lied.

"Thanks a bunch."

It takes legions of fools to sustain the sport of kings, their dreams dashed in less time than it takes to boil water for a cup of tea.

At a nearby grocery store I phoned Amanda Reynolds, hoping to stop her from mentioning Giovanni Alba to El Condor, but I was too late.

"Grandpa Claymore said he would look into the activities of Mr. Alba and make sure he no longer tries to follow you," she said.

"Thank you. That is indeed a kindness on his part."

"The reason the Old Man came to see me was to see if I thought a plea deal was a good idea."

"And you said --?"

"I told him the game was still very early innings and I had, as yet, no idea what I was up against. In fact, I told him that much depended on you at the moment. What you came up with."

"Thanks a lot. Still, all the more reason for him to get Alba off my back."

"By the way, the elder Claymore's son, Richard the Second, is against any attempt to plea bargain his son's crime down to sexual battery, even though, if that happened, Ricky could get off with just a fine."

"Could, but may not," I said. "As I recall, his agreeing to that could also get him six months in jail."

Amanda nodded. "That's why he does not want me to approach the prosecution. He doesn't want his son in jail even for one more minute. And I can understand that. Ricky is all he has left."

I understood the horrible root of Ricky's father's sentiment.

Nearly two years earlier Richard the Second had gone pheasant hunting near the tiny town of Shandon, in San Luis Obispo County, with his two sons, Ricky, who was sixteen at the time, and Robin, who was ten. Because it had been a hot, Indian-summer day in October, all three hunters wore light clothing.

When a pheasant was flushed nearest the father, Richard fired his double-barreled shotgun once, bringing down the bird. He then ejected the spent shell, the brass head of which was extremely hot from the gun's firing pin having hit it, causing the shell's powder to ignite and eject the shell's pellets. That's the way shotguns work.

However -- as reconstructed by the SLO sheriff's department afterwards -- the shell casing bounced off an oak tree next to which the father was standing. The hot casing then hit the father in the neck and proceeded to enter his open shirt, burning his skin. The senior Richard, caught by surprise and feeling the brass head of the casing searing his neck, began to hop about and scream. At that point the other shell in his gun somehow discharged, the pellets hitting young Robin in the chest. The boy was standing a mere ten feet away and died instantly.

Freak accident though it was, all three Richard Sylvester Claymores blamed the father, and, as one might expect, the incident weighed crushingly on the entire Claymore family. Then, just as the deep emotional wounds finally began to heal slightly, Ricky was arrested and accused of rape.

XVII

Next morning I found Ricky waiting for me at Millie's Pancake House in Goleta. He had already downed three Belgian waffles, four eggs, and three plates full of bacon. I ordered coffee and toast. After being arrested by Santa Julietta County sheriff's deputies on the rape charge -- the party where the alleged rape had occurred was not in any municipal district -- Ricky was out on bail faster than Superman racing that famous *speeding bullet.*

He got out on a weekend even. Amanda said there was a rumor that El Condor stopped some judge in the middle of his backswing on the fifth tee at Colonia Verde Country Club in order for him to hold an unprecedented Saturday morning bail hearing. Amanda was interrupted as well, having to change out of her gardening outfit into clothes suitable to plead before a very bewildered court staff and a judge who, though he made a valiant attempt to repress his irritation, was clearly annoyed, according to Amanda. And, though El Condor was not physically present, his specter was clearly an eight-hundred-pound gorilla in that courtroom.

"Grandpa says I gotta talk with you. So here I am."

Soft defiance.

"Did you rape Wendy Simmons?"

"No."

"Amanda Reynolds's attorney-client confidentiality privileges extend to me. I'm part of her defense team," I fudged. "So, if you did rape Wendy, it would help to know and we can work from there."

Ricky shook his head.

"My old man isn't going to go for any plea bargain. And he's right not to. I did not rape that chick." Pause. "Okay. I came close to fuckin' her. Really close. That's 'cause she was asking for it. And I don't mean that in some... what's it called?... metaphorical way. I mean she was literally asking me to do her. She had her panties down and she was strokin' me." Another pause. "I was just getting ready to slip it in -- and, boy, was she ready. I mean, wet and loose -- when *Whammo!* She tried to punch me in my nut sack."

He made a fist and demonstrated by shadowing-boxing a punch at my groin.

"Only her punch glanced off my thigh. Next thing I know she's screamin' 'Rape! Help! This guy's trying to rape me.' Man! Was I set up to take a fall."

I found myself reeling and at a momentary loss for what to say. Then I regained my verbal footing and asked the obvious question.

"Why would she want to set you up for anything?"

"'Cause she had just finished fuckin' her best girlfriend's boyfriend and she was afraid her girlfriend was about to find out. I mean, the girlfriend was at the party, too, and at least a couple people saw Wendy takin' it from behind, doin' it doggie style behind the bushes with Roxie's boyfriend. So she tries to make it look like somebody else -- me -- had been in her pussy instead. And she needed to draw plenty of attention away from the fact that she had been fooling around hot and heavy with Terry Morowitz."

"He's the boyfriend?"

A vigorous nod.

"Is Roxie who I think she is?"

"Roxanna Galboni."

Fruit basket upset.

If I smoked I would have been reaching for a cigarette right then. Instead, I took a deep breath and tried to size Ricky up quickly, estimate how much of a con artist lay behind his handsome, well-tanned face.

In my careers as cop and private detective my powers of discernment regarding people's honesty have ebbed and flowed. In Ricky Claymore's case I told myself to hold off trying to peg his sincerity, remembering Groucho Marx's infamous quip: *When you can successfully fake sincerity, you've got it made.*

Under indictment for rape, Ricky could hardly rate as having it made. Still, maybe he was right in claiming Wendy had made him her sacrificial pawn, thinking she had looked several moves ahead to avoid Roxy Galboni's wrath.

I asked, "Who are these friends of Terry Morowitz who might have seen him having sex with Wendy?"

"Harry Deemer and Chuck Paltzheimer."

"Are they students at UC?"

"Yeah. They're both in Terry's fraternity. The Kap Psi's."

"Kappa Alpha Psi?"

"Yeah."

"Have you told all this to Amanda?" I said. If so, I was both amazed and crushed that Amanda hadn't mentioned any of this to me.

"Is she my lawyer?"

My jaw dropped.

"You haven't met her yet."

"Nope. I think my grandpa is taking me to see her tomorrow. Like most everything else in my life, they kinda try to keep two steps ahead of me to try to keep me out of trouble."

Too bad his dad and granddad couldn't have been fronting him at the party when Wendy dropped her drawers. On the other hand, too many parents try to live their kids' lives for them. Their intentions in most cases are good, but kids aren't quarterbacks in need of parental offensive linemen blocking for them on every play.

My old man was pretty much the opposite. "You're on your own, Stu. But if you find you can't punch your way out of a predicament, reach for the phone and I'll be there to help you." Only twice -- that I remember -- did I ever have to call him for help. And when I called, he came running.

Ricky said, "I hear that Ms. Reynolds is a real ball buster."

"That's one way of putting it."

"Is she ugly?"

"Not at all. She's a bit old for you, but were she twenty years younger, you'd either ask her out or recommend her to one of your friends. By the way, is Terry Morowitz a friend of yours?"

"Nope. He's -- well, was -- in my English composition class. That's how I know who he is."

"What about Harry and Chuck?"

"Basketball players. Both play on the freshman team."

"Were they your buddies before the party?"

"No. My granddad arranged to pay for the team's uniforms and he asked me to be there to hand them out to the players. That's how I met them."

"How do you know they both saw Wendy and Terry going at it during the party?"

"Harry told me."

"Obviously you don't mind taking seconds then," I said.

"Hey! Harry didn't tell me until after --. Well, you know."

"Wait a second. I thought there was an uproar, you got pinned by several party members, and then the police arrived. How did Harry manage to talk to you amid all the hubbub?"

"He came up to me and whispered in my ear while a couple of guys were holding me down."

"I thought Harry was Terry's friend?"

"He is."

"Then why would Harry rat on his friend? And rat to you, of all people? Didn't he know why you were being pinned down by the police?"

"Yes, he knew. That's why he told me about Wendy and Terry."

"That still doesn't explain why a friend would rat on a friend," I said.

"Okay. Terry and Harry were high school buddies, but they had been on the outs a bit since arriving at UC."

"Why?"

The Comedian from Hellfire

"Because Harry had caught Terry plunking *his* girlfriend."

"Harry's girlfriend?"

A nod.

"When was this?"

"A week before school started. It happened in Salinas, which is where Harry, Chuck, and Terry are from. And Harry and Chuck's girlfriends."

"So did Terry and Wendy know each other before the night of the party?"

"I don't know."

"Did you know Wendy before the party?"

"No."

"How is it she grabbed onto *you*, so to speak?"

"She seemed to come looking for me."

"Did it ever occur to you that you were set up by a tag team to be a fall guy."

"Not at the time, but I am beginning to see it now."

"Where can I find Harry Deemer and Charles Paltzheimer?"

"Try the frat house."

XVIII

Up in Berkeley the spirit of "free love" was in full swing, but on the UC campus in Santa Julietta sex among students was proving to be more "uptight", to use the *au currant* phrase. At least among some students. I gathered that Roxanna Galboni would not approve of her boyfriend's *plunking* other coeds, to use Ricky's term. I guessed that Roxanna had been brought up Catholic, where the Church does not condone a woman's sex partner indulging himself with other women. But then the Church does not condone premarital sex either, and -- if I was reading between the lines correctly -- Roxanna, though unwed to Terry Morowitz, was treating him to her carnal favors.

Meanwhile, as men of draft age, Ricky Claymore, Terry Morowitz, Harry Deemer, and Charles Paltzheimer were lucky to be where there were young women to lust after and quarrel over. America's proxy Cold War battle against the Soviet Union was being waged on a sub-nuclear-weapon level in Southeast Asia and young men of college-freshman age were being sent to Laos, Cambodia, and South Vietnam by the tens of thousands to serve as mortar, land mine, and AK-47 fodder.

Yet, I was scarcely one to remark disparagingly. A decade and a half earlier, openings on the Burbank PD -- when I applied for a job -- had occurred in part because several men from that force found themselves in General Douglas MacArthur's US/UN Army in Korea, where they ended up on the wrong side of the Yalu River, facing vastly superior numbers of Chinese infantry charging at them again and again.

Jeff Ridenour

As a student at Long Beach State I was obliged to enroll in one credit hour of ROTC each semester and, in doing so, I could maintain my draft deferment. After I graduated my deferment expired. However, red-blooded American men from less fortunate circumstances than those into which I had been born volunteered in sufficient numbers that draftees became unnecessary.

You'd think "Lucky me!" -- but I enlisted anyway.

Ricky Claymore's account of how he fell accused of raping Wendy Simmons suffered from too many inconsistencies for me to think anything but that the whole was far less than the sum of its parts. Still, his claim that Wendy wanted to create a distraction to mask the fact that she was having sex with her girlfriend's boyfriend made a whole lot of sense, especially if Wendy supposed Roxanna might get wind of her betrayal.

But then a simple denial on Wendy's part made simpler sense. Still, a simpler explanation might not occur to someone in stressful circumstances. I had to wonder though if Wendy's choice of Ricky to be her fall guy was accidental or by choice. And if the latter, what reason lay behind her choice.

At the Kappa Alpha Psi fraternity house's lounge room I interrupted a chess game between two scruffy-bearded blond young men to ask where I might find Terry Morowitz, Harry Deemer, or Charles Paltzheimer. I might as well have asked them where to find the Ghosts of Christmas Past.

"Try the Student Intramural Building," came a voice that emerged from behind a Masked Marvel comic book on the far side of the room. Lowering his comic book, the young man offering me directions grinned and wiped a smudge from his horned-rim glasses.

"Look for a pickup basketball game. Harry and Chuck play a challenge game there every afternoon at this time," he said.

I barely had time to thank him before he re-engaged himself with the comic book characters.

Ten minutes later I found the Intramural Building. The basketball game consisted of six men a side and no referees. So no-autopsy, no-foul rules applied. The pace was hectic and soon one young man came limping off the court, his hands holding a small towel to his bloody nose.

I waited until he had stanched the flow, then asked him to identify any one of the three young men I was seeking. He shook his head.

"They didn't show up today."

"Know where I might find them?"

"Beats me. Try McDougal's."

McDougal's was a tavern two blocks off campus. I doubted the bartender would know the three amigos from the hundreds of other students who chugged suds in his establishment, but I had to be sure. Turned out I was right and I headed back to Amanda's office. I assumed she had finally met her client and I was right again.

She said she had listened to Ricky' story and shared my doubts about it. When I told her I had gone off in search of Terry, Harry, and Chuckie and came up empty, she explained how vital it was we find at least Harry Deemer.

"If Ricky is right about Harry's telling him about Terry Morowitz and Wendy, I can put Harry on the stand. That should set the jury's minds to spinning."

"And if Harry denies the story?" I said.

"Then we obviously need to find some other way to discredit Wendy."

"Terry or Chuck?"

Amanda shook her head.

"If Harry ducks, so too will the others."

"Ducks because there's no truth to the tale? Or ducks for some other reason?"

"We won't know until you speak with them," she said.

"And maybe not even then."

"You're pretty good at smelling out lies, Fletcher. And if one of them is lying, all of them are."

"Which makes the lie pretty smelly indeed," I said.

"Any more on why that Alba fellow was following you?"

"Apparently Paolo Galboni wants to know what I know."

"Ever drink any of his wine?" Amanda said.

"Yeah. He puts out a pretty good Pinot Noir."

"Maybe Giovanni Alba was merely trying to get you to take a survey on his new boss's products."

"You think?"

"Find those three kids."

"They're not kids, Amanda. They're all old enough to die in Vietnam."

"You think the chant 'Hey, hey, LBJ, how many kids did you kill today?' is only about Vietnamese kids?" she said.

XIX

I disliked stake-outs when I worked for the Burbank PD and my attitude hadn't changed. Ross Macdonald detective novels make for a pleasant distraction while waiting, and waiting, and waiting for a suspect or potential witness to show up. Still, when the sun sets over the Central California coast, damp, chill air settles in for the night.

Reading -- novels or anything else -- becomes impossible. Use of a flashlight, even a small one, is no good. Light after sunset draws bugs and curious two-legged creatures, violating the object of a stake-out: invisibility.

By 2:00 a.m. the bars had all closed and most weekday parties had wound down. Most of the upstairs lights had been extinguished, too. Kappa Psi men apparently were not ones to pull all-nighters in the name of improving their minds. And, as I squirmed in my car seat, no signs of my three potential witnesses came into view.

So I, too, called it a night and sacked out in a small apartment Amanda maintained in the north end of Santa Julietta, for my occasional use and for the utilization of other out-of-town guests when they came to see her on matters related to her criminal cases. Morning produced no frat men for me to interview. So I headed off to see Murky again.

The Santa Julietta County Jail is a crumbling adjunct to the County Courthouse. There had been talks for years, and maybe even some planning, regarding building a new jail, putting it somewhere between the current jail and Avenida de Libre, the UC student housing area, where over sixty percent of the crime in the county occurred.

As a pre-trial detainee Murky was being held in a separate part of the jail from those already convicted of crimes which didn't require their being sent to state prisons. Or so I thought. It turned out Amanda had already secured Murky's freedom. That puzzled me, given that murder suspects are always denied bail, even in California.

But the assistant jail warden who met me explained, to his obvious dismay, that Amanda had convinced the Chief County Prosecutor that the basis on which Murky had been arrested was far too flimsy and that the prosecutor had agreed. Someone's overhearing a murder threat isn't enough to arrest anyone for murder. I remember Amanda once explaining to me that, if every attendee at a baseball game who shouted "Kill the ump!" deserved to be arrested for such behavior, summertime would see our jails flooded with such people.

So, thwarted from seeing Murky at SJ's esteemed jail facility, I drove straight to Murky's ranch, where I found him already lolling in his hot tub. I didn't mind the mists that rose from Murky's indoor hot tub like steam from a cup of fresh, hot coffee. But the overwhelming smell of chlorine that rose with it nearly made me gag.

"You okay, Fletcher?" Murky said, after sipping from his ever-present tumbler of bourbon. He lay up to his neck in warm, bubbling water. So I couldn't see how pink and prune-like his flesh had turned, although his face was flushed. But that could have been from the whiskey.

"I'm fine," I lied as I slipped into the hot tub next to Murky. He had told me he kept extra bathing trunks in the dressing room next to the swimming pool. So I changed out of my street clothes, grabbed a towel, and returned to join Murky "leach out the cares of life", as he put it. I was convinced that whiskey served as a better agent for drawing off tensions than hot water. But, even so, I settled for a beer.

"If you tried to see me in that pig sty they call a jail, you, too, need to cleanse the filth of those dungeons from your flesh and from your soul."

I agreed.

"Did you talk with my neighbor yet?" he said.

"I did."

"What did he have to say?"

"Not much. Tell me again what you know of Cynthia's attempt to sell off your vineyards."

"She and that greedy bastard were colluding behind my back."

They could hardly have been colluding under his nose -- or so I imagined.

"So, how did you find out?" I said.

"Peggy Ann told me. She overheard Cynthia and that wicked sister of hers discussing it one evening -- over a bottle of wine no less. Peggy Ann was doing her usual eavesdroppin'. Damn that girl's sneaky. But sometimes that works in my favor."

And, no doubt, sometimes it didn't -- as in giving a blowjob to Murky's agent in Murky's private office on the evening of Cynthia Murtrans's murder.

"Then subsequently you met with Sam Rondle," I said.

"I did."

"And?"

"I told the sonuvabitch to stop talking to Cynthia 'cause such a sale wasn't gonna happen."

"And he said?"

"The cheeky fucker said, 'We'll see about that'."

"To which you responded?"

"I gave him the finger and left."

Bah! I would have expected a clever *verbal* riposte from such an eminent professional stage comedian. No doubt retirement was overdue for a man who had lost his oral insult skills.

"Mr. Rondle wasn't at your retirement party, right?"

"He most certainly wasn't. Why would he want to kill Cynthia, anyway?"

"She disappointed him badly by being unable to convince you, for one. My impression of him was that he wants your vineyards very, very badly, much as he tried to remain blasé about it. And for two, to get even with you by hurting you. Better yet, making it look like you killed Cynthia. You might even be next on his hit list. With you gone, maybe he figures he can deal with whoever inherits your property."

"Two verys, eh? Well, if he snuck into my party, I never saw him there."

I wasn't about to point out that Murky's failure on that score meant nothing. But I did at least get him to admit he was both busy with guests and woozy from swilling his usual intake of Wild Turkey.

"Who does inherit, Murky? I assume you have a will?"

"Of course, I do. With Cynthia gone, I've left the bulk of my estate, including the ranch, to Peggy Ann."

"Does she know she inherits?"

"Yep."

Those who stand to inherit wealth have always climbed to the top of my suspect lists, although sometimes someone with a deeper, darker motive has emerged as the culprit. Yet, prosecutors in cases I've been on have most often gone with the most transparent suspect and at least three times that I recall from my Burbank PD days the wrong person was convicted. And in two of those cases the state of California took three years to set things right.

Finally, I showered, dressed, and left Murky in his pickled state of hot-tub bliss, asking Armando, one of Murky's house servants, to keep an eye on his lordship, lest Murky literally drown his sorrows in his pool of bubbling water.

XX

Morning found me parked outside the gated estate of Paolo Galboni, in the prosperous Rancho Oro section of Santa Julietta, perched among the olive groves in the eastern foothills of that sainted city.

Without an invitation to pass beyond the wrought iron gates leading to Galboni Land, I waited for any vehicle belonging to one of the many vendors expected to deliver goods for a large lawn party the Galboni's were hosting the following day.

I learned of the party and pre-party preparations from Amanda Reynolds, who had tried to schedule a deposition with Roxanna Galboni for either day and was turned down because Roxanna told Amanda that she would be too busy helping her mother prepare for an elaborate birthday gala for Roxanna's younger sister, Sienna, who would be turning fifteen on the day of the party.

After nearly an hour of waiting, I was blessed with the arrival of three delivery vans at once. One truck belonged to a flossy local florist, the second one belonged to a caterer, and a third large one was a tent supplier. Once through the gates, the flower truck turned off early, toward vast colorful gardens. So I followed the catering truck up to the house.

The tent truck parked beside a cemetery-sized lawn of lush grass. The driver seemed to know what to do already, as he quickly gave hand signals to the two helpers emerging from the passenger side of the truck.

"Are you with Jacque, the caterer? Or with Tents for All Seasons?" a woman asked as I stood on the south portico of main house. She was in her mid to late forties, I guessed, with long black hair sparkling with strands of premature white. I hadn't seen her approach from the side of the house.

"None of the above, ma'am. I'm here to speak with Mr. Paolo Galboni."

"For what purpose?" she said politely, making me think she might not be a member of the household staff, but someone higher up the food chain.

"I'm here to discuss one of his employees, a Mr. Giovanni Alba."

"I know of no such man by that name working for us."

Us. The lady of the house.

"Mr. Alba only began working for you recently. Perhaps your husband hasn't introduced him to you yet," I said.

"Assuredly he has not," she said, eying me warily, as if 'Assuredly he has not' was assuredly not the right answer. "In any event, Paolo isn't here and won't be here the rest of the day.'"

"Does he have a business office where I might see him?"

"He conducts all of his business from...." She paused and her eyes narrowed. "I would have thought you knew where my husband conducted his business affairs."

"No. This is the first time I've had to have any dealings with him."

"Tell me what it is you want to know about this Giovanni fellow. I'll see what I can do."

Giovanni. But she knows of no such man.

"Alba is his last name," I said.

"Yes. Of course. Now please continue, Mister...?"

"Fletcher."

She took a step back and eyed me slowly from head to toe and back again.

Finally, she said, "You work for that attorney woman who defends my daughter's friend's rapist, do you not?"

"Accused rapist. That is why I am here. I wish to interview you husband and Mr. Alba."

She raided her voice. "I've already told you. My husband is not here. Nor is... the other man."

"Alba. Giovanni. I want to know why your husband has involved himself in this matter, actually both your husband and, by proxy, Mr. Alba."

"My husband is not involved in *this matter*, as you call it."

"I think he is."

"No! You are wrong! Now go away. Immediately. Or I will call the police. By the way, you should never have spoken to my daughter without her parents' permission. That was unconscionable of you."

I thought my speaking to Roxanna was hardly unconscionable, even though I knew Roxanna was only eighteen, when the age of adulthood in California was twenty-one. And I knew the courts would not ask permission from her parents to allow her to take the witness stand, should *this matter* come to trial.

I was returning to my car when I heard a soft female voice call out my name from behind me. I turned and saw Roxanna, wearing a turquoise muumuu and sandals.

"I apologize for my mother. My little sister's birthday party has her all stressed and making her behave badly. If you're looking for my father, I don't know where he is. And if Mother told you she didn't know where he is, she's probably not lying. Sometimes Daddy just disappears for days at a time without telling us where he is going -- or where he has been, when he returns."

I said to Roxanna, "Do you know anything about Giovanna Alba?"

"All I know is that he now does errands for our family winery, the kinds of errands he used to do for El Condor."

"And what kinds of errands are those?" I said.

A shrug before saying, "I don't really know. I think Daddy worries people are going to try to harm our family business in some way or other. "

"Do you think El Condor used Mr. Alba to try to hurt Galboni Winery?"

"I don't think anything, because I'm not allowed to know anything about the family business. After all, I'm just a woman. Or rather, a young woman, a little girl even."

Roxanna said this with an evident twinge of bitterness at the sexism. But then she belonged to a new generation, one that clearly lacked respect for "the old ways" of her parents and grandparents. Unlike Ricky Claymore, who seemed to embrace his father's and grandfather's traditions and way of life.

"So how does your family business survive if your father removes himself from the scene for days at a time? Who makes all the decisions that he normally makes?"

Another shrug, one she definitely learned from the male elders in her family tree. I had a hunch the shrug masked more than it told me. I was sure that, although there was much the young woman did not know, there were things she knew but was choosing not to share. Things that might be useful to my search for a defense for Ricky Claymore.

"Roxanna, I'd be grateful if you could provide me with some clues to where I can locate your boyfriend, Terry, and two of his mates, Harry Deemer, and Chuck Paltzheimer."

She gave me a weak laugh.

"Unless they all want to flunk out this term, they had better not have gone far. My guess is that they may have headed north for a long weekend in Santa Cruz. That's one of their favorite getaway spots. I'm also guessing that they'll be back by Sunday night. Or not. I don't think Terry wants to say anything that might hurt Wendy's chance to nail Ricky Claymore."

"He can't hide forever."

"He can try."

"Any particular spot in Santa Cruz?" I said.

"Try the seedy motels close to the Boardwalk. Neither Harry nor Chucky has a steady girlfriend now. So --. Have you ever been to Santa Cruz's Boardwalk district?"

I had and nodded in the affirmative. A previous case a year earlier had taken me to SC's Boardwalk area. My experiences from that case were still producing bitter and sorrowful memories. As with that case, in the Ricky Claymore case I had to remind myself that the Rich and Powerful really do live by a different set of rules, especially different laws, from the rest of us.

In my case a year earlier I knew a rich woman had murdered her husband. I even had what I thought was compelling, though circumstantial, evidence to prove her guilt. Yet the prosecutor and the police wouldn't bring charges against her. Instead, a kingpin from the criminal underworld framed her for an entirely different crime. So only then did she end up facing criminal charges. Now, though she was found guilty -- by a jury not exactly of her peers -- she has highly paid lawyers filing appeals on her behalf.

Meanwhile, the underworld kingpin who set her up was himself guilty of murder in Santa Julietta at the same time. His justice only came when I tipped off one of the sisters of an underling -- whom he had also killed. The sister fed my information regarding his temporary whereabouts in Mexico to her relatives there. Then, according to the sister, those relatives delivered justice to the kingpin. Unfortunately, shortly after the sister told me the local kingpin had been killed in Mexico, she disappeared -- permanently. There were no cozy endings to that case.

XXI

From Amanda Reynold's secretary's phone I dialed up the Kappa Psi house and was told my three guys had not returned yet. So where were they hiding in Santa Cruz, as Roxanna suggested? Or was she not to be trusted? Maybe she was just buying time for them as they headed toward the obscurity of Los Angeles. One thing I did learn was that none of them was bright enough to miss classes for any length of time and still manage to earn a passing grade. So the longer they remained missing, the greater their academic peril.

Hungry and frustrated, I decided "Screw 'em until tomorrow", drove back to Santa Maria, and grabbed a burger at Shelby's on Clark. After I had feasted on a greasy onion burger and over-salted fries, I headed home for a well-deserved shower and a couple of beers.

Seeing the barricades on my street, Third Street, reminded me of sewer construction that had been going on for at least two weeks. It seemed more like two eons. So I drove over to Fourth Street, planning to slip down the alley and park in my rear neighbors' extra parking space next to their garage. Sol and Noella had given me permission. Besides, I sort of remembered that they were off on vacation, puttering around the edges of the Mediterranean.

As I reached the alley I slammed on my breaks next to a car I was sure I recognized. It was a robin-egg blue 1966 Buick Electra, with tail fins streaming back like ribbons of fire. It belonged to Giovanni Alba. No doubts. He was looking for me, I was sure. And he had been sent by Paolo Galboni. But why?

If a man's home is his castle, mine is certainly a vulnerable one. On a previous case I was shot at as I sat reading in my living room easy chair with my drapes open. Luckily the shooter mistook my image in a mirror across from where I sat for the real me and my reflection took a bullet right between its eyes. The mirror and my picture window also suffered serious damage. I walked away unscathed.

I decided to avoid another encounter with someone known to have been following me. So I drove to a nearby drugstore and used the outside pay phone to call the police to report a burglar at my premises. I then drove back and parked where I could observe Giovanni Alba's car.

Three minutes later I saw the reflections of flashing red lights off windows between my house and where I sat parked. One minute after that Alba returned to his car, walking slowly, trying not to look suspicious, but giving himself away to me nonetheless. He drove north on Thornburg and turned on east after passing the junior high school.

I followed him, hoping he would turn back on Pine Street and drive past my house, pretending to be merely a curious onlooker, wondering what all the police lights were about. I had provided the police with a description of his car and hoped they would stop him. But I was wrong. He continued east to Broadway, a main thoroughfare, and then headed north, out of the city.

When I returned to my house the police were still there. Alba had attempted to jimmy my back door, but my deadbolt won that battle, though not without Alba's tearing a huge gouge in the casing. I guessed that my insurance deductible was going to run higher than the cost of fixing the casing. I told myself that when I found time I'd do the repair myself.

On my telephone call to them I had given the police the license plate number of Alba's car. So I left it to them to have further dealings with Signore Alba. I called my answering service and found out Amanda Reynolds had arranged an interview at ten o-clock with Richard Claymore II for the next morning in the Grill Room of the Alisal Ranch Golf Club, just outside of Solvang.

After the cops departed I decided to take a hot bath. And, on the chance Alba decided to return, I lay in the tub with my Smith & Wesson on the ledge and my living room stereo turned off. The latter represented a major sacrifice for me. Nothing complements a hot bath so much as the soothing tones of Gregorian chants, something my father taught me long ago.

With periodic police drive-bys throughout the night, Alba was wise to have stayed away. His car was found abandoned fifteen miles up the coast in the town of Pismo Beach with no sign of Alba. The Santa Maria police were kind to share info they were not obliged to disclose. Namely that no blood was found on Alba's car, nor had the Buick been damaged in any way. Alba had simply fled, they told me.

Well, at least I could take comfort that he wasn't going to pursue me on foot. On the other hand, when he changed cars I would no longer see him coming. I prefer being the pursuer, rather than the pursued. Pursuers almost always live longer.

XXII

Richard Claymore II was just finishing a plate of *huevos rancheros* when I slide into a chair across from him. He handed me a menu and gestured toward his empty highball glass -- which appeared to have recently contained a Gin Rickey -- by way of asking me if I cared for a morning cocktail.

"No thanks, sir. I just finished having coffee and a Danish at the bakery in Solvang."

Having read up on the middle Richard Claymore before I came, I knew him to be forty-eight years old, twice married, and the father of two sons, one of whom died of an accidental gunshot wound a year earlier. I had already warned myself to steer well clear of the topic of his dead son.

The man was trying strenuously to serve in his own father's immense shadow. By all accounts he was not succeeding -- at least by El Condor's standards. So the Old Man was refusing to let go, not allowing his son to take control of their wine empire.

"Mr. Fletcher, I hope you get the goods on that young woman, Wendy Simmons. Somehow prove she has fabricated this entire story about my Ricky's forcing himself on her."

I heard what he said, but he nonetheless stared over toward the bar, where a radio was playing Chuck Berry's "Promised Land" a tad too loudly. Mr. Claymore then stood and walked over to speak to the bartender, who, in turn, adjusted the volume of the music downward.

"Sorry about that," he said when he returned.

"Thanks. I was of two minds about the volume. I do want to hear everything you have to say without my straining to listen. On the other hand, Chuck Berry borrowed the melody for that song from 'Wabash Cannonball'."

I got a puzzled look.

I explained, "The Wabash Railroad is in Indiana, where my father grew up."

"Oh," was his only response.

So I said, "Giovanni Alba has been following me."

"Better watch out. Alba's a nasty piece of work."

"Do you know he's working for Paolo Galboni now?"

"No. I didn't know that."

"You do know your father fired him, right?"

He made a face before saying, "I didn't know that either."

Jeesuz! No wonder the Old Man wouldn't let him run his empire on his own. Either Richard II was deaf and blind, or else El Condor was a master at concealing matters from his son.

"So you warn me about the guy while supposing he is still working for Condor wines?" I said.

"Giovanni is dangerous no matter who he is working for. Let me tell you a story about Giovanni from when he was a small boy."

I was angry, but I let him continue.

"You've heard the accusation leveled at someone that goes 'He'd steal the pennies off a dead man's eyes', right?"

I nodded.

"Well, as a child Giovanni actually did it. And they weren't pennies either. They were two large pieces of gold." He paused, then said, "I'm a couple years older than Gio and we both attended a mass for one of my father's uncles. At a cathedral up in Fresno. While everyone else had his head bowed in prayer, I peeked and saw him run up, snatch the gold, then return to his place and pretend to be praying. "

"Did you tell anyone?" I said.

"No. Even then, as a young punk Gio had a mean reputation. I'm older than he is, but I was afraid of him. Rumor is that he's killed people." In a lower voice he added, "Killed them at my father's bidding. But that's just a rumor. I've never tried to confirm it. And I've certainly never asked my father."

"Back to your son."

"Yes."

I explained to him how I had been trying without success to track down the three potential witnesses who might corroborate Ricky's narrative. I also explained how I had interviewed both the alleged victim, Wendy Simmons, and her best friend, Roxanna Galboni."

"Roxanna is Paolo's daughter, is she not."

I nodded.

"I hear she's a nice young woman. I'm surprised she's giving her support to Miss Simmons, if Ricky's right that Miss Simmons was... well, you know... enticing Roxanna's boyfriend to cheat on Roxanna with her."

"Me, too. Unless she doesn't know yet," I said.

"I'd be surprised about that," he said and gave me a guilty look.

I made a mental note to go back to campus to see if I could tiptoe around the subject, yet still find out for certain whether Roxanna Galboni did indeed know that, according to Ricky Claymore at least, Terry Morowitz had been having sex with Wendy Simmons.

"Paolo Galboni is one of your company's chief competitors in this region. How does that fit into this equation?" I said.

"What equation?"

"Roxanna, Wendy, Ricky."

"Coincidence, I'm sure."

Yeah, right. The recipe for Murky Murtrans's murder case was beginning to look simpler by comparison. I left Richard Claymore to join three of his business friends for a round of golf and caught State Road 146 toward Sisquoc, where I finally ended up at Murky's ranch, after passing Ben Rondle's ranch along the way.

"Damned if I know where they went, Fletcher. Both of them have keys to my blue pickup truck. I don't ask either of them to check in or out. Last I knew Nancy was in no shape to drive. But then I've suspected her of faking whatever illness she supposedly has.

Can't say I recall her going anywhere to see a doctor, and I know there hasn't been any medical people come to the ranch to see her."

Murky was referring to his sister-in-law, Nancy Lorgran. Peggy Ann Lorgran's mother, and to Peggy Ann.

"By the way, my son's witch of a wife, Genesis, was just here. My God, if there is a Hell, I'd love to sit on a picnic blanket and spend a lazy afternoon watching her dance on a bed of red-hot rocks."

"Pissed you off that badly, did she?" I said.

"Damned right she did. She came her to snivel and drivel about how I should feel obliged to honor my dead wife's commitment to give Jess the money to build his new church, blah, blah, blah. How my not writing her husband a check for a quarter of a million dollars would be a disservice to poor Cynthia's memory."

I chuckled.

"Precisely. What utter horseshit!"

"What if she had asked you nicely? Said 'Please, Mr. Murtrans.'"

Murky slapped his thigh and said, "I'd still have told her to go fuck herself. Mercy, that woman is a walkin' billboard for abortion. Her mother has a lot to be held accountable for."

"I've met her, Murky. She strikes me as no more than a typical True Believer. She doesn't know any better. I'm sure she thinks the hand of the Lord is pressing gently on her back."

"Well, when she left here the toe of my boot was pressing not so gently up her ass."

"Could she have killed Cynthia?"

"She wasn't even here." Murky paused, then added, "At least I didn't invite her."

"Easy enough to slide in among all your hard-drinking guests and host. One door into the billiard room opens from the outside of the house. And, you've already allowed, is never locked."

Murky thought for a while, a task made more difficult for him without his usual tumbler of whiskey in one hand.

"Jeezus, Fletcher! What kind of heart of stone would it take for that woman to kill my wife, then come back and plead with me to 'honor my dead wife's commitment' to build her and her husband's holy mother-fucking church?"

"The magnitude of such audacity doesn't rule it out," I said.

"The hellishness of such atrociousness is what you mean."

"Okay."

"How can we catch her out?"

"I need to think on that."

"I'm willing to beat a confession out of the shrew."

"No, No. She may even be innocent, you know."

"Who's more likely than she is?" he asked.

"Peggy Ann is the primary beneficiary of your will."

XXIII

"Yeah, as I told you already, Peggy Ann gets the ranch and most of my money, but I can always change that if it turns out she killed Cynthia."

"Unless she kills you first."

"You really think she'd kill her Old Uncle Murky, Fletcher?"

"Lots of people have killed in anticipation of a whole lot less."

"Yes, but you'd prove her guilty, Stu. And then all she'd inherit is a couple of whiffs of cyanide, courtesy of the State of California."

"In that case, maybe her mother killed Cynthia and plans to do you in next, all in the name of delivering your pots of gold and the land you've buried them in over to her daughter."

"You've got a point. Nancy's always been a treacherous fiend. I swear, sometimes I've thought she'd just as soon shoot me as look at me."

"Well, you're not much to look at."

"Okay. Enough of this talk. You prove Nancy is Cynthia's killer and I'll write you a check for fifty grand."

That sounded good to me, but I wasn't about to frame Nancy Lorgran in order to fatten my bank account.

"By the way, I want you to stay for dinner. I'm grillin' some steaks. Besides, I've invited a couple of guests who will surely tickle your detective buds. Among the four of us we should stir up some spicy conversation."

I left Murky to tend to his dinner preparations and sat comfortably on his back porch, nursing a Budweiser. Next thing I knew, I heard a familiar voice.

"Well, well. The clever sleuth is among us. Figured out who killed Cynthia yet?" Jocko Silverado walked out and occupied the chair across from me.

"You'd save me time by confessing," I said, omitting his name in my reply. I wasn't sure quite how to address him. *Mr. Silverado* struck me as too formal, *Jocko* as too informal. After all, I had only met him once and that occasion had been for official business.

"Confessing to what? Standing in need of a tall whiskey? I confess. Where's the waiter?"

"Don't look at me," said Betty Sue Murtrans, waltzing onto the porch as though making a Broadway stage entrance. "I never played step-n'-fetchit roles in my career."

"At least that might have made you memorable, Sweetheart," Jocko panned.

"I'm sure the value of fifteen percent of my royalties and residuals is profoundly memorable to you, Mr. Silverstein."

Jocko's eyes narrowed, but he said nothing in response to Betty Sue's reminder that Jocko was Jewish.

Thankfully, Murky appeared to announce, "I'm ready to put on the ribeyes, folks. Jocko, you want medium rare; Betty Sue wants well-done, I know. How about you, Fletcher?"

"Medium well," I said.

Murky then retreated to the kitchen again.

Betty Sue said, "I thought you Jews didn't eat beef, Jock."

"I think that's Muslim's, Betty Sue," he said.

"Well, what's all that business about rabbis blessing stuff? Oh never mind. I wouldn't understand it anyway."

Jocko looked at me and shrugged.

Murky returned with a platter of steaks and walked to the end of the porch, where his grill was smoking. While Murky flung our steaks onto the grill with gusto, Jocko went into the house and returned quickly with a Highball glass full of Wild Turkey. He hadn't bothered to ask Betty Sue if she cared for a drink, so I did.

"Why, thank you, Mr. Fletcher. I would like a Manhattan."

Over his shoulder, as the meat sizzled, Murky called out to me, "Whiskey, vermouth, and bitters. Heavy on the whiskey for Betty Sue." Then he added, "Betty Sue, Fletcher ain't no bartender. It's all he can do to remember to pop the cap on a beer."

I winced.

Murky then added, "Remember the ol' line: *Git away from that wheel barrel, Pancho. You don't know nuthin' 'bout muh-sheenery?* That's the way Fletcher is about bartendin'. Dumb as a dead goat."

I responded, "The next time you want me to pour you a whiskey neat, Murky, I'll pretend to forget how to."

"One Fletcher ribeye, burnt to a crisp, comin' up," Murky said, then guffawed.

After we were seated and eating our salads, Jocko said, "Where's Peggy Ann. I thought she might be here."

Murky said, "Sorry, Jock. You're out of luck." Pause. "Or maybe not." To Betty Sue he asked, "Hey, Betty Sue. Did you give Jocko a blowjob while he was driving you here?"

Betty Sue said, "Now, Murky. I told you when we were still married that I do not engage in such behavior in a moving vehicle."

"So you did, Sweetie." Pause. "Reckon you're SOL, Jocko. Unless you can talk Betty Sue into takin' you into my office and doin' you on my castin' couch the way Peggy Ann did you on the night of my retirement party."

"Did Peggy Ann do that, Mister Jocko Silverado? Why, shame on you," Betty Sue said.

"She ought to mean shame on Peggy Ann, shouldn't she, Jock? I'm sure it was Peggy Ann's idea," Murky said, and punched Jock on a shoulder.

Jock failed to blush, I thought, though it would have been hard to tell with his deep tan.

He did, however, remain silent and stare off into the Middle Distance.

Murky continued. "Hey, Jocko. Think of it this way. Peggy Ann gave you one hell of an alibi for your not murderin' Cynthia. And gave herself one as well, eh?"

Betty Sue said, "Shame on you anyway, Jock."

Murky then said, "Fletcher, did I ever tell you the story about Judy Garland and her producer, Arthur Freed?"

"Yes, you did. At least part of it."

"Well, here's the rest. Ol' Arthur used to make Judy stand naked on a chair in his office and sing "Over the Rainbow" to him. At least that was the scuttlebutt back then. Now whether she gave him a bj before or after she sang to him still has folks divided. But no one questions the fact that she sucked and sang naked for him. No question of it because we all know the story of poor Shirley Temple and Arthur, when he had twelve-year-old Shirley in his office alone with him."

Actually, I did not know the Shirley Temple story. But I was not about to ask Murky to fill me in on it.

XXIV

After dinner the four of us retired to Murky's living room, where he had a crackling fire burning in his huge fireplace, even though it was summer. Drinks for Betty Sue, Jocko, and Murky switched from wine to bourbon. I stayed with another beer.

Sinking into one of Murky's overstuffed leather chairs, Betty Sue said, "Got any more questions for me, Mr. Detective?"

I listened to her clink the ice cubes in her tumbler before answering. Betty Sue, unlike Jocko and Murky, didn't drink her whiskey neat. Finally, I said, "Sure. Remind me where you told me you were around the time Cynthia got beaned in the billiard room."

"You mean right after she slapped me?"

"You can start there," I said.

"I went straight to the ladies' room to see if the slap had left a welt on my cheek."

"And did it?"

"Sure it did. She really let me have it."

"Did you learn your lesson?" Jocko asked snidely.

"I'll never know, will I? Cynthia will never catch me and Murky French kissing again. Isn't that right, Mr. Murtrans."

"I consider that highly disrespectful, Betty Sue. Knock it off," Murky said.

"Oh, now since when did you consider French kissing disrespectful?" she said.

"You know what I mean."

I said, "So you went to the powder room to examine your face. What next?"

She thought for a couple moments before saying, "I guess I went out onto the back porch to get some air. The atmosphere was kinda steamy in the piano parlor, if you know what I mean."

The back porch. Well now. The billiard room was directly accessible from the back porch. And, according to Murky's account, the back porch was left dark after the sun went down.

"Did you see anyone else out on the porch while you were there, Betty Sue?" I said.

"I heard Nancy talking with someone, but I couldn't tell who was with her. She's got a real distinctive voice, you know. And loud."

"Was the voice besides Nancy's male or female?"

"I can't say for sure. I was still smartin' from that slap, you know. So I wasn't thinkin' all too clearly."

"Take a guess."

"One of the servants. Nancy's always so demanding of them. She probably wanted a refill on her drink without having to go back into the house to get it."

Jocko sat looking like he felt left out of the conversation, so I fired a question at him.

"Jocko, Murky's retirement has surely left a large gap in your life -- both your private and your social life. How have, had, you made plans to fill those empty hours and days?"

Murky's retirement party was, I now realized, symbolic. Pretty much everyone in the Murk's immediate orbit had lost his or her continuing sense of purpose and I had been trying to determine how that was playing out with each of those characters. I wanted to gage Jocko's self-estimate of his life after Murky. He immediately grasped where I was fishing and bit on my bait.

"Gap? Yes. Leaving me unemployed? Hardly. I'll miss trying to wheedle Murky into accepting new roles. But don't think for a moment,

Mr. Fletcher, that my financial condition has ever depended on the small percentages I collected from Murky's contracts."

"No deep letdown? No feeling that, with Murky out to pasture, you might be viewed as a has-been agent? And with that your other signings might fall off dramatically?" I said.

Jocko gave me a small shrug.

"Oh, I'm sure I'll loose a few bookings I might have lassoed if Murky was still in my corral. But not enough to make me contemplate murdering Cynthia." He then grinned and added, "At least I wouldn't kill her for that reason."

"What would have been an adequate motive?" I said.

"Banning Peggy Ann from coming to the ranch, like she threatened a time or two lately. Or banning me."

"Why would she ban you?"

"Two reasons. For my continued harassing of Murky to stay in show business. *Harassing* was her repeated exaggeration. And for my continued pestering of her niece. Again, *pestering* was her mis-description."

"Tell me, Jocko. Did you ever screw Cynthia? Either before or after she married Murky?"

My question stirred Murky from his semi-slumber. He ever spilled a few drops of his precious Wild Turkey down the front of his shirt.

"Easy does it, Fletcher. Jocko's too good a friend for me to shoot him between his eyes," Murky said. "If you think you need to know the answer to that question, ask him when I'm not around."

"I didn't think you were around, Murky. You were beginning to snore, which strongly suggested to me that you had drifted out to sea."

"Nope. My anchor is still dug into the sea floor, even if I'm three sheets to the wind."

My youth was spent as a part-time sailor, learning "the ropes" from my father. But I was unaware that Murky was familiar with nautical terms, although *three sheets to the wind* had already entered general English usage as a metaphor for drunkenness.

Murky sat up and brushed away Miss Kitty, much to the calico cat's annoyance. She had been asleep on Murky's chest. The cat staggered away as though either it was not yet fully awake or else it was drunk from inhaling Murky's bourbon breath. Miss Kitty, Murky once told me, was named after the female saloon owner on the TV Western *Gunsmoke.*

Jocko said, "Mr. Fletcher, I was the man who introduced Cynthia to Murky."

Murky objected. "You got that backwards, Jocko. You introduced me to her."

With that piece of farce I decided to take my leave, only Murky objected to that, too.

"Spend the night, Fletcher. You may not have sucked as much juice out of the whiskey bottle as I have, but I declare you unfit to drive. I don't want one of Sheriff Cuddly's brown shirts to pull you over for DUI and jail your ass. You still gotta find Cynthia's killer."

So I agreed -- reluctantly -- to spend the night in one of Murky's guest cottages. Not since 1946, when I was a teenager, had I slept on a ranch. WWII was over and I was living in San Diego with my parents. My dad had just mustered out of the Navy, where he had served as a pilot trainer. A fellow trainer, Heinie Walters, from a rich Kansas family, had bought one of the Navy's now obsolete PV-2 Harpoon aircraft, a medium-sized, two-engine, twin-tail utility plane.

Heinie offered to let my dad fly the plane to southern Arizona for a week, even offering to pay for the fuel the plane would use. Apparently, Heinie felt he owed my dad for getting him out of some scrape or other with Navy MP's a year back. Dad refused to tell Mom and me the story, but my father did accept Heinie's offer.

The KRK Ranch lay one hundred miles southeast of Tucson, in the Sulphur Springs Valley. To the west of the ranch lay the Dragoon Mountains and the Cochise Stronghold. Just to the west of that lay the town of Tombstone. It was a working ranch of six hundred acres, and eighty to ninety head of cattle at any given time. But it was also a dude ranch with room for twelve guests at a time. Mom wasn't took keen on the idea of going there but, because I was excited to go, she agreed to go.

Dad flew the Harpoon right to the ranch, which had a twelve-hundred-foot-long hard-pack gravel runway. The ranch's owner, Kyle McLaren, was a flying enthusiast, as well as a rancher and owned a Piper J-3 Cub, plus a brand new model Cessna 140. Kyle's son, Seth, met us when we landed and drove us to the ranch house in a Jeep station wagon. The trip took us over a stretch of washboard dirt road, which caused my mother to squeal and fear the rattling was going to cause her teeth to fall out.

I got to ride a horse ever day and help with branding five new calves that Mr. McLaren had just bought. Plus, the ranch had a swimming pool and two billiard tables and a horseshoe pit. I had a grand time, while my parents took it easy, mostly eating and rocking in porch rockers while they read the latest best-seller novels.

Murky's ranch was bigger, had hills and trees, and was almost as remote as the KRK Ranch. Yet, as I lay in bed listening to a coyote bark and howl nearby, I didn't feel the thrill I felt back in 1946, when it seemed as though I was part of the Wild West of Wyatt Earp and Geronimo.

Gustavo, Murky's personal chef, had prepared a breakfast fit for royalty. Alas, his patrons were a pair of hungover low-lifes. Still, Murky and I both ate with gusto and the Murk drank pink champagne from a beer mug.

"Bubbly is the best cure for a bourbon headache," he muttered as he polished off a plateful of scrambled eggs and two plates full of crisp bacon.

I chose strong coffee topped with frothy cream to treat my own brain damage. Whether it helped or not, I wasn't up to judging.

Between gulps of wine, Murky told me, "Jocko and Betty Sue trotted off to their cabin shortly after you left us, Fletcher. Knowing Betty Sue, I suspect she took Señor Silverado for a ride into the sunset." When I failed to respond, he added, "Her ass gives a ride as smooth as a Cadillac's."

For background noise Murky preferred listening to a police scanner over listening to any type of music. So it was that, as he and I were finishing our breakfast, excited voices on the scanner told of a pair of automobiles just discovered off Highway 146 between Sweetwater Canyon and Sisquoc Falls, both cars appearing to have gone off the highway and settled near the bank of the Sisquoc River.

The description of one of the cars made me stop eating Gustavo's fresh strawberries and listen more closely. It was a robin-egg blue Buick Electra. Maybe Giovanni Alba's. But was he in it? I moved my chair closer to the scanner, taking my bowl of berries with me. The second car, a policeman said, was a Sheriff's Department cruiser. Soon another voice announced the driver of the cruiser was dead. The cruiser's number was 218. The same sheriff's car that had stopped me after I had left Murky's on the day after Cynthia Murkans had been murdered. I told myself that, with luck, Colby Gray was the dead man in the cruiser.

In any case, I excused myself -- or tried to.

"Where the hell you goin', Fletcher? We got things to discuss, ground to cover," Murky said when he realized I intended to leave.

"I'll be back in an hour," I told him as I opened the door to leave. I actually supposed I'd be gone at least twice that length of time.

XXV

The road was blockaded at the town of Sisquoc, deputies explaining to drivers that a multiple-vehicle accident a few miles ahead was the reason for closing the highway. Flashing my PI license was not going to gain me a special dispensation to enter the police-only zone. So I did what any self-respecting progeny of Sam Spade and Philip Marlow would do. I performed an end run -- taking gravel-packed ranch roads and Forest Services dirt roads through the Los Padres National Forest until I finally reemerged onto Highway 146 some five miles southeast of Sisquoc. Sheriff Sam Cuddleston himself was on the scene when I pulled up behind a cruiser with its red lights flashing.

"I suppose I shouldn't ask how you got past my men," Cuddleston said when I approached him.

"Via the magic of narrow, rattletrap, back roads," I said.

"Why the effort?" the sheriff said.

I pointed to the Buick, where paramedics were extracting the driver from a car that now looked more like Lawrence Welk's accordion.

"The medics say the guy might live. Know him?"

I explained what I knew of Giovanni Alba, assuming that was who the sheriff's men were now loading onto a gurney.

As the men with the sheriff's medical aid car passed by, the sheriff motioned from them to stop.

"Is that your guy?" he said to me.

"I can't say for sure. I've never seen him up close.," I said.

Sheriff Cuddleston roughly emptied the man's pocket, causing the man to groan.

"Yep, this is your guy, Fletcher. But you can't talk to him now."

With a nod of his head the sheriff told the paramedics to load Alba into the ambulance.

To me Cuddleston said, "You can speak with him -- briefly -- in the hospital. Tomorrow. Maybe. That's actually up to the docs."

"Which hospital?"

"The new one. Marian."

Santa Maria's Sisters of Saint Francis Hospital had served the city well for decades, but with Vandenberg Air base causing a rapid increase in population in recent years, the city needed a new primary medical facility. Remarkable -- and surprising -- community cooperation resulted in the Marian Regional Medical Center.

I turned to leave when one of Sheriff Cuddleston's deputies approached him, looking somber. I paused long enough to hear the deputy whisper to the sheriff, "Colby was breathing when I got here, but not now. He's gone. I tried to get him out to do CPR, but he's pinned against the steering wheel."

I turned and walked back to my car, thinking Colby Gray's death made for one less asshole cop on California's highways. No doubt I should have felt more charitable. The guy probably had a wife and kids. Still, now, after a suitable period of grief, she could surely find herself a better husband, find a decent step-father for her kids. I couldn't imagine any woman being happily married to Colby Gray. I was willing to shed a tear for Mrs. Colby Gray -- but not for him.

With most of the day ahead of me, I decided to drive to Santa Cruz. But first I swung over to Pismo Beach to ask among the "bushy blond hairdo" surfers referred to in the 1963 Beach Boys' *Surfin' USA* song if they had seen any of the three young college men I was seeking. No one acknowledged seeing any of them.

Two days earlier I had clipped a photo of the three from a yearbook I had found on a shelf at the UCSJ campus library. I knew my act to be utterly rebarbative, but I did it anyway, desperate as I was. My next door neighbor in Santa Maria, Mary Ann Chase, would never forgive me, were she to find out. Murder she could pardon. Defacing a library book? Never.

She was sixty-eight years old and a retiree from the Santa Maria Public Library. Five-foot two, with an impish smile, she had worked there as a reference librarian for forty-two years and had lived in the house next to mine for thirty-six of those years. She was the only person I knew, besides a handful of experts in Central American archeology and me, who knew that the name of the Aztec god Huitzilopochtli meant *left-handed hummingbird.*

I arrived in Santa Cruz in mid-afternoon, checked into a bedbug motel well south of the Boardwalk, unpacked my razor and my comb, then headed out to the pier, where I eased myself into a corner booth at the Tia Lopez Eclectic Cantina and ordered a Tecate beer. If I had said that life was good at that moment, I'd have been a liar. I was getting the proverbial "nowhere fast" on both my cases.

I began by showing the photos of my three amigos around to employees at the Cool Breeze Motel, which featured prominently in my last visit to Santa Cruz. Kimberly Hardy, the motel's owner, claimed not to remember me when she invited me into her office, though the flash of recognition in her eyes was palpable. I had spurned her advances when I had last sat in her office interviewing her about a missing woman. So maybe she had worked hard on suppressing all memory of my face after that little encounter.

I showed her the photo of the three college men.

"Handsome-looking studs. I doubt if they came here looking for whores. There's plenty of free pussy floating about this town."

That I already knew. And, in fact, I was staring at some of it.

Then she pointed out, "Plenty of freebies in Santa Julietta, too. Why come up *here* looking to get laid? Especially when they're as good-looking at those young gentlemen."

"Sex isn't the only way to have fun," I said.

"It's not? Who says?"

I didn't have time for her mocking game. So I stood and took my leave, much as I did the last time I had sat in her office.

Sam Williston's The Beach Browser Bookstore was still open for business, not that it seemed to attract much business. Sam looked at the photos I showed him and shook his head.

"Boys that age aren't interested in anything I sell. I don't stock *Playboy* magazine," he said, smirking.

"And you're sold out of copies of *Peyton Place*, right?" I said. A reference to an exchange Sam and I had the previous year.

"Probably."

I moved on to Truda Novotny's flower shop, but the sign in the window said that Truda would be closed for two weeks while she went back for a nephew's wedding in Czechoslovakia.

When I went around the corner to the Saintly Mission for the Homeless, the used clothing store where I had met Sandra Kraszynski a year earlier, the young woman who ran the store now told me she had no idea where Sandra had moved to. San Jose maybe. Or was it San Francisco?

I strolled over to the Boardwalk, but no one there had seen my three young men. I received the same answers from the shopkeepers out on the wharf. So I went back to my motel and sulked.

XXVI

"I wasn't expecting you back so soon. I thought you were up in Santa Cruz,"

Murky said when he saw me pull into his driveway.

"A short, unhappy, unfulfilling trip," I said, following him into his house.

"That must mean you didn't get laid, eh? Jeezus, Fletcher. In a town crawling with horny young coeds, you come up empty. I'm beginning to think you're queer."

"No time for women. Not when I'm working for Amanda Reynolds."

"Tell Amanda you were working for me and that required interviewing lots of hot, young cheerleaders."

"Amanda wants me not only to put your case on a back burner, she wants me then to turn that burner off."

"The Old Man get to her?" Murky said.

"What old man?" I said.

Murky fetched me two Buds and poured himself a double whiskey. He plopped himself into his easy chair in front of the fireplace and gestured for me to sit across from him. I complied.

"The guy they call El Condor."

"Oh, him."

"You know, Fletcher, sometimes I think you can't tell a schlemiel from a schlimazel."

"Enlighten me."

"Okay. Imagine you are sitting in a cafeteria full of people everyday and you see a woman walking from the coffee urn back to her seat. And every day that same woman trips and spills her coffee on somebody or other. That woman is a schlemiel, a bumbler, a klutz."

I nodded.

"Now imagine that woman always trips and spills her coffee on the same person every day. The same poor guy. Well, the person she spills her coffee on is a schlimazel, an unlucky person. An extremely unlucky person."

"The way you put it, I'm guessing the spillage is deliberate," I said.

Murky shrugged.

"Makes no difference," he said. "Accidental? Deliberate? The guy gets spilled on, time after time."

"Maybe he deserves it," I said.

"That makes him a schmendrick. A schmuck. A loser."

"And this Yiddish point of yours is?" I said.

"My point is this: That kid you are working so hard to absolve of his crime. Sorry. Of his *alleged* crime. Is he a schlemiel? A perpetrator? Or a schlimazel? A victim?"

"I'm hoping to prove he's a victim. Prove that he's been set up."

"Okay. But let me assure you of something. The family that kid comes from is a clan of perpetrators. Starting with the Old Man himself."

"You seem to be rather knowledgeable about the Claymores, Murky. Tell me about it."

And he did. But not before fetching the half-empty bottle of Wild Turkey and taking a long draw on it. He then placed the bottle carefully in his lap, nursing it like a newborn.

"If you want to know Ricky Claymore inside out, you need to speak with Peggy Ann. She'll tell you all about him. And about his family. Cutthroat pirates they are. Any one of them would just as soon slit your throat as look at you."

"How does Peggy Ann know Ricky?" I asked.

"Peggy Ann met Ricky through a mutual friend at Fresno State. Ricky's a gun enthusiast, just like Peggy Ann. Peggy's known him for a couple of years. A bunch of shooters, including the two of them, even drove down to LAX to welcome back that young man who won the three-hundred meter rifle gold medal at the Tokyo Olympics in '64. Gary Anderson, I think was the fella's name. Anyhow, Peggy Ann and Ricky Claymore were gettin' it on for several months. Then something happened. Peggy Ann wouldn't say exactly what. But suddenly the Claymore kid became anathema. She never brought him here to the ranch, but if the two of them were here right now, you can bet Peggy Ann would cut that kid's *cojones* off and pop 'em on the grill."

"Has Peggy Ann said anything about Ricky's arrest in Santa Julietta?" I said.

"You bet she did. Why, she laughed her fool head off. Said she hoped he gets what's comin' to him."

"How close did they get?" I said.

"Don't make me be crude, Fletcher. You've seen Peggy Ann. Use your imagination. But put a cap on it. You're too old for her."

"So they are not together any more. Why?"

"Peggy Ann got dumped. Finally got fucked without getting kissed. And why, you ask? Because Ricky is a dutiful boy. Dutiful grandson, that is. Peggy Ann claims the Old Man told Ricky that she wasn't good enough for him. Warned him that she lacked the class necessary to hob-nob with the Claymores."

"What was Peggy Ann's response?" I said.

"He broke her heart. That's what Ricky Fucking Claymore did to her. Put her ox in the ditch."

"Somehow I can't picture Peggy Ann crying in her beer... or, for that matter, come crying to you," I said.

"You're right. Peggy Ann is as solid as a bulldozer. Still, even bulldozers have feelings. Right?"

"But if Peggy Ann wasn't good enough for Ricky, Wendy Simmons wouldn't be good enough for him either. Her parents are as middle class as they come. No posh estate, no stable of polo ponies, no yacht with a clever name. Certainly no acres of grape vines."

"Watch yourself, Fletcher, when you're speaking of ponies and grape vines."

"That's what I don't understand, Murky. Peggy Ann is every bit as upper middle-class American as Ricky Claymore. You own horses and vineyards, same as El Condor. And, as I understand it, she inherits. Faster than Ricky, even. I imagine Richard the Second becomes El Condor Two when the Old Man dies."

"Maybe El Condor imagines himself to be descended from Julius Caesar, whereas I'm just a half-assed comedian from Hellfire, Alabama. Maybe it's me he resents, not Peggy Ann. I've even heard a rumor that Condor Wines is behind Sam Rondle's attempt to buy my vineyards. Now that will truly singe my hairs, if true. First, piss on Peggy Ann. Next piss on me."

I could see that Murky was working himself into a volcano. But then he cooled off -- at least for a moment.

"Ricky could haven been trying to dip into that Wendy chick just to defy his grandfather and his dad," Murky said.

"But, in that case, he might well have clandestinely tried to hang onto Peggy Ann," I pointed out.

"But he didn't. He dropped her straight down in the mud. Peggy Ann was the one who tried to hang on. Christ, that girl still burns a candle for that little shit. But, at the same time, she'd just as soon cut his balls off as kiss him. Spews unrequited love for the bastard one minute; screams at his photos the next. Whenever you get the urge again to try to figure out women, Fletcher, just go sit on a sharp stick instead. You'll find that more enlightening."

"Don't you think we are obliged to keep trying?" I said.

Murky laughed.

"What if God turns out to be a woman, Fletcher? Not only will I go to hell, I'll never know why."

So Murky's story was that Peggy Ann was a victim of El Condor's snobbishness. Ricky made a commitment to abide by his grandfather's false sense of class superiority and hence break up with Peggy Ann. But then Murky made it sound as though Peggy Ann was not going to accept Ricky's decision quietly. Oh boy. Now, not only were my two cases connected, but not in a good way. I got the impression Peggy Ann was quite keen to have Ricky Claymore be convicted of a rape charge, whether he deserved to be or not. The question now was: What might she do to abet Ricky's conviction?

Back in Santa Maria, I went to the hospital to see how Giovanni Alba was faring. Sheriff Cuddleston had green-lighted me to check in on Alba, but that turned out to be a revenge joke the sheriff had decided to play on me. Alba was in a coma. I was told he was lucky to be alive and there was no telling when, or if, he might become conscious again. No matter. I wasn't sure what to ask him. Nor whether I could trust whatever he told me.

Murky called me at home to tell me Nancy had returned to his ranch. Peggy Ann had not. But it was Peggy Ann I wanted most to speak with. Still, Nancy would do for a start. Perhaps she could tell me what both she and her daughter knew about Murky's making Peggy Ann the secondary beneficiary of his estate, after Cynthia.

When I arrived I found Murky in his favorite easy chair, nursing a tumbler of Wild Turkey. I had no idea how far down Whiskey Road he had traveled before my arrival, but he seemed reasonably coherent. Lucky me.

"Before that bitch, Nancy, strolls in here, Fletcher, let me tell you something about her I think you ought to know. First of all, Peggy Ann will fuck a snake if she can hold it still. But -- and this is important -- she learned that skill from her mother. And, unlike Peggy Ann -- Peggy Ann's too young -- Nancy can be a cradle-robber. And has been."

I could only guess, but my first guess was, "Ricky Claymore?"

Murky nodded, then grinned.

"Nancy taught Ricky most of what he knows," Murky said.

"Does Peggy Ann know?" I said.

"Nope. And don't you go tellin' her, Fletcher."

"I wouldn't think of it."

"Sure you would."

Murky didn't know me very well, and I intended to keep it that way.

"So, Murk, what does what you've just told have to do with Ricky Claymore's innocence or guilt?"

"Just that you can't trust women."

"If you have some proof that Ricky raped or didn't rape Wendy Simmons, please be forthcoming. But spare me your broad theory on the untrustworthiness of any and all females."

"I think if you dig deeper, you'll find that Ricky Claymore is a queer."

"Who told you this, Murky? Peggy Ann?"

"No."

"Nancy?"

A nod.

He said, "She can't think of any other reason for Ricky's turning his back on Peggy Ann. She refuses to believe that El Condor ordered him to drop Peggy Ann."

I shrugged.

"Could be so, Fletcher. Livin' in them fraternity houses can do it, I'm told. Hell, I didn't even go to college, but ...."

"But what?" I said.

Murky took a deep breath and looked all around slowly.

"One year when I was doin' stand-up in the Catskills there wasn't --. I mean there weren't any *shiksas* around. Christ, the only women -- single or married -- were Jew women. So what were guys like me to do?"

I sat quietly.

"Come on, Fletcher. There weren't any goddamned women."

"Except Jewish women."

"Exactly. So this other comedian --. I can't even remember his name. Anyway, we started to --. Oh, hell. You figure it out."

"So you're suggesting that fraternities and sororities are hotbeds of homosexuality," I said.

"Precisely! You figure it out. The numbers add up, don't they?"

"What numbers?"

Murky waved his arms as though what he was saying was obvious.

"You throw forty, fifty, or more horny young kids together like that, kids of the same sex, and... whammo!"

"Whammo, eh?"

"Yes, siree. It happened in the Catskills. Boom! Just like that."

"Why didn't it last?" I said.

"Are you mocking me, Fletcher?"

"No. But whamoo, you're gay; bammoo, you're not. Your transformations sound like Alice after she fell down the rabbit hole. One pill to make you queer; one pill to make you straight again. The Pope will want to know where he can buy a truckload of the latter pills."

"Beats me how any of it happened," Murky said, looking sheepish.

"Right. It's all a miracle. Or several miracles. God works in mysterious ways, eh?"

"Now I know you're mocking me."

"What I'm doing is letting you know I don't believe a word of this bullshit you've been feeding me."

"No. Wait! It's true. I did spend several nights in bed with some guy. Leonard was his name. I think."

"Okay, okay, Murky. I believe you. But what does this have to do with Peggy Ann and Ricky Claymore? I'm pretty sure Ricky isn't queer. And as for Peggy Ann --. Oh, forget it. None of this proves anything regarding whether Ricky could have raped Wendy Simmons."

"Sorry," Murky said.

"Does Peggy Ann know Wendy Simmons?" i said.

"She's never mentioned her."

"Too bad. I was thinking that maybe Peggy Ann encouraged Wendy to imagine that Ricky Claymore had raped her."

Murky laughed. "You haven't asked me if I know Wendy Simmons."

"Okay. do you?"

"No. But I know her girlfriend's dad."

"Paolo Galboni?'

"He's the one. I met him last year at a Santa Julietta Vintners' Association gathering. Paolo is a bit of an ass, but he has a gorgeous wife and a charming daughter."

"Yeah. I've met both the wife and the daughter. His wife is attractive all right, but a bit stern and curt," I said.

"I suppose if you had to put up with a guy like Paolo you'd lose your sense of humor fast enough."

"Supposing she had one to begin with."

"You're seldom one to give anybody a break, are you, Fletcher?"

"Not when I'm wearing my imaginary pork pie hat, I'm not."

Murky laughed, then said, "Stern and curt? It takes one to know one, right?"

"*Touché*, my friend. The muse still sticks with you, doesn't she?"

"Do you mean Thalia, the muse of comedy? Yes, she became my first true love, and we've been lovers ever since."

What could I say to that?

Murky continued, "The Greeks, you know, possessed a far richer set of stories about their gods, their demi-gods, plus the mortals who played among them -- both mortal fools and mortal wise men -- than any of the three religions derived from Abraham. Yahweh of the Old Testament is a vindictive monster and the Trinity of the New Testament only pretends to be kinder and gentler. Pretends because Hell is a horrific place and most of us are destined for it -- to the glee of those counted as Saved."

"Go on, " I said. "You're on a roll."

"The Greeks laugh and satirize their Underworld. Christians have no sense of humor about theirs at all. But then for them it's a torture chamber for non-believers. First of all, the kingpin of the Greek under-world was actually a queenpin, Hecate. She was queen of all the darkest forces in the universe. And how is this for worship? At the full moon meals made up of garbage, including rotten eggs, were offered up to appease her."

"I thought Hades was the king of the underworld."

Murky mumbled, "You're right. He was also called Pluto. and the Romans called him Dis. Wait. Pluto is a Disney character. Anyway, King of Hell? Queen of Hell? What the hell. The Greeks no more believed in consistency than Christians do."

I figured Murky had had enough whiskey that he was not only drifting off into the land of ancient mythology, but was likely to be firmly entrenched there for a while. Meanwhile, I had to deal with dark forces in the here and now.

XXVII

I had reached my car when Nancy Lorgran drove up and parked beside me.

I told her, "I'm looking for your daughter. Do you know where I can find her?"

"Jesus Christ, Mr. Detective. Not you, too."

"Me, too? Me, too, what?"

"Lusting after Peggy Ann. You're a bit old for her, aren't you?"

"Sorry. I don't have time for lust at the moment."

"I bet I could change your mind about that," she said, giving me her best mid-forties come-hither look.

"Some other time maybe. Right now you can tell me about your relationship with Ricky Claymore."

She laughed.

"Relationship? Is that what I had?"

Another laugh, this one filled with sadness and self-pity.

"If only, Mister. If only."

"Meaning what?"

"Ricky Claymore used me in order to piss my daughter off. He wanted to be able to say to Peggy Ann, 'Hey, Sweetie, I fucked your mother. What do you think of that?'"

"Why did he want to annoy Peggy Ann?" I said.

Nancy shrugged.

"Who knows? Maybe my daughter's a bum fuck, though I doubt that. Maybe he was jealous."

"Jealous of whom?" I said.

"Not who, but what. They first met at the local horseback riding club. Afterwards Peggy Ann also joined the local rifle club that Ricky belonged to. It wasn't long before Ricky Claymore discovered my daughter could not only outride him, but outshoot him as well. That didn't go over well with his male pride. And, given that, I imagine it didn't matter how good Peggy Ann was in the sack, it was her performance in a real leather saddle that doomed her to being dumped by Ricky."

"People tell me that around the time your sister was murdered you were outside, in the back of the house, talking with someone. Is that correct?"

"People?"

"Yes. My sources tell me they recognized your voice but were unable to determine who was with you. They thought maybe the other voice was female."

"Oh, yes. One of the female caterers Murky hired for the party was on her way to Murky's equivalent of a wine cellar. Murk has a small blockhouse set back from the main house. I'm sure you've seen it. That's where he keeps all of his liquor. Well, nearly all. You've also seen his main-house bar."

"Yes. It rivals the bar at Hotel Belmond El Encanto."

"Oh, you've been there? I didn't suppose anyone of your stature was allowed inside the gates."

I passed on that remark.

"Speaking of gates, I'm surprised Murky would allow a caterer to go out alone to his alcohol cave," I said.

"You're right. Little CJ went with her and he held the keys to Murky's Fort Knox. On the way out I spoke to the caterer, telling her I wanted a bottle of vodka delivered to my cabin after she finished retrieving whatever booze she was collecting in order to keep the party on an uneven keel."

"Anything else you can remember?" I said.

"Oh, yes. Vividly. On their return from the liquor shed I detained Little CJ and performed an act of pity sex on him. Poor creature! Such a pathetic, guilt-racked man. And, on top of that, he's married to that wretched harridan. God, she's a hound from hell."

"The billiard room has an outside entrance, not all that far from where you were... let's say, ministering to Little CJ. By chance, did you see anyone come in, or exit from, that door?"

"How could I? I was on my knees, with my back to that door."

A Santa Julietta sheriff's car pulled into Murky's driveway so I abandoned my questioning of Nancy Lorgran. I was afraid the police had come to re-arrest Murky, based on some new piece of evidence. Thankfully I was wrong. The visitor was Sheriff Cuddleston himself, come to tell Murky that the police were dropping the murder charge -- for the moment. The sheriff humbly admitted that he and his staff were back to square one in their investigation into the murder of Cynthia Murtrans.

Before Murky could say something snarky, I said to the sheriff, "Dropping the charge against Murky is good news, but that you don't have a replacement suspect is definitely not good news."

I signaled to Murky not to say anything unpleasant and hoped he understood my gesture. He apparently did.

"Sorry about your loss, Cuddly. You think he was pushed over the embankment?" Murky said to the sheriff.

"Yeah. Some heavy-duty truck hit him hard from the read, pushing both our cruiser and the Buick over the edge. It must have hit Colby's car just as soon as Colby stopped the Buick, because both the Colby and the driver of the Buick, a man named Giovanni Alba, were still in their cars."

"Giovanni Alba?" Murky said to the sheriff as he looked toward me. I stared back blankly.

"Yeah. Some guy who used to work for Richard Claymore, the elderly gentleman who owns Condor Wines. Do you know him?" the sheriff asked.

"Nope. I mean Alba, naturally. Of course, I know who El Condor is. I've even met him a time or two at local wine events," Murky said.

The sheriff then said, "We'll be holding a high-profile funeral for our slain officer, Colby Gray. A week from tomorrow in Santa Julietta. At The Church of the Holy Cross. Colby was Catholic. I do hope you will attend. My invitation includes you, Mr. Fletcher. We want as big a gathering as we can pull together. I've already sent out messages to all police agencies in surrounding counties to send official representatives, plus as many other officers who are able to get away to attend."

Murky hesitated and I said nothing.

"Well, gentlemen, you don't have to decide immediately."

The sheriff then turned and left.

Inside, Murky walked straight to his liquor stock behind the bar and poured us each a double whiskey. He then motioned for me to plop down in my usual seat across from his.

"Now tell me, Fletcher, are you up to attending a funeral for your buddy, Colby Gray?"

"I am not."

"Nor am I. Good riddance to the little shit," he said.

"Mustn't speak ill of the dead, Murk. I'm sure you don't want anyone pissing on your grave when the times comes," I said.

"Let 'em try. I'll be up the fuckin' chimney."

"Now, now. Don't go all somber and bitter on me. Sometimes I think you've begun to lose your sense of humor."

He drained his tumbler.

"You're wrong, Fletcher. I can't lose what I've never had."

"You? The comedian from Hellfire never had a sense of humor?"

"Nope. I just faked it. Or rather... I have been a skillful actor. Not just when I was performing serious parts in films, but even when I was on the Borscht Belt, doing stand-up comedy."

"Oh, come on."

"It's true. Telling jokes is no different from reading lines from a stage play or a screen play. Is an actor who plays Iago or Macbeth, or an actress who plays Lady Macbeth, evil as a person based on his or her belting out the lines Shakespeare wrote for his evil characters?"

"I see your point. Still, I think you're a funny guy. Or used to be," I said.

"Well, obviously I've had a lot of heavy shit on my mind lately. Sorry if I've slunk into becoming such a cranky old bastard."

"Let's talk some more about Peggy Ann. Can you be sure she's not trying in any way to stitch you up for the murder of your wife? I mean, standing to inherit all of this --. I gestured broadly. "-- is a powerful incentive to hasten matters along."

"No! I don't want to hear it. Get out of here, Stu, and find out who did kill Cynthia."

XXVIII

From Murky's ranch I headed home to shower and change into my best gentleman sailor's costume. Amanda Reynolds had invited me to a dinner onboard her yacht, moored at the Santa Julietta Yacht Club. The boat, built in 1964, was a beauty, a fifty-foot-long, wooden-hulled, Kettenburg-design sloop Amanda named *Shanghai*. Her choice of name, she said, had to do with the fact that she almost always served her yacht guests Chinese food.

I had dined on her boat twice before, each meal superb, even though she had brought the entirety of each feast from home and then heated up the entree and vegetables in the vessel's propane-fired ovens. I assumed this night's layout would be cooked the same and my expectations were for a gourmet repast, something I never get when left to my own devices.

When she purchased the boat two years earlier Amanda barely knew a sheet from a halyard. As a teen in Seattle during WWII -- where my father was a Navy flight instructor at Sand Point Naval Air Station at the north end of Lake Washington before he was transferred to San Diego -- I had learned to sail skillfully, under my father's tutelage, when he would rent a thirty-foot Islander sloop from the Kenmore Marina on his days off.

Feeling more comfortable teaching Amanda on a smaller sloop than *Shanghai*, I asked her to rent one of Santa Julietta Yacht Club's thirty-two sloops that were available for members' use.

Amanda was a quick learner and before long she was at the helm on her own, as well as working winches to raise and lower sails at the beginnings and ends of our hour-long sessions between Channel Island oil rigs and the mainland. Having long ago mastered the arcane Latin of the law, she also quickly picked up sailboat and sailing terminology, until, after a few weeks, a stranger might have judged her to be an old salt.

Finally, I decided the time had arrived for her to take *Shanghai* out, with her at the helm and with me taking her orders. I expected her to be nervous but she wasn't.

As we motored out beyond the protection of the yacht club's rock jetty, Amanda said, "I vividly recall my first criminal defense case. I was trying to get off a truly execrable douche bag from a charge of exposing himself outside a public restroom at a state park's beach. The night before the trial began I convinced myself that I was going to puke on the courtroom floor. So, of course, I failed to sleep a wink all night long."

"What actually happened the next day?" I asked.

"I puked on the courtroom floor," she deadpanned.

"Really?"

"No. Of course not. I was as composed as could be. I even got the shithead off, by convincing the jury he accidentally dropped his pants while trying to unzip his fly, because he feared he would pee his pants if he didn't start unzipping before he reached the door to the restroom. I even brought in a physician to testify that my client had chronic urinary tract issues."

"And your career has been on the ascent ever since," I said.

"Sometimes it feels like a descent."

Ascent or descent, Amanda Reynolds's career earned her a reputation as one of the top criminal defense lawyers on the Central Coast. The money wasn't what it should have been for someone of her caliber, but she did all right. A fifty-foot yacht costs several bags of peanuts, as does a four-thousand-square-foot home on Colonia Verde Country Club.

I arrived at the *Shanghai* expecting dinner for three, but Amanda surprised me. Sofiya Karenrova Vilenskaya stood on the dock near where

Amanda's boat was moored. She leaned with one hand on a piling, her other hand wrapped around a martini glass. From a distance I was unable to tell if she was already drunk.

Sofiya was a model and would-be actress whose father was a Soviet trade official based in Los Angeles. *Trade official* was her description. I liked to suppose he was a high-ranking KGB officer, though I had only met him once -- at an event hosted by an American Undersecretary of Commerce at the lah-dee-dah Beverly Wilshire Hotel in Beverly Hills. I found him far too charming to be a trade official. Every government trade official I had ever met -- and I had met several when I pulled off-duty guard duty while working for the Burbank PD -- reminded me of used car salesmen, smarmy to a fault. Every one except Alexi Fydorovitch Vilenskov.

"Well, well, well. Amanda's favorite private dick. How's it hangin', Fletcher?"

On a scale of one to ten Sofiya rated between nine and ten in the categories of beauty and intelligence. But, when it came to charm, she only scored between zero and minus one.

"I'm just peachy, Sof. And you?"

"My fruit's hangin' higher than yours, Baby. I've got prospects."

"And your prospects are?"

"I'm almost engaged."

"Is that like being almost pregnant?" I said.

"Hell, no. I'm still on the pill."

Okay. Maybe I overrated her intelligence. But, damn, she was good-looking. Enough to sway my judgment elsewhere. Except for her charm. I was bull's eye on that she lacked the power to enchant. Beguile me, that is. I know, because two years earlier she had tried. and I mean tried really hard.

Amanda had introduced Sofiya to me while Sofiya was in Santa Julietta for beach shoots wearing skimpy swimwear. Several big-name companies peddling sundry brands of cosmetics had joined to offer her a contract to model for them. The photos would then be parsed out among the companies for use in their women's magazine ads. A fake merging of photos of Sofiya holding this or that product up would be created later in the photographers' studios.

A bit of a *yenta*, Amanda hinted that there could be more at stake in my serving as Sofiya's date than mere beautiful companionship. I told my lady lawyer that marriage held no interest for me, but I would be glad to chaperone a lovely young woman about town for a few days. And so I did just that.

Sofiya and I had a splendid week together. But, at the end, when she found out I was not interested in being her permanent ticket out of LA and out of her father's house, she cooled on me dramatically.

"You pig! How could you lead me on like that? And now you dump me like I am a sack of rotten potatoes," I remember she had said to me.

And now, on Amanda's dock, she looked at me slyly and said, "I hope you are not counting on many more blowjobs from Sofiya, Stu Fletcher, because --."

"Because you're almost engaged," I said.

She nodded.

Her Russian accent was still a bit thick. So I wasn't entirely sure whether she had spoken of *many* more or *any* more. Then, too, I wasn't sure Sofiya understood the contextual difference.

"Who is the lucky man?"

"Lucky?"

"What is the name of your almost fiancé?"

"His name is Jason Arthur Kohlvester."

"And his line of work?"

"He works at the US trade mission in Los Angeles as a commercial attaché. He is looking forward to becoming my husband."

"And then you can both engage in pillow talk," I said.

"What is pillow talk?"

"Pillow talk is where you are in bed and you whisper to one another. You are not allowed to keep any secrets from one another. None. Is that understood?"

"Da! Oh, excuse me. I mean yes. I understand. No secrets," she said.

I was certain Sofiya's father looked forward to his daughter's passing along Jason's half of the conjugal pillow whispers. No doubt the Politburo in Moscow also eagerly awaited news gathered by Comrade Vilenskov's daughter. Given that the California's economy was larger than all but four countries in the world, trade secrets emanating from Los Angeles would be highly prized in the Kremlin.

By contrast, during our week at a Santa Juliette Biltmore beachfront resort two years earlier, Sofiya and I shared no pillow talk. Neither one of us, we both quickly discovered, is much of a conversationalist. Still, we shared other activities which proved her to be a good, above average even, bedroom playmate.

"Where are you staying, Sofiya?" I asked, trying to sound casual.

"At the Biltmore again."

"Is your fiancé with you?"

"Oh, no. Jason is much too busy to take time off from his important work right now."

"Too bad."

"Why is it too bad?"

"Santa Julietta is so lovely this time of year," I said.

"This city is handsome at all times of the year, not so?" she replied.

"She is."

"Do you know who is our fourth dinner partner tonight?" Sofiya said, standing on her tiptoes and looking over my shoulder toward the parking lot.

"I do believe Amanda mentioned inviting Everett Cole. Do you know him?" I said.

"Everett Cole," she repeated slowly. "No, I don't think so. What kind of position does he hold?"

"He's a judge. Or rather an administrative court arbiter."

"I do not understand."

"He's a kind of referee."

"He wears a black and white striped shirt?" she said sincerely.

"Not exactly. He tries to get companies, corporations, that are suing each other to settle their differences without going to a court trial."

"Is this an important position?"

"In what way do you mean?" I said.

"Do I have to be very, very nice to him so as not to get Amanda in trouble?"

"No, No. Just be your own loveable self."

"That will be easy."

XXIX

Sofiya then saw Amanda and Judge Cole emerge from a gunmetal blue Mercedes in the yacht club parking lot and pointed. I turned and waved. Within minutes Amanda and Everett Cole arrived to join us at the *Shanghai* and Amanda formally gave each of us permission to board her boat.

While her three guests were seated in the cockpit, Amanda went below to pour wine. While she was doing that two of her office secretaries arrived wheeling a cart loaded with the entree and side dishes wrapped in foil, plus hors d'oeuvres. A local Pinot Noir served, Amanda announced that dinner would consist of lasagna, fresh green beans with pine nuts and cranberries, and garlic bread. Not Chinese, as usual.

On the previous day Amanda had joked that she planned to serve us In-N-Out burgers, adding that she had read that Julia Child -- the famous TV chef, and Santa Julietta resident -- knew the location of every In-N-Out Burgers emporium between Santa Julietta and San Francisco.

We all headed below deck and seated ourselves around her small table with its built-in breakfast-nook-style seats. The two secretaries served up the food and then left. The older one -- Ruth, I think she said her name was, Bridget might have been the younger one -- announced to Amanda that she would return later to collect dirty dishes, silverware, and any leftover food.

Dinner conversation centered on the performance of our new governor, Ronald Reagan, who had trounced the incumbent, Pat Brown, in the prior November's election. Amanda and Judge Cole both allowed that they had voted for the new governor and thought he was doing a splendid job. Sofiya played "dumb Russian" and asked who we were talking about, although I, at least, knew perfectly well she was *au courant* on American politics, at both the federal and state levels.

At any rate, I was Reagan's sole detractor, pointing out how indistinguishable from Goldwater he was on nearly every issue. I tried not to demean the man based on his undistinguished movie-star past, though I did get in a dig about his starring role in *Bedtime for Bonzo.*

Judge Cole pointed out, "Reagan's fairly flexible on taxes. He's likely going to raise them on several fronts."

Lamely, I said, "I'll not be affected by that, given I earn so little I scarcely pay any taxes."

Amanda retorted, " Oh, come now, Stu. I pay you a fortune every year. Are you announcing that you don't claim on your tax returns any of the millions in earnings I shovel your way?"

I said, "No, Ma'am. Everything you pay me is unearned, given I just make up stories about whatever information it is you want me to unearth."

Amanda and Judge Cole laughed at my joke, but Sofiya said, "Isn't unearned income also taxable in America?"

"Very good, Sofie. You're not as dumb as you like to pretend you are," I said.

"I still have much to learn," she said.

Amanda said, "Well, Sofiya, don't depend on Stu to teach you much."

"Oh, no. Miss Amanda. Stu, he has taught me a lot about --." she paused. "Excuse me. It is not polite, I'm told, to talk about you know what."

"What is not polite to talk about?" Judge Cole stupidly asked.

A day earlier Amanda had hinted that her male dinner companion, though sociable enough, lacked acumen when it came to knowledge the rest of us took for granted.

"Home schooling and a feckless wife," was how Amanda explained away the judge's being un-attuned to conversational nuances. I began to think she was being charitable.

"Sex is what Stu has taught me all about," Sofiya blurted out. "But am I correct? Sex is not a proper topic of conversation during mealtimes?"

That put the kibosh on any dinner conversation, polite, proper, and otherwise. While my face turned several shades of red, I helped clear away the entree plates and stack them in the small sink. Then I stood aside so Amanda could get into the half-fridge and tiny freezer. We were just finishing our dessert of local strawberries topped with vanilla ice cream when the intruder appeared.

He was dressed all in brown, including wearing a brown porkpie hat. His hair was black and the pencil-thin mustache he wore was a mixture of black and white. He was holding a handgun that appeared to be a WWII-vintage Mauser. At first I thought this was some kind of surprise joke Amanda had prepared for the rest of us, and that all that was missing was a large red clown bulb on the end of his nose -- until I saw the look on her face. Genuine fright.

"Who are you?" Sofiya asked.

"No one you are expecting, Signorina," he said with a heavy Italian accent.

"What is this all about?" Judge Cole said as he started to rise.

"Sit down, Signore. Sit, before I must shoot at you."

Cole sat.

I sat nearest the man, but I was not within reach to be able to try to grab his gun.

Amanda said, "Get off my boat immediately," as if the man were a witness she could badger.

The man with the gun merely chuckled.

"No, Signora. It is I who give the instructions."

"What do you want?" Sofiya said.

"I want Signora Reynolds and Signore Fletcher to come with me. We are going to start the sailboat engine and go for a little ride out into the bay. This other man and the Russian spy will stay below and behave themselves."

"I'm not a spy!" Sofiya shouted.

The gunman shrugged.

"But you will still do nothing to stir trouble. Otherwise I might have to shoot the lady lawyer and the detective."

Topside Amanda pressed the ignition button for the diesel engine, while I was told to release the mooring lines from the docking cleats. I then returned to the cockpit.

"Now, Signore Fletcher, you will maneuver us out past the jetty and into open water," the gunman said, waving his pistol in back of Amanda's head.

As I began to comply, the gunman forced Amanda to sit next to him on the starboard-side cockpit bench. He pressed the gun into her ribs. Amanda stared intently at me, her eyes teary, her hands trembling. I knew if I did nothing, the outcome would be all too predictable. Action was risky, but inaction would be fatal -- times four.

I looked about to see if I could see anything lying around the cockpit with which to try to hit the gunman. Amanda was such a tidy person, I didn't expect to find much, if anything. But, lucky for me -- or so I hoped -- the winch handle for the left foresail winch lay misplaced. It perched on the stern transom, next to the mainsail sheet traveler.

So, as we rounded the end of the jetty, I slowly brought the bow around ninety degrees to port, using one hand on the wheel. With my left hand I reached behind me and loosened the cam cleat that kept the mainsail sheet firmly locked in place. I then quickly loosened the traveler lock with kept the main sheet block and tackle from sliding either to the left or right.

"What are you doing?' the gunman demanded.

"Transforming the boom hash so you won't get hit in the head when it foozles," I said, hoping he understood nothing nautical, because I had just made up a sentence filled with gibberish to explain my movements.

"Do it slowly," he responded.

I then said, "Open sea ahead. Which direction now?"

In the fraction of a second he turned his head toward the bow, I cranked the wheel hard to port, simultaneously reached over my head to swung the main mast boom as hard as I could to starboard, then grabbed the winch handle and rushed the gunman, swinging the handle wildly and screaming at him as I charged toward him.

As I knew he would, he turned his pistol toward me, rather than shoot Amanda. Shooting her would not stop me from hammering his head with a solid steel weapon. So, as his gun came up, I swung down hard onto his gun wrist with the winch handle. With my free hand I grabbed for one of his ankles and tipped him backwards as hard as I could, sending him overboard. His gun fell to the deck, where Amanda picked it up, turned and fired wildly into the water.

"Whoa!" I said and took the gun from her.

"I want to kill that bastard!" Amanda screamed. "Give me back the gun."

Sofiya and Judge Cole emerged from below deck.

"Kill him! Yes! Kill him!" Sofiya shouted.

"Let him drown!" the judge said.

I thought: At last. A judge who truly believes that justice delayed is justice denied.

From the darkness off the stern came a cry.

"Help me, please. I cannot swim."

Sofiya broke into laughter, before saying, "Listen to that piece of shit. He was going to kill us, but now wants our help."

I said, "We don't even know who he is."

"Who cares?" Sofiya said, looking at me incredulously.

"I want to know," I said. "I want to know who he is and who sent him."

Judge Cole said, "Let divers fish out his corpse in the morning."

I shook me head. "The tide will drag him out to sea. He'll sink and may never emerge."

Amanda said, "Stu's right. He'll become crab meat and we'll never know."

"Maybe his car is in the car lot," Sofiya said.

That made sense, but I still said, "And maybe not."

"Help! Please. Save me. Do not let me drown."

"Who sent you?" Sofiya called out.

"Not until you save me," he called back.

The sloop's engine was still running and, with my sharp turn to port on the wheel, the boat was, in fact, circling back toward the gunman. I handed the pistol back to Amanda.

"Promise not to shoot him," I said to her. "Judge, when we're along side of him you hold onto my belt and I'll reach down to grab him and try to pull him up into the boat."

"What should I do?" Sofiya said.

I thought for a second, then said, "Amanda, give the gun to Sofiya and you go below. Bring me a flashlight, then go back to radio the police. Do you remember how the radio works?"

"I'll figure it out," she said.

I grabbed the wheel and stopped us from turning in a tight circle. I then called out to the gunman, "Move your arms like a hummingbird and keep shouting. You need to keep your head above water and allow us to locate you. Can you still hear me?"

Moments of silence. Then, "Come fast. I do not want to drown."

Sofiya shouted, "Beg, you bastard. I want to hear you beg."

Silence. Amanda returned and handed me a heavy-duty nine-volt light with a wide beam.

"Shout!" I yelled.

"I am here," came a cry. I moved the flashlight's beam systematically until I spotted him. Then I had to bring the sloop full circle to put the gunman on the starboard side of the boat, so we could try to haul him up into the cockpit.

I cut the engine fifty yards short of the man in the water so the sloop would slow down and glide toward him. When we were within twenty yards of him I thrust the engine into reverse momentarily, then into neutral. Finally, I tied off the wheel so I could leave it without the boat changing course.

"Okay, Judge. Grab my belt with one hand and hold this flashlight with the other."

Judge Cole nodded.

Bracing my belly against the starboard gunwale, I reached over to grab onto the gunman as the boat eased up to him. While he thrashed about in the water, I reached past his sports coat and grabbed onto his wet shirtsleeves to keep him from slipping away from me. Then, one hand at a time, I let loose for a moment to grip his forearms.

I called over my shoulder, "Judge Cole, start tugging on my belt to try to pull me back into the boat, while I hold fast to this jerk."

"Will do." I felt him pulling at my waist.

I pulled on the gunman, the judge pulled on me. No progress. We tried again. No progress.

"He's too much dead weight, Judge, especially adding the weight of his sopping wet clothes. I have another idea," I said over my shoulder.

To the gunman I said, "Try to hang onto the side of the boat while we slip a rope under your armpits." I had start to say *sheet* in place of *rope* before I realized that this sleazebag wouldn't recognize a sailor's term for the rope I was going to use to try to haul him aboard.

I returned to the starboard side, pulling the portside jib sheet with me as I returned to the starboard side. With great difficulty I managed to work the rope around the man, then knot it. I then explained to the judge and the gunman what I intended to do. They both nodded that they understood. That the gunman appeared so hopeful annoyed the hell out of me.

Even so, I returned to the portside jib winch and gave the jib sheet two turns around the winch, popped the winch handle socket into the winch, and began cranking. I had made four slow turns when Judge Cole called out, "Stop, Fletcher! He went limp and slid out from the rope."

I thought the need for the judge to pull on the man simultaneously with my winching would have gone without saying, but obvious my telling the judge that was something I should have done.

"Is he back in the water?" I called to the judge.

"Yes!" came the answer.

"Keep a light on him and tell him to keep his arms out," I said.

Hoping he wouldn't sink, I quickly went to the wheel and cranked it to port as hard as I could in order to make as tight turn a turn as possible. I called for the women to come up on deck with flashlights -- Amanda had found two more -- and for them also to keep their lights aimed at the gunman as he floated. Or try to. He was flailing so much that I was afraid he would sink.

XXX

Judge Cole managed to grab the gunman again by his sports coat as the cockpit section of the sloop came even with him. Sofiya even reached down into the water to try to help.

"Are you able to hang onto the rope?" I called out. "Do you have enough strength left in your hands?"

I realized I was asking too much. The man was scarcely alive. But I was unwilling to let him simply drift off and sink. I wanted the sonuvabitch alive.

Sofiya and the judge both had hold of his sports coat, but the coat was again proving to be an obstacle to my working a line around him. But I wasn't about to jump into the water. I had leaped before thinking while on a previous case and I had nearly drowned. I had been warned at the time that, when in a man-overboard situation, do not put more bodies into the water.

So, on this try, I worked the rope over the sports coat and then under his armpits. After what seemed like hours I managed to get the line completely around him and tied off. Then, with that done, I told Judge Cole and Sofiya to hang onto the drowning rat so I could return to the portside winch and begin reeling him in.

Amanda's boat's sheet winches had two speeds. The lower gear provided a mechanical advantage of roughly nine to one. The upper gear ratio's advantage was forty to one. So, because I was knackered, as the Brits would say, I slipped the winch into the higher gear and began turning the handle slowly.

I estimated the gunman's weight, including his wet clothes, would offer less resistance on the rescue line than would a large jib in a moderate breeze.

"Doing okay?" I called out.

"Just fine," Judge Cole responded.

So I cranked and I cranked and I cranked -- using very little effort, yet gasping for air anyway.

At last I heard Amanda cry out, "Okay, Stu. You can stop. He's onboard."

I tied off the sheet on the port stern cleat, stood, then slowly made my way to the rescued gunman. What I saw sent shivers through my entire body. Somehow the rope had slipped from the gunman's armpits and had wrapped around his neck. So, as I was reeling him in like a marlin, I was simultaneously strangling the man.

Hastily, I unwrapped the roped and felt his neck for a pulse. Then I grabbed his wrist to try to find a sign of life. Finally, I straddled him and began pressing on his chest repeatedly.

I then cried out, "Someone help me. Blow air into his lungs. Come on. Do it, while I keep pressing on his chest."

But no one offered to help.

"Okay, Judge Cole. Take over what I'm doing and I'll blow air." I slid off the man and the judge replaced me.

Giving mouth-to-mouth resuscitation to a man bent on killing me was repellent, yet some misplaced pang of conscience told me I was doing the right thing. I tried to focus on filling the man's lungs with air and force myself to forget who he was, what he was.

Minutes passed and the gunman showed no signs of resurrection from his near-drowned, almost hanged state. I was about to give up. The judge was nearing exhaustion, I could tell. His efforts at pressing on the gunman's ribcage had both weakened and slowed.

As I stood, I gestured for Judge Cole to cease his efforts. And then, unexpectedly, the gunman coughed and spit up water. The son-of-a-bitch was still alive. Oh, well, I thought. I looked at the judge, whose face registered a mixture of disappointment and disgust. Whether his disgust was directed at the gunman for having the audacity to stay alive, or directed at me for trying to keep the man alive, I could not tell.

I dropped to my knees again, rolled the gunman over, and began pressing down on his back, hard and rhythmically, causing him to cough up more water. When I stopped pushing down on his back he began to gasp for air -- on his own. Once again I was torn between thinking I had done the right thing and wishing the man had died.

But now I began to ponder how the jib sheet had managed to slip from under his arms to around his neck. I was certain I had secured the line tightly enough around his chest that it couldn't slip. My worrying about that issue ended with the gunman's heavy coughing, followed by shallow, labored breathing.

"I'd still like to toss him back into the ocean," Judge Cole said, still scowling.

I ignored him and called out to Amanda and she quickly appeared from below deck.

I asked, "Figured out that radio yet?"

"I think so."

I said to her, "Call the Santa Julietta police."

She said, "Shouldn't I call the Coast Guard instead?"

"Do you really want to take this to a federal level?" I said.

She thought for a moment before saying, "No. I don't. Please steer the boat back to my slip. If the Coast Guard later screams that we should have called them because we're in their crime jurisdiction, I'll apologize and tell them we weren't thinking clearly. By then this guy, whoever he is, will be in the hands of the city police." She shrugged, then added, "Let the police and the Coast Guard fight it out over whose investigation this is."

Later, I realized I should have kept my attention on the gunman because, while I was contesting with Amanda which cops to hand the gunman over to, he died.

My own investigation began by checking the gunman's pockets. In his right front pocket I found a set of keys, one of which was definitely a car key. I didn't worry about what the other three might unlock. In his right rear pocket a soggy leather wallet produced a fist full of hundred-dollar bills, each one making Ben Franklin look less bright-eyed than the engraving was meant to portray.

The jackpot was the gunman's driver's license. I could now put a name to the dead man: Antonio Bardello. And an address: San Francisco. Little Italy, was my best guess, after staring hard at the damp license's crinkled street address.

Amanda's sloop was still performing tight, lazy circles in the water just beyond the jetty. So I stepped away from Mr. Bardello's corpse and spun the wheel, watching the bow slowly nose around to port. When we were parallel to the jetty I placed the diesel engine gear in slow forward and headed back to the marina.

Five police officers awaited our arrival as I eased the boat into its slip. By the time the officer in charge, a man who introduced him-self as Lieutenant Matt Accarro, stepped aboard, Judge Cole had unwrapped the jib sheet from the corpse's neck, which may or may not have constituted tampering. I'd leave that to the judge and the police to work out.

Photographers arrived -- police, not press -- and flashbulbs began to pop. Amanda went below and began to try to clean up the dinner scene, but Lieutenant Accarro told her to leave it. Amanda, fusspot that she is, looked dismayed, but complied. She looked dazed as she emerged topside. So I helped her step off from her yacht and steadied her as we walked up the dock toward the parking lot.

The police had commandeered two rooms inside the yacht club to use for interrogation.

Sofiya and Amanda were taken in first.

"Who do you suppose that Bardello guy is?" Judge Cole asked me, as we sat outside on a bench, awaiting our turns to have our accounts recorded by Santa Julietta detectives.

"No idea," I said, although in fact I had several ideas about who might have sent him.

"I didn't realize Amanda had any vicious enemies among those who dislike her," the judge said.

"Otherwise, you'd have stayed at home tonight, eh?" I said.

"I've gone to dinner at her house several times and nothing like this ever happened," he said.

Making me think Bardello had been hired by a recent enemy. Paolo Galboni was the first name to come to my mind. Unless Amanda had done something unknown to me to piss off El Condor. Maybe he thought Amanda and I were doing too little to keep his grandson from going to jail. Or... maybe we were doing too much to keep Murky out of jail. In which case Peggy Ann and her mother might want us out of the way.

If Peggy and Nancy had hired Bardello, how would they know enough to go about it?

Then I recalled reading something offhand when reading up on Peggy Ann. Her roommate at Fresno State was a young woman named Ginger Frichetti. Now I had to wonder if she was any relation to one of the San Francisco Frichettis, three brothers whose reputations were that of being thugs in three-piece suits. Kingpins of prostitution and the numbers racket in Oakland and San Jose, competing with San Francisco tongs in the latter, with black gangs in the former.

"Honestly, the rope slipped, Fletcher," the judge said.

Honestly. In my experience most claims preceded by that word ended up being not true at all. As in, "Honestly, Mom, the dog ate my homework."

If Judge Cole wished to be known -- if only to himself -- as a hanging judge, I had little quarrel with that sentiment. But, if that were so, I would have gone to less trouble exerting myself trying to save Bardello for the State of California's hangman. Well, metaphorically anyway. In California the death penalty is invoked using cyanide.

Still, Bardello had not, at least in our presence, committed a capital crime. It wasn't even clear in my mind that a prosecutor could win a conviction for attempted murder. But maybe his taking us out beyond the jetty suggested he wanted to kill us. Or not. His waving a gun at us constituted what? Attempted robbery? He hadn't even asked for our wallets. Maybe that he was a hungry Italian robbing us of lasagna and garlic bread would be his lawyer's tongue-in-cheek defense.

Anyway, the man was dead and we had no clue why he had boarded Amanda's yacht.

Knowing who had hired him would surely explain why he had showed up. On that note I intended to go looking for Paolo Galboni as soon as the police were done questioning me.

XXXI

Judge Cole appeared consternated when he emerged from his police interview. I had finished a couple minutes earlier and I felt comfortable with what I told the police. My account of events was accurate, but then I only told the cops what I saw and heard. No extrapolation. I told them that my winching the gunman onboard was probably what killed him, but that obviously a coroner's examination might prove otherwise. I claimed -- truthfully -- that I was unaware the jib sheet had been wrapped around the man's neck, given that was not where I had secured it. I also said the light was so poor -- the sun had long since set -- that I could not see the man's body while I was winching him in.

I wasn't sure how a jury would react to that story, if it came to my having to repeat my story in court. And I didn't know what Judge Cole had told the police that might not agree with my explanation. But then I decided I didn't care. I had told the truth and I didn't even want to stay around to listen to what the judge might or might not have told the cops.

"Stu Fletcher, remember me?"

I turned and was facing Santa Julietta's chief of police, Wallace Fry.

"Yes, sir. I do. The Hogswood business a couple years ago."

"That's right, although you might better call it the Hogswood Barbecue," he said, laughing.

"Too grim for me to make light of it, I'm afraid, sir. Ned Hogswood and Bonnie Slaeger both died in that fire."

"But you nailed Billy Slaeger for it. Caught him with the empty can of gasoline still in his hand."

So I had, thanks to Leeann Hogswood's suspicions that Ned was being unfaithful to her. While spying on Ned and Bonnie having a romp in Ned's brother's guesthouse, I watched Bonnie's husband emerge from the trees behind the guesthouse, quickly circle the building, pouring petrol as he ran, then toss a match on the fuel.

Flames erupted like Roman candles, blocking both the front and rear doors of the guesthouse. Why Ned and Bonnie failed to escape through a window no one ever figured out. Whatever the reason, their charred corpses were found in the bedroom.

Meanwhile, I had been hiding in among the trees on the far side of the house from where Billy had been watching. The bedroom window was open -- given the unseasonably warm night for Santa Julietta -- so I easily snapped photos of the embracing couple to show to Ned's wife.

Now, however, I thought I'd best let that story die and said, "Chief, do you know anything about this guy, Antonio Bardello?"

"Sure. But he's better known as Tony Whores."

"And why is that?" I said.

"Oh, come on. Bardello morphs into Bordello and there you are. Easy peasy."

"Okay. So what can you tell me about him?"

"He's a thug for hire, as you might guess. He's from Little Italy up in San Fran. He mostly works the docks all over the Bay Area as an enforcer for the Bigliasi family, knee-capping stevedores who don't want to pay their union dues. Or fall behind. But sometimes he branches out. Numbers-running, prostitution. Beats up other people -- or kills them. Hookers in the Bay Area don't need pimps to keep them in line. Tony loves slapping the ladies around."

"So how do you know him? No stevedores in Santa Julietta. And this place is a long way to come for whore-enforcement," I said.

"Before I came to Santa Julietta as Assistant Chief I headed up the vice squad in San Jose. Tony and I were on a first-name basis. From our being in court together, that is. Unfortunately, the bastard had damned clever lawyers." He looked over his shoulder, then whispered to me, "And no doubt the Bigliasi family had a few judges in their pockets."

Judge Cole was nowhere in sight.

Then the chief asked, "Why do you suppose Tony was in Santa Julietta? And why come to Miss Reynold's boat to threaten you all?"

"He didn't show up to steal her stainless utensils and her K-Mart stemware."

"Is Miss Reynolds defending some enemy of the Bigliasis?" he said.

"Two of her main clients at the moment are Ricky Claymore and Murky Murtrans," I said.

"Ah, yes. The rapist out in Avenida De Libre and the actor."

"Alleged rapist and retired comedian."

The chief gave me a crooked smile, before saying, "Okay."

Just then Sofiya walked out of the yacht club's ladies' room.

"Stu, darling, I'm still shuddering from this horrid business. I can't possibly sleep alone tonight. Will you please come back to my hotel with me, buy me a strong drink, then take me to bed?"

Lucky me!

"Of course, Sofiya. I can't allow a poor girl to spend the night shuddering all by herself. That's probably against the law," I said to her, and glanced over at the dumbstruck chief of police.

In the morning the phone rang just as Sofiya and I were stepping out of the shower.

"Got any energy left, Fletcher?"

The caller was Amanda.

"Some. How much do I need?"

"Murky's back in jail. I need for you to drive up to his ranch and see for yourself what is happening," Amanda said.

"What's the rumor I need to confirm or disconfirm?" I said.

"Two bodies are being dug up on Murky's property. The sheriff's boys think the corpses belong to Harry Deemer and Chuck Paltzheimer."

"What about Terry Morowitz?"

"As I understand it, they're still digging," she said.

"I'm on my way."

Sofiya was shuddering again, this time from insufficient toweling wrapped around her still damp body. I took care of that, dressed myself, and kissed my young Russian lover goodbye.

"You'll come back soon, Stu?" she said in almost a whisper.

"As soon as I am able."

> *Row, row, row your boat*
> *Gently down the stream.*
> *Merrily, merrily*
> *Merrily, merrily*
> *Life is but a dream.*

Perhaps last night had been a dream. Maybe, too, the boat I had been "rowing".

Still, the contrast between my dream night with Sofiya and my night-mare night on Amanda's sloop were worlds apart. Both were *Life*, both were dreamy. Yet... hedonism and homicide.

XXXII

The Beach Boys less-than-a-year-old hit "Good Vibrations" was playing on KXDKAM as I exited Hwy 101 and drove toward Sisquoc. With Murky in jail again I was going to miss the vibrations of Murky's ice cubes in his tumbler of Wild Turkey. I thought to myself over and over again: *Jeezus! What new hole has he dug for himself?*

When I reached Murky's ranch I saw Sheriff Cuddleston standing beside a cornoner's wagon talking to two men in white coats. I recognized them as coroner's assistants. Coroners plus cops almost always spelled murder.

"I reckoned you'd show up sooner than later, Fletcher, although I'm surprised Wally Fry let you off his hook so quickly."

I said, "He expects to see me again soon. I'm not off the hook, as you put it. What's going on here?"

"I thought you'd know, Fletcher. You're a five-star shit-magnet. We've got more bodies to deal with. A pair of teenagers found here in Murtrans's grape plantation."

"Who found them?"

"Murtrans's vineyard manager, a man named --." The sheriff had to look at his notes. "Yeah. Here it is. Ernest Stellhorn. Know him?"

I allowed that I had never heard of the man.

"Actually, Mr. Stellhorn's dog, a German Shepard named Quagmire, found the bodies." Pause. "Oh, don't worry. Stellhorn will tell you all about the name. And the next question on your mind is: *Where* did he find the bodies, right?"

I nodded.

"Buried beneath a pile of fertilizer next to a tool shed at the far end of the grape orchard."

I saw no point in telling the sheriff a grape orchard is called a vineyard. For a man whose county contained a sizeable number of vineyards, the man showed an unwarranted obtuse side to his character.

"Mind if I have a chat with Mr. Stellhorn?" I said.

"Sure. Go ahead. Your Ms. Reynolds is going to have a tough nut to crack with this one."

I laughed to myself. If anything, by the time Amanda got done stomping on Sam Cuddleston he'd be reduced to a thick mash of grape juice.

"By the way, Fletcher, that dog of his looks nasty enough to chew you to rags, but he's actually as friendly as a teddy bear."

"You can call me Ernie," he said when I found him snipping dead grape leaves from vines growing next to a fence overgrown with blackberry bushes. "I've already told the cops my story."

I explained that I represented his boss, the man who had just been jailed, presumably for two more murders.

"When Quag started goin' berserk I thought he was after a gopher, although he's never been noisy like that before when he'd cornered a little animal."

"Quagmire?' I asked.

"That's not the name the Army gave him, but every pot-smokin' grunt below the rank of second lieutenant knows what a snake-eyes roll of a war we're fightin' against Victor Charles and his northern cousins. Quag and I did two tours together in The Nam. He saved my platoon's asses more than a dozen times, he did. Why, not once did he miss finding one of them sly bunch of slant-eyes' hidden arms caches whenever we 'coptered into a village up in the highlands."

He hesitated, then continued.

"You know why I took this job for Mr. Murky?"

"Tell me."

"Because it's quiet here among the vines. Peaceful. Listen. Not a sound. Now don't get me wrong. A lot of guys, they came back to the States scared to death of silence. That's 'cause they spent too many long, long nights doin' night patrol."

"Go on."

"At night we had to be attuned to every sound the dark threw at us. We'd listen till we swore our ears were gonna bleed. But I never worried about the difference between a whisper of the wind and sneaky Charlie crawling ever closer to our lines. I had Quagmire by my side and he knew. He could smell black pajamas from half a mile away."

Ernie paused.

"At the end of our two tours the friggin' Army was going to just turn Quag loose in the streets of Saigon, saying his usefulness to the Army was over. Rotten bastards. But I put up money out of my own savings to pay Quag's way back to the States. No way was I gonna let the Army abandon him for dog meat. Fuckin' shithead Army brass!"

Ernie knelt down to hug and stroke his loyal companion. I was looking at two inseparable war buddies who had earned their vine-filled acres of peaceable quiet.

Sheriff Cuddleston had told me the two bodies Quagmire found buried under the fertilizer were Harry Deemer and Chuck Paltzheimer. The coroner estimated they had been dead less than two days. Further digging had not produced another buried corpse.

Ernie turned his mind to the dead fraternity lads. "Yesterday was my day off. So I wasn't around. As I told the sheriff, I was in San Luis Obispo on church business all day. My preacher can vouch for me. He's Mr. Murky's son, CJ."

I walked the mile or so back to Murky's house. Two deputy cruisers were parked out front. Inside, I saw one of Murky's maids, the one named Mirasol, standing tapping one foot and angrily twirling a feather duster as she watch two deputies rummaging through drawers in the living room.

"They've taken Mr. Murky back to jail, Mr. Fletcher. And now this is going on," she called out when she saw me.

The deputies paid no attention to her, although one of them took a brief glance over his shoulder toward me before resuming his search.

"What the hell are you guys looking for?" I called out, although I was sure they were digging through Murky's closets looking for a gun or guns.

"Stay out of this, Mister," the closer deputy said to me.

"They've got no idea what they're after, Mr. Fletcher. They've just come here to make a mess of Mr. Murky's belongings." Mirasol balled her fists in anger, but made no move toward the cops.

"Is anyone else here?" I said.

"You mean Miss Peggy or her mother?" Mirasol said. She obviously took it for granted I didn't mean any of the hired help when I said *anyone*. I hadn't intended any disrespect and she clearly took no offense. Still, I regretted my phrasing.

"Yes, I'd like to speak with Peggy Ann."

"Sorry. She and her mother have both gone north. They say they board the train at Santa Julietta. Mrs. Lorgran, she goes to San Francisco. To North beach to visit friends, she say to me. And Miss Peggy, she goes to Monterey to some kind of big music gathering. I don't remember what name she called it."

The *big music gathering*, as Mirasol called it, was the three-day The Monterey Pop Festival, starting June 18th. Performers scheduled to play included Jefferson Airplane, The Grateful Dead, Canned Heat, Ravi Shankar, Simon and Garfunkel, The Who, and Otis Redding, along with a pair of relative newcomers to the scene -- Janis Joplin and Jimi Hendrix.

I knew this because I had seen fliers for the festival posted everywhere, along with the fact that the most-played new song on my car's radio for at least a month was Scott McKenzie's tune, the first line of which was, "If you're going to San Francisco, be sure to wear a flower in your hair." But the real destination of the moment, for those who were finely tuned to the lyrics, was not San Francisco. It was Monterey. The festival was being called a *love-in*.

XXXII

According to Sheriff Cuddleston the two young men had each been shot behind the left ear, then dragged to the pile of fertilizer, where burying them was easy enough. The ground was soft and the shed provided ample tools for digging shallow graves. The sheriff added that they apparently had not been shot at the tool shed but rather somewhere else in the "grape orchard", because searchers found one of Harry Deemer's red tennis shoes two hundred yards and many rows of grapevines, away from the shed.

I had asked Ernie Stellhorn why Quagmire hadn't smelled the tennis shoe and gone to it before digging at the fertilizer. Ernie's answer was that he had been far from the shed in the other direction, sitting in his small John Deere tractor, pulling a dead eucalyptus stump from the ground at the southern border of the sprawling vineyard, while Quagmire watched with his lips curling every time Ernie floored the tractor's accelerator and sent black smoke spewing into the air. Only when Ernie and Quag had headed back toward the tool shed did the dog begin to react.

Execution-style murders now were supposedly Murky's method of choice for killing two young men who had come in search of Peggy Ann. At least that was the explanation Mirasol told me she overheard the boys tell Murky when they had arrived at his ranch. Of course, all this presupposed Murky had in fact been the one who murdered Harry and Chuck.

I doubted that. Why would he? True, for Peggy Ann's sake he might prefer they not testify so as to exonerate Ricky Claymore. But *kill* them so they couldn't testify and allow Peggy Ann's arch-enemy off the hook from a rape charge? That seemed far fetched. Still, many a genuine murderer had killed from a seemingly weaker motive.

One question I had forgotten to ask Sheriff Cuddleston was: Where had he found the young men's car? The answer to that might be important, I decided. I doubted it would turn up squirreled away in one of Murky's barns.

I also decided my next stop would be at the Marian Regional Medical Center. If he had regained consciousness, Giovanni Alba might tell me who in the neighborhood might be able and willing to put a gun to young men's heads and pull the trigger. Given that he would have been unable to perform the task, he would surely know who would have been able. My guess was his answer was going to be Antonio Bardello, aka Tony Whores.

The next obvious question was: Who had hired Tony? A less obvious, yet lingering question was: Where was Terry Morowitz? Was he another victim? Or a participant in his friends' murders?

One my way to Santa Maria to see Alba I reflected on the death of Antonio Bardello, still feeling queasy that Amanda, Sofiya, and Judge Cole allowed me to strangle him without saying or doing anything to stop me. Did they not know the jib sheet was wrapped tightly around his neck? How could they not? And I remained puzzled how the rope came to be at his neck when I had secured it decisively around his chest. Unless one of the three confessed to having rearranged the rope, how it came to be around Bardello's neck will remain a deep mystery to me. Oh, well. It wasn't one I was being paid to solve.

The police showed no curiosity why the gunman had been "saved" in such a fashion. For them a criminal had been subdued, apprehended, brought to quick justice -- and at a modest cost. Investigation closed. In the morning newspapers the four of us were being hailed as heroes.

Both Amanda and the judge were being swamped with calls for interviews. Luckily, the press could not find Sofiya or me. I intended to try to keep it that way. Sofiya, I was sure, had made a mad dash for LA and to the safety of her father's diplomatic protections.

I felt a mild kinship with Ernie Stellhorn. We both had experienced what many stay-at-home saber-rattlers call "The Yellow Swarm". And we both knew that a "line drawn in the sand" represents an unrealistic metaphor. From the Yalu River to the Mekong we committed and were committing troops in numbers immeasureably too small, counting instead on sophisticated weaponry and superior tactics. Condescendingly counting on American technical genius and superior firepower to prevail. It's as if West Point had never heard of Hannibal and the Punic Wars.

With a whisk broom I chased the dust from my black marryin'-'n'-buryin' suit. I examined it for moth holes and found none. I never understood the science behind putting cedar chips in a zippered garment bag to ward off moths and crickets from eating suit fabric. But if it was good enough for my mother, it's good enough for me.

After showering I put on a white tee shirt, then, with my back to the bathroom mirror, I pulled on a white dress shirt backwards., buttoned except for the top one. I then struggled for several minutes to get the top button fastened at the back of my neck. The contortions required seemed hardly worth the strain on my arms.

To complete my caring-priest look I found a pair of old horn-rimmed glasses with plain glass lenses, a simple stage tool my father wore in amateur performances by a community theatrical-production group in Torrance. My dad liked to play parts where he could be an elderly gentleman, either wise or foolish. Or in between. I remember seeing him playing Willy Lohman in *Death of a Salesman* shortly after I came back from Korea.

At Marian Regional Medical Center no one paid me any attention as I made my way to Giovanni Alba's room in the ICU ward. My decision to dress like a priest was based on my belief that only putting the fear of God into Giovanni, *literally* the fear of God, would entice him to talk about his mission in Santa Julietta County.

A nurse was attending him when I stepped quietly into his room.

"Sister, is Mr. Alba conscious?" I said softly.

"Eek! You scared me, Father," she said, turning white.

"I do apologize," I said, feeling smug that I had deceived her. I then pointed toward her patient. "Is he --?"

She nodded. "But barely. Make it quick."

"I will."

She left the room.

I bent forward over the patient and was immediately repelled by his body odor. But I decided that, if Satan was up to receiving this man in his current condition, then I could bear him for a short while.

His eyes were closed.

"Giovanni, can you hear me? I am Father Flecchorini and I'm here to see if you are prepared to meet your Maker. If so, you must cleanse your soul by unburdening yourself of the horrible secrets that you hold."

I felt awkward doing this, not only because of my uncomfortable costume, but because I hadn't seen the inside of a church since I was eight years old, when my Aunt Millicent dragged me to some red brick Pentecostal edifice whose literally Bible-thumping minister shook the mortar in the walls with his remonstrations against Satan and the fallen angels.

I assumed, too, that a mobster like Giovanni hadn't attended mass since he was an acolyte being buggered by his parish priest. But I was hoping that he had not abandoned God as quickly as he had escaped from the black-robed monsters masquerading as holy men.

"Giovanni, your immortal soul is at risk, unless you quickly confess your sins and agree to atone for them before you depart this earth. Do you understand me? Only by telling the truth will God grant you entry into Heaven."

Voila! He gave me a wan nod.

"Who sent you here? And why?"

No answer.

"Remember, Giovanni. God is listening."

"The woman."

"Yes, yes. The woman," I repeated.

"The woman whose --."

"Go on."

"The woman with the daughter --."

"Yes?"

"The daughter with two names. The woman whose sister --."

"Whose sister --. Go on."

"Whose sister was murdered."

Voila again!

"What did this woman want you to do?" I said.

He whispered, "Send old man to jail. Grapes. Vineyards. For herself."

Just then a different nurse popped in.

"Father, what are you doing? You must stop pestering my patient. This is Intensive Care after all. Now please leave."

And I complied immediately, thrilled I had pulled off my ruse.

XXXIII

While driving from the hospital to my house I tried to decide who best to share my new information with first. Amanda? Sheriff Cuddleston? No one? Maybe the latter, even though I found it hard to imagine that Giovanni Alba would lie when his eternal salvation was on the line. Or so he imagined.

Yet, what had he told me really? Not that Nancy or Peggy Ann Lorgran had actually killed anyone. Nor did Alba say anything to substantiate the likelihood that the two women had hired Tony Whores to take over Alba's tasks. And Alba didn't confess to killing Cynthia Murtrans. No one placed him anywhere near Murky's ranch that night. Not that he couldn't have been there anyway. Nor could Alba name the killer or killers of Harry Deemer and Chuck Paltzheimer. Tony Whores, most likely.

So what if anything substantive did I have that I could go to any law enforcement agency with? *Nada.* Nancy and her daughter hired Giovanni Alba to do jobs he apparently didn't get around to doing, before --. Before someone shoved him and Colby Gray over an embankment. Who could that have been? Murky? Maybe he caught on to what his sister-in-law and her daughter were up to. Or maybe the elusive Paolo Galboni, who feared if Peggy Ann became owner of Murky's vineyards, she'd sell them to El Condor for more money. Except... except she would not likely do that, if for no other reason than to spite Ricky Claymore.

Maybe Murky was a more violent man than I credited him to be. I now began to think the competition for killing Cynthia and the two fraternity lads narrowed down to Murky versus Nancy and Peggy Ann Lorgran. But which competitor?

Or was I wrong to lump Nancy and Peggy Ann together? No. It seemed on that score Giovanni Alba was clear. He was hired by both. Or was he? I tried to replay his whispers in my mind. Was his naming Peggy Ann merely by way of clarifying who Nancy was? In the same way he added that she was the woman whose sister was murdered? Possibly.

In any event, both Nancy and Peggy Ann were like two needles who had disappeared into two separate haystacks. The Monterey Pop Festival would have tens of thousands of attendees, all wearing flowers in their hair. And Nancy would have by now disappeared into the alleys of San Francisco's Little Italy. Unless one knew of her connections there, she would be impossible to find.

When I returned to my house to shed my priestly garments I placed a call to my answering service. I had two messages. One, from Amanda, asked me to visit Murky. Her message said she had already seen Murk in his jail cell, but she got the feeling he was holding out on her. So maybe I could be more successful in getting him to open up.

I told Amanda what I had coaxed out of Giovanni Alba, although I chose not to mention how I had succeeded in doing so. When I finished she agreed that Nancy and Peggy Ann were, if not prime suspects, at least what police call *persons of interest*. Amanda said she would phone Sheriff Cuddleston and pass along what Giovanni Alba had told me.

The second message from my answering service was from a Floyd Carlisle, a lending officer with San Luis Obispo County Ranchers' Bank and Trust, requesting a visit from me to talk over a very private topic. He said he tried to contact Mr. Murtrans but had been told Mr. Murtans would be unavailable for quite some time and that he was to contact me instead.

Amanda's wishes always trumped everybody else's, given that she was the one who contributed the most toward my monthly mortgage payment. So I drove to Santa Julietta to visit Murky in his jail cell. Along the way I stopped at a Walgreen's pharmacy, then at a liquor store.

My knowing the jailors' pat-down procedures proved greatly to Murky's advantage. I hid the condoms filled with cheap-grade whiskey in places where I knew the guards wouldn't check very closely, if at all. I had purchased cheap whiskey for two reasons. Not because I was a piker or because the liquor store didn't stock Wild Turkey, but because I figured Murk, finding himself more than a quart low on the oil that kept his engine running, was probably ready by now to swill high-octane moonshine, and I wanted him better to appreciate his circumstances, realize fine whiskey was not available everywhere in the world, especially in a jail cell meant to hold an accused murderer.

"I may not believe in God, Fletcher, but, by God, I believe in you," he told me after the guards had departed and I had pulled a condom out from the front of my underpants.

He downed the entire contents of the prophylactic, then sat down and threw his head back, and closed his eyes.

When he finally opened his eyes he said, "Salvation may not be eternal, but that will get me through the next few hours. Thank you."

I pulled out three more whiskey-filled rubbers and we concealed them as best we could under his bunk.

"When's Amanda going to spring me?" he said.

"I doubt if you're going to get bail, Murk. The charge is murder. Times two."

"It looks bad, doesn't it."

"I'm sure Amanda has dealt successfully with worse. But tell me about those boys. Did you see them? Did they come to the ranch?"

"They did. They came looking for Peggy Ann."

"What did they want with her?" I said.

"They wanted her to testify on Ricky's behalf. They said it would look good if a woman spoke up regarding Ricky's character."

"I bet that went over well with Peggy Ann."

"She wasn't even there. Peggy Ann and her mother went hell-catting off up north before those boys ever showed up."

"Did you explain to those frat men that Peggy Ann would not make a suitable character witness for Ricky?"

"I most certainly did. But they said Peggy Ann had Ricky all wrong, that he still loved her, that his having to break off with her was entirely his grandfather's idea."

"And nobody but nobody goes against the wishes of El Condor," I added.

Murky said, "At that point I told the boys that, if that was the case, Peggy Ann wouldn't want a gutless wimp for a boyfriend and was unlikely going to want to stand up in court in his defense and claim he was an honorable man."

"What then?" I said.

"They were determined they were still going to try to persuade Peggy Ann to vouch for Ricky. But I told them she had gone whooping off to Monterey to the music festival and good luck finding her in that crowd."

"Go on."

"That's it. They turned around and left. That was the last I saw of them."

"Obviously they didn't get far."

Murky nodded.

"See anybody lurking around the ranch?"

"Nope. But then I wasn't on the lookout for frat-boy murderers."

"I'm still not clear what reason the county prosecutor is going to give for why you killed them. Did Sam Cuddleston or any of his detectives say anything to you about why you might want to harm them? I saw Sam when I came here looking for you and he gave no explanation. And I don't think Ernie Stellhorn knew anything."

Murky said, "I hear Ernie found the bodies."

"Well, Quagmire did and Ernie reported the finding."

"That dog of Ernie's is something. Quag once ran off a pair of coyotes that were trying to attack a newborn colt out in my horse barn. He didn't just run them off. He caught one and ripped the coyote to pieces. No wonder Ernie didn't come back from frontline combat in Vietnam filled with nightmares and uncontrollable shakes. That dog preserved his sanity."

"Does Ernie own a gun?" I said.

"Now wait a minute, Fletcher. Ernie Stellhorn is a good citizen."

"Somebody shot Harry Deemer and Chuck Paltzheimer, then buried them far, far off any well-traveled trails."

"But then Quagmire --."

"Many a murderer has been first on the scene to discover the corpse or corpses he or she laid low."

"But why would he do it?"

"Maybe Ernie thought he was protecting you. He hasn't been home from the war all that long."

"Yeah, but when they came to the ranch, those frat boys were definitely not wearing black pajamas."

"Ernie may not suffer from nightmares or the screaming meemis, but I bet he still has a pretty vivid imagination, possibly a warped imagination. In which case, he might easily have pictured Harry and Chuck wearing coolie hats and black pajamas."

"I know I'm not guilty, Stu, but I'm not ready to point a finger at poor old Ernie."

"Let me remind you, Murk. Somebody in close proximity to your ranch killed those two young men. Who else could it have been?"

I was hoping he would bring up Peggy Ann and her mother. After helping himself to another pop of whiskey, he did just that.

XXXIV

"Who do you think killed those boys?" Murky asked me.

"You'd know better than I would."

"Do you really think I'm capable of murder, Fletcher?"

"Capable? Yes. We all are. Even the nuns of Vedanta ashram are not exempt," I said.

"You know about them?"

"Yes. I had to go there once in search of a teenager who had run away from home. From a note and some readings I found stashed away deep in the desk in the teenage girl's bedroom I decided to go to Montecito to ask the nuns. And, sure enough, she was there."

"Was she given sanctuary?" Murky asked, perhaps hoping he might make a dash for the ashram if he got the chance.

"There is no immunity inside a church, Murk, despite what you might have seen or read. The nuns had to give her up."

"Then what?"

"I took her home. Child Protective Services finally showed up ten days later to check on her. Her parents had gone back to New York City to a wedding, leaving the girl behind, which they said is what she demanded of them. When CPS broke in they found her dead. Apparent suicide. Hanged herself in the garage."

"Jesus! How'd that make you feel?"

"Like a hangman."

I steered Murky back to the murder of Harry and Chuck.

"Shit! I don't know, Fletcher. I can't picture Peggy Ann puttin' a gun to those guys' heads. But her mother? Yes. That bitch would not only steal the pennies off a dead man's eyes, she'd be the one who caused them to be there in the first place. Medusa incarnate! A man-hatin' bitch with a capital 'B'."

"Okay."

"By the way, Fletcher, while my mind is on bustin' out of this crap place, what do you call a clairvoyant midget who has escaped from jail?"

I shrugged.

"A small medium at large."

You can take a comedian away from vaudeville, but you can't take vaudeville away from the comedian. Maybe telling jokes kept his mind off the predicament he was now in.

I asked him "Why do you think Nancy would kill two young men she hardly knew?"

"Hardly knew? You are clueless, Fletcher. That was not the first time those two, along with another kid, came to the ranch looking for Peggy Ann. And damned if Nancy didn't try to seduce all three of them. Right in front of Peggy Ann no less."

"How did that turn out?" I said.

"Them boys weren't the least bit interested in humpin' an old sow when they had hopes of jumpin' the sow's piglet. And, brother, did Peggy Ann lead them boys down Cocktease Lane. Afterwards Peggy Ann was pleased as punch with herself, while her momma threw a shit-fit to beat all tantrums."

He laughed at his own story.

To change the subject, I then asked him, apropos of nothing, "Do you know why Nancy went off to San Francisco?"

Murky pondered for a moment, then said, "Probably to see some of her former Eye-Tie relations, I reckon."

"I don't understand."

"Of course, you don't. The guy Nancy was married to, Al Lorgran, was a wop mobster. Ties to trucking. Teamsters. Jimmy Hoffa. Those connections. His real last name was Lorgranetti, but he dropped the 'etti' so he would not sound like the Sicilian thug he was."

Nancy Lorgranetti, eh?

Murky went on. "Anyway, Al was killed in a motorcycle accident back in 1962. Speeding down Highway 17 from San Jose to Santa Cruz when he lost control. CHP had to scrape him off a boulder at the bottom of a canyon."

"But Nancy has kept in contact with Al Lorgranetti's relatives?" I said.

"Kept in touch doesn't begin to describe it. She loves those guinea fowls, especially all the women. And they reciprocate, I understand."

So I was right. Likely she, not Paolo Galboni, hired Giovanni Alba. And Tony Whores.

I then asked Murky, "Does Peggy Ann still have warm relations with her father's side of the family?"

"Not that I know of. No, wait. Peggy Ann's roommate at Fresno State was, is, one of her cousins from the Bay Area. Ginger Frichetti. In fact, Peggy Ann was going to meet Ginger when Peggy Ann got off the train in Salinas. Then they were going together in Ginger's VW van to the music thing in Monterey."

A cousin's name and a VW van's license plate number might help authorities track down Peggy Ann -- if it comes to that, I thought. Also, looking for Lorgranettis and Frichettis in North Beach would help immensely in narrowing down a search for Nancy -- if it comes to that.

I left Murky to his balloons of liquor and his fantasies of becoming a large comedian at large again. Amanda, I was told by her cute secretary, Felicity, was in judge's chambers arguing -- fruitlessly, I guessed -- for dismissal of the charges against Ricky Claymore, on the grounds that three witnesses absolutely essential to the defense's case were now either missing or dead. Terry Morowitz still had not shown up anywhere -- dead or alive.

I told Felicity that I had fulfilled my charge from Amanda to pay Murky a visit in jail and that I was now on my way to San Luis Obispo to listen to a banker pass on news he considered urgent for Murky to hear.

I could imagine the news, but wanted to hear it in person. But, when I stepped outside, a City of Santa Julietta police detective I recognized, Jason Patterson, approached me.

"Chief Fry would like a chat with you, Fletcher. We're still trying to clear things up regarding the Tony Whores incident."

So, fifteen minutes later, I sat across from the chief, with Patterson sitting in on our exchange as well.

"Who do you think hired Tony to take you all for a little boat ride?" Chief Fry asked to start things off.

"Any why?" Detective Patterson threw in.

I said, "Amanda Reynolds has had me doing background checks trying to push back against the charge that Ricky Claymore raped Wendy Simmons."

"Yes, we know a bit about that already," the chief said.

"The only explanation that makes sense to me is that Amanda or I or both of us were getting too close to getting Ricky off the hook, and somebody desperately wants Ricky to be convicted."

"Who is that desperate?" Patterson said.

"Besides Wendy Simmons?" I said.

The chief said, "You don't think Miss Simmons hired a goon like Tony, do you?"

"No, but maybe her dad, an uncle, some family member on her behalf."

Patterson said, "You don't just place an ad in the 'Thugs for Hire' section of the *LA Times* or *SF Chronicle*. You have to know someone who knows someone."

I said, "I understand. But you asked who badly wanted Ricky convicted. Wendy should be at the top of anyone's list."

The chief said, "Okay. But who's second on your list?"

"Peggy Ann Lorgran."

That name took both policemen aback. So I gave them a short version of 'Peggy hates Ricky'.

Pattern asked, "So do you think Miss Lorgran is capable of hiring Tony Whores?"

I said, "No, but her mother is."

I then explained Nancy Lorgran's connection to San Francisco Italian Teamster thugs.

"You've been doing some homework, Fletcher. Congratulations," the chief said.

I nodded and remembered back to how hard it often was to get people to open up to cops who are investigating crimes. But private eyes were usually less intimidating. There was no way Murky would tell a cop about his sister-in-law's late husband's connections to shady characters. And Murky didn't even like Nancy.

"Which chick do you favor for hiring Tony, Fletcher?" Detective Patterson said.

"Right now I favor Peggy Ann's mother. It may turn out Peggy Ann doesn't even know Harry and Chuck are dead. But the reason I favor Nancy Lorgran over Wendy's mother, father, aunts, or uncles is because I haven't investigated Wendy's family yet. For all I know at the moment, someone in Wendy's family may have mob connections, too. Connections tighter than Nancy's Lorgran's, though I seriously doubt it."

By the time I left Chief Fry's office it was too late for me to drive to San Luis Obispo and arrive before the banks closed. So I headed home to Santa Maria with a plan to drive to drive to San Luis in the morning.

XXXV

As I was unlocking the front door to my house I saw my next door neighbor Mary Ann Chase come around from the side of her house. She was holding a pair of pruning shears in one hand and a handful of pale pink hydrangeas in the other.

"Good afternoon to you, Stu. Did you catch any bad guys today?"

"I'm afraid not, Mrs. Chase. They were just too clever for me. And how have you been since I saw you last?"

"Well, you know, if it's true that one is as young as one feels, why today my age would be hovering somewhere near one-hundred forty."

"So, tell me, Mrs. Chase, how a hundred forty year old woman feels?"

"Like Hell, only hotter."

"You don't look flushed to me."

"I'm sure I don't. But I'm burning up inside."

"Do I need to rush you to emergency?"

"No, no. I'm sure the feeling will pass."

"Are you sure?"

"I'm sure."

"So what's the good word today?" I said.

"How about *chatoyant.*" She then spelled it for me.

I shook my head.

I said, "It sounds lovely, but is it a curse word?"

"No, no, no. You have a naughty mind, Stu Fletcher. It comes to us from French and means 'to change luster, like a cat's eye'."

"You are amazing, Mrs. Chase."

"Thank you, Mr. Fletcher."

"Mrs. Chase, how would you like a library-research challenge?" I said as she put her nose to her hydrangeas.

"I'd like nothing better. As you know, I miss the library."

"Well, what I have in mind will keep you there for a few hours."

Wendy Simpson's family lived in the Los Angeles area, not one of my favorite places to go anymore. So it occurred to me I could have Mrs. Chase check out any potential mob connections to Wendy's family. She could find information that I could not find and find it faster, at least if any connections or hints of connections had ever been published.

But perhaps it hadn't been published, in which case I would have to use my connections with LA area policemen and former policemen to try to find out. However, by using -- rather by employing -- Mrs. Chase first, I might save myself some phone calls and lots of footwork.

After dinner I invited Mrs. Chase over for some cake I had bought at a local favorite of mine, Patti Cortez's Confectionary, and afterwards laid out my task for her. She agreed and said she would start the next day. I didn't hold out any hope of success for her, but I didn't tell her that. Maybe she'd surprise me.

In the morning I drove to San Luis Obispo, taking my time, so that bankers at The San Luis Obispo County Ranchers' Bank and Trust could, like bankers everywhere, loll in their scented bathtubs until the sybaritic hour of ten.

A loan officer named Lyle Etteron welcomed me into his office and closed the door. He was a young man who wore a bespoke three-piece suit of light gray, which made my off-the-rack, brown Sears sports coat look shabbier than ever. His hair was better kept than mine, too. Had I been there for a loan, I imagine I would have been turned down on appearances alone.

"Have a seat, Mr. Fletcher. When I called to speak to Mr. Murtrans I was told he might be unavailable for quite some time and that I was to contact you."

"That is correct. Mr. Murtrans has been jailed on a charge of murder. So, yes, if the charge sticks, he will be unavailable for a very long time."

I had intended my remark to be a sophomoric joke, but I failed to elicit some much as a tiny smile from the man.

"Quite so, Mr. Fletcher. Mrs. Murtrans's murder was what prompted me to make my call in the first place. Only day before yesterday did I happen to read about Mrs. Murtrans's unfortunate demise."

Of course. San Luis Obispo is on the far side of the planet from the Sisquoc Valley.

So I said, "Yes, news does travel slowly these days."

He missed my irony.

"Especially when the news article was on page four of our local paper."

Page four. Right. I was willing to bet the comics page was deeper than that. Still, at least he had made the call instead of chucking the newspaper without another thought. In fact, I wondered about that.

"What prompted you to call, Mr. Etteron? The newspapers are full of murders these days."

"The name, Mr. Fletcher, the name."

"What name?"

"Murtrans, of course. I read that Cynthia Murtrans is -- well, was -- the wife of the TV actor and comedian, Murky Murtrans. Why, I have seen Mr. Murtrans appear on TV many times. He's very funny, but he's also a highly talented character actor. I was unaware he lived nearby."

"So you hoped to meet him? Offer your condolences in person?" I said.

"Oh, no. I wanted to talk to him about his son."

"Little CJ?"

He nodded. "I guess that is what many people call him. To me he is the Reverend Clyde J. Browning."

"Okay. What about him?"

"Are you aware of his pending loan with us?"

"Yes," I lied. "But tell me more. What's at issue?"

"Why, the loan itself, of course."

"Go on."

"Well, Mrs. Murtrans was supposed to come in to put her signature to the loan. That is, she would provide collateral in the form of backup cash. But she kept postponing when she would come in to sign. She claimed she had to sell off some property first in order to have the cash on hand."

"How big a loan are you talking about?" I said.

"Two hundred fifty thousand dollars."

Puzzled, I asked, "Why did she need cash? Wouldn't the property itself serve as collateral?"

"Yes, but, may I remind you: California is a community property state, in which case we would also need Mr. Murtrans's signature."

"The loan is to build CJ's new church, right?"

"That is correct."

Of course. Murky would never sign for a loan to build a church, even his son's church.

I said, "Obviously Mrs. Murtrans's signature is now going to be somewhat difficult to obtain."

"Totally impossible," the banker said, again missing my attempt at humor. I suddenly wondered if Murky might be able to get this guy to crack a smile. I don't think I'd bet much money on it.

"Okay. So two days ago you find out Cynthia Murtrans is dead. I assume that kills any possibility of CJ's getting the loan. I assume you won't accept God's signature."

All that remark got me was a puzzled look. Talk about a tough audience.

"So why the urgent call?" I said.

"Because Reverend Murtrans came in here yesterday positively beside himself. He demanded that the bank issue him the loan. He claimed the contractor he had hired was already purchasing building materials and lining up sub-contractors. So now the contractor was demanding payment."

"And you told him --."

"I said to him that our bank was unable to complete his loan application without guaranteed collateral. At which point, I must say, the pastor became very, very angry."

"So how did you console him?"

"I couldn't. He was beside himself. He began picking up objects from my desk and throwing them. The he began to shout and curse and pound his fists on my desk."

"Did you call the police?" I said.

"Oh, no. I wouldn't want my minister arrested. Our bank manager heard Mr. Murtrans yelling. So he came in to try to calm the man. But to no avail. In fact, the man's behavior turned worse. He screamed obscenities directed toward both Mr. and Mrs. Murtrans. And, oh, if looks could kill. I was positively taken aback that such language and such conduct could emanate from a man of God."

"What happened next?"

"He stormed out, slamming the door behind him."

If looks could kill. Maybe they already had.

I doubted if CJ was much of a history buff. Too bad. He could have learned a lot from San Luis Obispo's original church. The Franciscan mission of San Luis Obispo de Tolosa, built in 1772 and named after a bishop from the Basque town of Tolosa, was a humble edifice, built of logs. However, after repeated attacks by the local Chumash Indians, who used burning arrows, tiles were added to the church's roof, the first roof tiles used on any California mission. So, then again, maybe CJ did know local history and it was this upgrade that inspired him.

On my drive to CJ's Church of the Holy Redeemer Resurrection, a few miles south of San Luis Obispo, I wondered if I really ought to confront CJ alone. Murky had told me of a previous violence, but swore his son had no other history of it. However, from what the banker told me, CJ had a hair-trigger for explosive behavior. I promised myself I would be cautious. I also assured myself that I had no hard evidence whatsoever to pin on CJ for Cynthia Murtrans's murder.

Still, he was now my prime suspect, given Cynthia's failure to come through with the quarter million dollar loan she had, in effect, promised CJ she would back, pledging hers and Murky's vineyards as collateral.

Severe disappointment wouldn't begin to describe CJ's reaction toward not getting the loan. He had already exploded while in the bank office. I'm sure if I were in his shoes, I'd be pissed off and ready to crush someone's skull. Rather, one skull in particular. Maybe two. I tried to imagine why he hadn't attacked Murky. Maybe he had and Murk chose not to tell me.

XXXVI

I found CJ polishing one of the six candlesticks on his altar. He was not whistling while he worked. His face was a fixed grimace. Music was present, however. In the room beyond us I saw Genesis Browning tapping a baton on a music stand as she tried to shepherd several young girls through the opening strains of "Swing Low, Sweet Chariot".

"Detective Fletcher. If you've come looking for a donation toward bail money for my father, you're wasting your time."

"The charge of murder doesn't warrant bail, CJ."

"Oh. I didn't know that. Then how may I help you?"

"I'm hoping you can answer a biblical question about murder," I said.

He stopped polishing and I sat down in a front pew.

"I'm sure I can," he said.

"Okay. The question is this: Does your God grant murderers entry into Heaven?"

"My God? I take it you are not a Christian."

"No."

"What are you then?"

"Let's just say I worship one god less than you do."

"Ah! A heathen, like my father."

"Heathen, pagan, infidel, heretic."

"An atheist."

I said, "I prefer secular humanist."

"A distinction without a difference."

I shrugged.

"Back to my question, CJ. What is the answer? Is your God so forgiving that he is willing to populate His paradise with murderers?"

From behind me came the voice of CJ's wife, Genesis Browning. I turned to see she had dismissed her small youth choir.

"The answer to your question, Mr. Fletcher is *Yes*. Emphatically. All murderers are welcome into God's kingdom. Remember: *Whosoever believeth in Me shall not perish but have everlasting life.*"

"Then why aren't deathbed conversions as many as grains of sand on a beach?" I asked.

"Because God would know they are false conversions. Acts of dishonest desperation," she said.

I looked at CJ and asked, "But a lifelong true believer who is also a murderer will be granted entry through the Pearly Gates?"

CJ hesitated, then said, "For certain if his motive was not sinful."

I arched an eyebrow.

"A sin-free murder?" I said.

CJ's voice changed. He spoke rapidly, excitedly. "Yes. The man was doing God's work. He was slaying a sinner, a sinner who failed to fulfill a promise to carry on God's work."

"Shut up, CJ," Genesis called out. "That's enough!"

But CJ went on.

""Fulfilling God's goals sometimes calls for his most faithful worshipers to step outside God's normal limitations on us."

"CJ, shut up! Now!" his wife implored.

"Just as David violated God's commandment not to kill by slaying Goliath, I was incited by God to strike down that wicked, wicked woman for her treachery, for turning her back on God. Yes, for that she had to die! God himself ordered me. God understands."

I was certain the State of California would not be nearly as understanding.

Genesis had worked her way to the altar, where she embraced her husband for a moment. Then she grabbed an unpolished candlestick from its base and charged toward me, holding it high above her head, prepared to slay yet another pagan who failed to grasp the Grand Calling her husband had been invited to. Only with a worthy temple could CJ properly perform his duty to God and his service to his flock.

I easily ducked her swing, the blow of the candlestick striking the back of the wooden pew. I gripped her candle-holding wrist and bent it backward until she winced and finally dropped the weapon. I took a quick look at CJ to see if he intended to attack me, too. But he stood leaning against his pulpit, looking for all the world like a saddened clown, a mime whose role had ended.

I waited until deputies from the San Luis Obispo County Sheriff's Department had taken my statement before leaving CJ's small, now-even-more-diminished sanctuary. CJ and Genesis had each been driven off in a cruiser, CJ to face a murder indictment, Genesis looking at doing time as an accessory -- after the fact for sure, and maybe before the fact as well.

So God called upon CJ to slay Cynthia. Or rather, CJ saw murdering her as part and parcel of his holy calling. Hmm. The concept of callings has always bothered me. People who believe they have been *called*, most often by God, to this or that life's work always turn out to be people who end up as doctors, ministers, teachers, or in other lofty professions. I have never heard a cocktail waitress, a grocery clerk, or an assembly line worker speak of having been called to his or her blue-collar career job.

Funny how the calling God metes out -- for example a preacher -- always manages to coincide with what the person who is called wants to be. Of course, no one wants to be a cocktail waitress or a bus driver. So, not so amazingly, people who end up doing those tasks never end up being *called* to them.

I made two more phone calls from CJ's church office before heading back to Santa Maria. Because I wanted to shake Murky free from his jail cell before he got the D.T.'s, I first called Sheriff Cuddleston's office to let him know Murky's son, CJ, had confessed to killing Cynthia

Murtrans. After I was told the sheriff was unavailable, I called Amanda
Reynold's office to get her to free Murky.

"CJ actually confessed to you?" Amanda said.

"Yes."

"You didn't have him in a half-nelson when he squealed, did you?
Because, if you did, his confession won't be allowed to stand."

"No, but I gave Genesis Browning a sprained wrist. Does that count?"

"Of course not. Good for you, Stu. I am impressed," she said.

"Thank you."

"Now I am going over to the county jail myself to make sure someone
there has spoken to the SLO sheriff. Thanks again."

"By the way, Amanda, tell Murky to pick up his empty condoms,
please. Tell him to be a tidy boy."

"Condoms? What *are* you talking about?"

"Murky will explain."

XXXVII

At home in Santa Maria I showered, poured myself a double Jim Beam over ice, then turned on my TV to watch the Vietnam War, where American success was being measured by Viet Cong body counts. If our Vietnamese enemies were anywhere near as numerous as our Chinese enemies had been in North Korea, the Pentagon and American generals were fooling themselves badly.

I remember the joke in Korea when I was there. If just one Chinaman stepped off a cliff every second, there would never be an end to the process, because there were so many of them. At the Battle of Osan in 1950 that had seemed all too true, when what seemed like never-ending waves of Chinese troops attacked us, until our lines broke and we retreated in disgrace. Behind us we left mountains of dead Chinese soldiers. Thousands, maybe tens of thousands, more of them dead than of us. So how many times in the history of warfare had body counts proved meaningless?

When my doorbell rang I cheerfully turned off Walter Cronkite. My caller was Mrs. Chase.

"Was your trip to San Luis successful, Mr. Fletcher?"

"Yes. Sit down."

I told Mary Ann about my adventure inquiring into God's forgiveness of murderers.

"What a wonderful result. So God tickled a confession out of your man of God. And now, if memory serves, in lieu of forgiveness God will subject the poor man to eternal, fiery torture," she said.

"Maybe. But only after the State of California treats him to a whiff of cyanide," I added.

"So he was desperate for this woman's money, was he? Odd, don't you think? Money, many of these people say, is the root of all evil. Yet they all covet it. In fact, every last denomination of them, I do believe, passes a collection plate on Sunday mornings."

I nodded and tried hard not to laugh.

"It's a grim business when man, God's most enlightened creature, is also his most devilish, don't you think?" Mary Ann said. "Why didn't God simply have us all start out in Heaven and then keep us there?"

"And deny us opportunities to pillage, plunder, and murder?" I said.

"You left out rape, Stu. And that brings me to why I am here. I've been rummaging through the darkest corners of the local libraries, both here and in Santa Julietta. And what I've found will curl your hair," she said, smiling.

My hair was already curly, which was why she smiled.

"So the Simmonses are Devil worshippers, are they?"

"Oh, no. Quite the opposite. Dull as dish water for the most part. Wendy's father is an accountant, her mother a nurse. They work hard, save their money. Then spend it on vacations to Yellowstone and the Grand Canyon. However --."

Given her dramatic pause, I knew something juicy was coming.

"Go on, Mrs. Chase."

"Well, let me preface my next remarks by saying my conclusions are not based on photographic evidence. Don't I wish. Instead, I have carefully pieced together times, places, money coming and going, that sort of thing. What I have come up with is not just guesswork, but conjecture based on lots and lots of facts."

"Is this going to end up in court, Mrs. Chase?"

"I don't know, Stu. You'd be a better judge of that."

Judge of that. Clever.

She went on. "My findings have mostly to do with Wendy. She's the wayward one."

"Ah ha! That's precisely what I'm looking for. Behavior that will discredit her."

"Well, you'd better listen, because it's not very pretty."

"All the better." I grabbed my pen and notebook.

"Wait until I've finished. Then make your judgments about good, better, and so on."

"Very well."

Then Mary Ann Chase began her story about what she had unearthed about Wendy Simmons.

"It began when she was sixteen and had just completed her sophomore year at Culver City High School. Near the end of her second semester of her sophomore year she had acquired a boyfriend, a young man named Simon Fineman, who was a junior. Well, to make a long story short, in early August of that year --1964 -- she and her girlfriend, Roxanna Galboni, took an overnight trip to Tijuana. Apparently they told their parents they were going to the San Diego Zoo."

"Tijuana? To buy cheap bumper stickers for Goldwater?" I said.

"Now why do you really suppose young girls would go alone overnight to Tijuana?"

"To buy booze? To experience Tijuana's night life?"

"Maybe. But think harder," Mary Ann said quietly. "New boyfriend in April."

"No! Not our sweet Wendy!"

Mary Ann nodded solemnly.

"Don't they sell condoms in Culver City? Jesus! When I was her age every Chevron gas station in Garden City had a condom dispenser in the men's restroom. Twenty-five cents apiece."

"I wouldn't know anything about that, but apparently Simon Fineman did not buy his gas at a Chevron station. He drove a 1960 Chevy station wagon, by the way."

"Double-sized bed on wheels. Perfect for drive-in double-features," I whispered to myself.

"I'll pretend I didn't hear that," Mrs. Chase said.

"Hear what?"

"There's more," she said.

"By all means, continue."

"By following bank transactions, among other things, I discovered that, beginning in October of 1964, Wendy and Roxanna Galboni returned to Tijuana regularly -- always on weekends -- not only up until the time they graduated, but into the summer afterward and then into when they began attending UCSJ."

"So that first visit wasn't for Wendy to have an abortion?" I said.

"Yes, I think it was. No, I mean I'm sure it was."

"Then what were the other visits to Tijuana all about?"

"Think about it, Stu. Surely you don't imagine Wendy was the only high school girl in the Los Angeles area having sex without protection. And where better for these young women to turn for help than one of their own kind who already *knew the ropes*, to use an totally inadequate metaphor."

"So Wendy Simmons was taking other girls to Tijuana to have abortions?"

"Wendy and Roxanna. And they were getting paid to do it. Each girl received fifty dollars from the girl in need, plus another fifty each from the abortionist, who raised his fee to cover the kickback. They always went to the same woman. Yes, a female abortionist in Tijuana. An abdominal surgeon from Buenos Aires, by the name of Monique Dubois. Father's French, mother's Argentinean."

"Wow! You dug really deep."

"I forgot to add that the girl in need paid for gas and one night's lodging for three."

"From her mother, the nurse, Wendy would know all about how to hold a patient's hand. Two girls along to be comfort girls," I said.

"No, Stu. A *comfort girl* is the euphemism the Japanese military in World War Two used to refer to prostitutes who accompanied their military officers on the front lines."

"I knew that. My dad explained that to me when the war was going on."

"But, yes," Mary Ann said. "Two women the same age as the woman about to have an abortion would provide about as much stress relief as would be possible under such horrifying circumstances."

"Wendy and Roxanna were making a hundred bucks clear for every girl they took to Tijuana, is that right?" I said.

"Correct."

"What about Roxanna? Did she have an abortion as well?"

"No, I don't think so."

"Terry Morowitz must have bought his gas at Chevron stations," I muttered.

"Perhaps he did," Mary Ann said.

"Please allow me to pay you for all your time and hard work, Mary Ann."

"The answer to that is a firm 'No'. Oh, and by the way, during all my hard work and time, I discovered another tidbit that might interest you."

"Go ahead."

XXXVIII

Before she continued, Mary Ann asked for a glass of water. I poured her a glass of sherry instead.

"Not exactly thirst-quenching, " she pointed out, "but it does sooth the soul, does it not, Mr. Fletcher?"

"Indeed, it does, Ma'am. So you still want a glass of ice water?"

"No, but another sherry would be wonderful," she said as she drained her small glass.

Her soul now doubly soothed, she went on.

"In 1935 at the Big Game, held at Stanford that year -- where Stanford shut out Cal 13-0, by the way -- a group of young coeds from Cal attended the game, then attended several fraternity parties on Stanford's campus afterwards. Well, one of those girls turned up dead the next morning, both murdered and raped."

"Oh, my."

"And the man charged with those crimes was none other than Richard Claymore II."

"Jeezus!"

"Indeed! Joseph and Mary, too, for that matter. But, in any case, I made copies of all the headline articles throughout the case, including the trial."

"I never heard about any of this," I said.

"Of course not. Once it was all over, Richard's father did his best to bury the whole episode."

"El Condor."

"Yes. That is mostly what he is known by now."

"Obviously, R Two was not convicted. Otherwise --."

"El Condor hired the best lawyers he could find and, according to news articles and editorials I read, the defense lawyers simply overwhelmed the prosecuting attorneys. It took the jury less than five hours' time to acquit Richard the Second, who was, of course, a big-name fraternity man at Stanford."

"I'm sure."

"The women in the group to which the dead woman belonged were crushed. Absolutely devastated by the verdict. The dead woman's sister, who was herself a freshman at Cal and a member of the group that attended the game and the parties, had to be hospitalized because she was so distraught."

"What was the dead woman's name?" I said.

"Roxanna Coangelo."

I went limp before I asked, "And her younger sister's name?"

"Gianetta. She's now married to --."

"Paolo Galboni."

"Why, yes," Mary Ann said, seemingly surprised that I knew what was now suddenly obvious.

I had it all wrong. In part because I had been misled by Giovanni Alba. Not intentionally misled, but misled anyway. Sister murdered. Okay. Had a daughter with two names? Not okay. Giovanni thought Roxanna is two separate words. Rox Anna. Roxi Anna. Or some such. As far as I was concerned Nancy Lorgran and Peggy Ann were no longer *persons of interest.* Gianetta Galboni was.

Tempted as I was to ask Amanda to send out word to call off the searches in Monterey and San Francisco, I held off. I wanted more on Roxanna and her mother before I recommended that. But I called Amanda anyway and told her I would meet her at her office and explain why I wanted her to join me on a short trip to the Galboni Estate, just south of Santa Julietta.

Amanda agreed and an hour later I found
of her Shaffler, Klein & Reynold's office, on S;
main square. She clutched her purse so tightly
ined she had just burgled the exclusive luxury jewel y
law office.

"Require a getaway car, Lady?" I asked.

"Depends. How big a cut of my heist do you expect?"

"Only ninety-nine percent."

"Well, all right. I am in a hurry."

"Hop in," I said.

"You trust me to pay you later?"

"Nope."

"Just drive, Fletcher."

"Yes, Ma'am."

I explained to Amanda everything I had written down about what
Mary Ann Chase had dug up for me in her library research.

"Jeez, Fletcher, maybe I should fire you and hire your neighbor for
my detective."

"Who just coaxed a confession out of CJ Browning, eh? A confession
that got your client out of jail."

"*Our* client. He hired you first to find Cynthia's killer."

"Okay. In either case, credit goes to me for CJ," I said. "And now that
we no longer need consider the motives Nancy and Peggy Ann might
have had for killing Cynthia, I'm mostly convinced they didn't kill the
frat boys either. It makes more sense to me now that Gianetta had Tony
Whores kill them. For her they could provide an account that would take
Ricky Claymore off the hook for raping Wendy Simmons. And Gianetta
Galboni wants Ricky to be found guilty in the worst way."

"All right. You can keep your job."

"Thanks."

"What if the gates leading to Casa Galboni are shut and locked?"
Amanda asked.

guess we wait for Sam Cuddleston to show up with a search warrant and a bullhorn."

Via either divine intervention or plain dumb luck the gates were open. So I hastened through before our luck changed. As it turned out, maybe I should have waited for the sheriff. Actually, there was no *maybe* to it. I should have waited. Period. But I didn't. If it's true that fools rush in where angels fear to tread, and that there is a very fine line between bravery and folly, I led the kind of charge for which no medals are awarded.

XXXIX

"You're comfortable with this, Fletcher? Just walking up to the front door?" Amanda said, once I had driven up the long driveway to the main house and parked in one of the many spaces provided for guests.

"She hasn't killed anyone herself... that we know of," I said defensively, knowing that Terry Morowitz remained unaccounted for.

"So you're eager to be her first victim. Is that right?"

"Preferably not."

Amanda just stared at me like I was a creature she didn't recognize.

"Feel free to stay here in the car until the sheriff arrives," I said.

"Sure. And spend the rest of my life hearing people snicker about what a paper tiger I am outside the courtroom."

"While you sit here having a three-way argument with your conscience and your good judgment, I'm going in to rattle Gianetta Galboni's psyche to see what wicked little ghouls tumble out."

By the time I reached the front door Amanda was right behind me. I could hear the doorbell ring inside the house when I pressed the buzzer twice. A short, middle-aged woman wearing a maid's uniform answered the door and spoke to us in a Hispanic accent. I asked to speak to the lady of the house and the maid invited us into the foyer and asked our names.

"I will inform the señora you are here to see her."

A minute later the maid returned.

"Follow, please."

We were led into a library with dark, wooden bookshelves on each of the four walls. Mrs. Galboni sat at a large desk with her back to us. The desk faced a window with opened curtains and through the window in the distance I could see a hillside garden filled with larkspur, delphinium, and Bells of Ireland.

Turning slowly in her chair to face us, Ginetta Galboni took the measure of Amanda, then said, "I know you by reputation, Mrs. Reynolds. You are a great defense lawyer, one whose services I hope never to require."

Amanda nodded, ignoring the flattery and the presumption that she was married.

"So why are the two of you here?" Gianetta said.

I said, "For one, we're looking for Terry Morowitz."

"Roxanna broke up with him."

"Why is that?' Amanda said.

Gianetta shrugged. "You'll have to ask my daughter."

"No. I'm asking you," Amanda said sharply.

"They had a fight."

"About what?" Amanda said.

"Typical young people's spat. Terry stormed off in a huff. Roxanna told him never to come back."

I changed the subject.

"Do you know a man named Antonio Bardello?"

"Tony? Sure. We went to grade school together in San Leandro. That's --."

"I know where it is. Just south of Oakland," I said.

"Yeah, right. Jeez, I haven't even thought of Tony for years, let alone seen him."

Amanda said, "You don't watch the local news on TV?"

"No. I pretty much keep to myself. I don't care what goes on beyond my front gate."

I said, "That means you don't even know that Tony died right here in Santa Julietta just the other day?"

Her eyes betrayed her, but she said, "Oh, my God. No. I didn't know."

Amanda and I both waited for the question that didn't come.

I finally said, "Aren't you going to ask how he died?"

"Well, uh, sure. It's just that I'm having a hard time taking it in that Tony's dead. Good grief! He's only my age."

Amanda said, "Tony died trying to kill me on board my sailboat. Kill Fletcher here, too."

"That's terrible! Why would he want to kill you?" she deadpanned.

"You tell us," I said.

"What do you mean?"

"You know what we mean," I said.

While verbally in denial, Ginetta began slowly to edge back toward her desk.

"As I said, I haven't even thought of Tony for years and years."

"You were the one who hired him to kill us. And to kill two young men, friends of Terry Morowitz named Harry Deemer and Chuck Paltzheimer."

"Now you are accusing me of ordering even more killings?"

I said, "Two murders. Maybe three. And four attempted murders."

"No!"

"Try this on, as well. The first thug you hired to do your dirty work, Giovanni Alba, proved to be even a bigger bungler than Tony. But at least Giovanni confessed to a priest, when he thought he was on the verge of dying, that it was you who hired him to murder everyone who was working successfully toward freeing Ricky Claymore from a rape charge."

"I've never heard of this Ricky Claymore."

I said, "There you did it, Gianetta. You tripped yourself up -- badly. Of course, you know who Ricky Claymore is. He's the son of the man who was found not guilty of raping and murdering your older sister, Roxanna Coangelo. You couldn't get to Richard the Second, so you decided to go after Richard Number Three, even after you found out Wendy lied about Ricky's raping her."

"Lies!"

"Alba was on his way to kill Harry and Chuck but took a wrong turn. Then El Condor, Richard the First, tried to stop Alba by running him into the Siquoc River. After that you hired your friend, Tony, to do the job. First he killed the two young men, then he came to Amanda's boat to kill us. You wanted anybody dead who could help free Ricky. Which brings us back to: Where is Terry Morowitz?"

I drew my gun when she reached for the desk drawer. But then I hesitated. I had never shot a woman. At least knowingly. In Korea Chinese soldiers, wearing their *ushanka* hats and winter coats, all looked alike when they swarmed toward our thinly manned lines. Rumors placed women in the ranks of Chinese infantry. But I scarcely had the time to sort through the piles of enemy bodies we left behind as we retreated through a field of our own dead. Maybe there were dead women there. Or maybe not. I never thought about it. I was just a kid, ten thousand miles from home, and in the middle of a war that made no sense to me.

Later, as a cop with the Burbank PD, I once drew on a Mexican woman who drew a knife on me. But she had the good sense to figure out she was holding the wrong weapon to face me evenly. She dropped the knife and put up her hands.

Other cops in my ranks had shoot-outs with women. Some women in those fights died. Two of the shooters I knew personally and both of them felt more than a twinge of guilt for killing a female. Others I knew who had killed women, nearly all in gang-related gun battles, shrugged and thought nothing of it. Killing bad guys included killing bad gals.

My hesitation allowed Gianetta to open the drawer, pull out a revolver, and begin to turn around. With my left arm extended, gun in my left hand, I swept all of the tschotskes from a side table not far from the desk. The knick-knacks hit her as her gun came up. The surprise barrage sent her reeling backward into the desk. But the gun went off and the trajectory of the bullet was unclear.

At the sound of the gun's discharge I heard a distant scream, somewhere beyond the room. I rushed Gianetta before she could recover from her surprise and shoot again. Grabbing her right wrist, I squeezed hard and hammered her right elbow and forearm with my .38. She clawed at my face with her left hand, so I swung my left elbow hard into her head several times. When she grabbed at my gun I squeezed the trigger, blowing a hole in her hand. She screamed, dropped her pistol, and clutched her bleeding palm.

I kicked her gun away and watched her flee. Just then Roxanna appeared.

"Mama, what's happening?"

"Run, Roxy, run. Come. Quick. The car," Gianetta cried out as she fled.

Roxanna looked into the study, saw me, and shouted, "You!", then followed her mother. The maid appeared, let out a squeal, then she fled, too.

When I looked for Amanda my heart nearly stopped. She lay curled up on the floor, clutching her left thigh. Gianetta's deflected gunshot had hit her and blood was oozing steadily through her trouser leg.

As I ran to her I whipped off my belt. I knelt, fumbled for my pen knife, then cut into her pants and tore at the material until it gave way. Finally I spoke to her.

"I'm going to put at tourniquet on you to stop the bleeding."

Amanda nodded wanly, but continued to clutch her leg. I wrapped my belt around her thigh above where she clung to her leg. Then I picked up Gianetta's revolver and used the barrel to wrench the belt tighter and tighter.

Shuffling sounds from the door through which Giantta, Roxanna, and the maid had fled made me look up from the bloody mess on the floor. When I saw it was Gianetta's gardener, looking confused, I motioned for him to come in.

"What's going on?" he said in a low voice.

"My friend here has been wounded. She needs an ambulance." I pointed to the telephone of Gianetta's desk. " When the gardener hesitated I shouted, "Now! Do it!" When he still just stood there, I shouted even louder, "Don't you dare let her die!"

With that he hastened to the phone and dialed.

My circumstances triggered a flashback to Korea, 1950, Osan. Wounded GIs everywhere. Cries of "Medic! Over here!" crisscrossed the battlefield. Where were our medics? Dead, most of them, I imagined.

Then, as I bent down over our platoon sergeant, Forrest Heckler, staring at what I knew was a fatal chest wound, I felt a tap on my left shoulder. I looked up to see our platoon medic, Arnie "Band-aid" Blevins, motioning for me to move aside.

"Hold this, Fletcher." He handed me his first-aid bag.

"He's done for, Arnie," I said reverently.

He whispered back, "I can see that. He's going to bleed out. So move over while I administer his tranquil slide into the next world, wherever that may be."

Arnie held a needle full of morphine, preparing to jab it into the back of the sergeant's right hand.

Finished, he said, "There. He'll be dead before he knows it. Now get outta here before you are, too."

"What about you?" I said.

"I'm too friggin' busy to die. Now go!"

My next encounter with Arnie was 1961, eleven years later, when I heard a whisper from behind me as I was walking out onto the Santa Monica Pier.

"Stu Fletcher, why aren't you dead, my friend?"

"More by luck than by design," I said as I turned. That had been our platoon's motto in Korea.

He shook my hand and said, "Wasn't it our plan to strangle MacArthur by the time the war was over?"

"Your plan, not mine. Well, okay. I wasn't going to try to stop you. But, of course, you're a slacker as always. Dugout Doug only died three years ago."

Calling Arnie Blevins a slacker had been a platoon insider joke. In fact, he never slowed down on the field of battle. He was everywhere. No bullet ever had Arnie's name on it, although he dutifully administered to dozens of our soldiers who had literally been ripped apart by bullets with their names on them.

Arnie told me he had used the GI Bill to complete an undergraduate degree at the University of Cincinnati, then had gone on to Chicago University Medical School. Now he served as an emergency-room doctor at LA General Hospital.

"My job now is second nature after doing triage in the trenches," he said.

I told him my post-war story.

"So you're a cop now, Fletch? You put bullets in the bad guys, I pull the bullets out."

"Only if I'm a bad shot, Arnie. Otherwise, the pathologist extracts my bullets."

"Keep on kickin', Fletcher," was Arnie's heartfelt wish for me as we parted ways that day. Two months later I read in the *LA Times* that Arnie had died of an aortic aneurism. What a thousand bullets couldn't do, a weak blood vessel could.

Those thoughts of Arnie Blevins flashed through my mind in seconds. Then quickly I turned my attention back to Amanda.

XL

Amanda was reduced to painful moaning. I'd never heard that in a woman before, but I'd heard it often in Korea. It didn't sound any better in contralto that it had in male tenor or bass. Despite her agony I twisted hard on the tourniquet.

To the gardener I called out, "What's downstairs?"

I got a shrug.

"Maybe a basement? I don't know. I've never been in the house much."

"Find out!" I shouted, then backed off and said a quiet, "Please."

I could hear sirens in the distance, but, even as a cop, I never paid enough attention to distinguish a police siren from a fire truck's siren from an ambulance's siren. As I tried to listen harder, Amanda passed out.

My first thought was: *She's going to bleed out. Bleed out! Damn it, Arnie! Where are you when I need you? Medic! I need a medic over here. Now! Don't die on me, Amanda. Don't you dare.*

In the near distance the sounds of sirens stopped. What was going on? Where were they? *Ambulance! Medics? We have a serious wound here. Arnie, bring your kit!*

At the library door the gardener appeared again. He was helping a young woman who was wrapped in a burlap sheet the size of a blanket. As they slowly edged into the room I could see the girl had badly disheveled hair and her face was covered with dirt. She was sobbing loudly.

"Call for another ambulance!" I shouted to him. "And see what's holding up the first one you called for."

"Yes, sir," the gardener said, letting loose of the burlap and heading for the phone.

As the girl's blanket hit the floor I recognized the woman to be Wendy Simmons. The gardener picked up the telephone receiver, then turned to see Wendy had become uncovered. He hastily returned to her and pulled the blanket -- such as it was -- over her again. He then urged her to curl up on the floor. Once she did, he returned to the phone and made the call.

"No! We're inside the house. Please, hurry," the gardener said into the phone. Then turning to me he said, "The ambulance people thought the wounded woman was in the car that sideswiped them and then went into a ditch just outside the gate."

Wounded woman. Gunshot. Galboni Estate.

How would they know Gianetta Galboni was not the victim the phone call was about?

Just then Sheriff Cuddleston walked through the door with two deputies, all three with guns drawn. The look on the sheriff's face indicated he didn't begin to comprehend what had happened.

Whatever the sheriff thought, he took one look at Amanda and turned to one of his deputies. "Call for a backup ambulance. Top priority." To the other he shouted, "Water, salt, and sugar cubes. In my cruiser trunk. Be quick."

Cuddleston then knelt down beside Amanda. "Let me take over, Fletcher. You look too beaten down to maintain the tourniquet."

I nodded and allowed him to take the gun barrel.. I went to Wendy Simmons and sat down beside her as she continued to cry and shiver. I told the gardener he was free to leave and he rose, shaking his head.

Sheriff Cuddleston called out, "Give a statement to one of my deputies. Don't worry. Just tell them what you saw and heard."

The gardener nodded and left.

"I'll get your story later, Fletcher. I'm sure it's a doozey."

I said, "Don't let Ginetta or Roxanna Galboni get away. Ginetta is behind the murders of Harry Deemer and Charles Paltzheimer. She hired Tony Bardello to kill them. And she told him to kill Amanda, me, and whoever was with us on her yacht."

I pointed to Wendy. "Also, Roxanna may be guilty of trying to abuse Wendy here."

Wendy looked up briefly and nodded.

At that point two ambulances arrived together and the next few minutes involved taking both women away to hospitals. I noticed the ambulance attendant left my tourniquet in place, allowing the sheriff to maintain the tension on my pants belt as the slowly wheeled Amanda away. I offered to ride with her to the hospital, but Sheriff Cuddleston said not. I was to remain behind to give my statement.

An hour and three bottles of orange juice later I pointed to the grand, spacious flower garden sprawling just east of the Galboni mansion.

"I think you'll find Terry Morowitz buried over there somewhere. 'Twould be a pity to dig up much of such a gorgeous garden. Do you have a cadaver-sniffing dog, Sheriff?"

"No, but LA will cheerfully loan me one of theirs for a day or two," he said.

I added, "There's a chance you'll also find Paolo Galboni, Ginetta's husband, in there. Turns out Gianetta wore the pants in the Galboni family. All through this Paolo has been nothing but an apparition, a ghost, a chimera."

"A what?" Cuddleston said.

"A figment of the imagination."

"Oh, right. Lately my imagination has been full of figments. Little fuzzy, flithy chunks of debris. Just like rocks in the...the...what's that belt of rocks floating out there in space somewhere?

"The Kuyper Belt," I said.

"If you say so."

"I say so."

"Oh, by the way, *belt* reminds me: You'll get your belt back at the hospital. It'll be cataloged along with all of Miss Reynolds's other belongings. Might not be much good anymore, but you can hang it in your living room as a souvenir."

"Do I get to keep Ginetta's gun, too?" I said.

"I switched it out with a long dowel already. It will serve as evidence in the...uh...uh...earlier events that happened here," he said.

"But you didn't want my belt?"

"Hell, no. I didn't see any trophy notches on it."

I said, "You know, I think you'll find this whole business amounted to a new version of an Old West range war, except now, instead of fighting over cattle, sheep, or water rights, Gianetta was fighting El Condor over grapes. And Ricky's alleged rape of Wendy turned out to be a sharp weapon in that war."

"Feed me your theories some other time. Right now my head is spinning."

"Am I free to go?" I said.

"Not very far. Stay in the county."

"Has Murky been freed?"

Cuddleston gave me a snarky look.

"He will be."

"Soon?"

"Yeah, soon."

XLI

Arriving at Santa Julietta's Waverly Hospital -- the largest and best in the city -- I learned from a sheriff's deputy that Sienna, Gianetta Galboni's other daughter, was in the custody of the State of California's Child Protective Services, after being picked up at her school. Whether the poor girl was bewildered by current events I had no idea. Maybe she was in on them. Maybe not.

Amanda had an IV in her when I reached her room. She also appeared to be sedated. A nurse told me she had just come out of surgery and that I was not allowed to enter the room or try to speak her. I was assured she was in good care and that the surgeon had saved her leg. As I stood staring at Amanda and being thankful she was alive, the nurse told me I would not be allowed to see the patient until tomorrow.

The patient. How readily and often we depersonalize each other. Then sometimes the next step is to pull a trigger. However, the reason I put a bullet through Gianetta's hand had nothing to do with my depersonalizing her. She in fact was a person who was trying to kill Amanda, kill me, had in fact ordered the deaths of three young men. She was a very real, very monstrous person.

When I reached Wendy Simmon's room she was sitting on the edge of her bed with a tray of food in front of her. She held a spoon awkwardly while picking at a dull half pear drifting in a puddle of juice, accompanied by half a marachino cherry.

I riveted my gaze on the pear. I'm not sure why. It was innocent of any crime other than ending up on a hospital dinner tray. Maybe I was looking for innocence. The young woman on the bed was not going to provide me with any.

"Five minutes," Her nurse said. "And don't make her cry."

I was to be kind to a woman whose own twisted mind had started a string of lies that ended in three deaths and nearly more. I was looking at another moral monster.

"Oh, Mr. Fletcher, I'm so glad you and that other man saved me." She said and put down her spoon.

"The other man's name is Fred Donaldson. He's the gardener at the Galboni Estate. Be sure to thank him later."

"Oh, I will. I will."

"Are they taking good care of you here? I know from seeing other people here in the past that it's a very good hospital."

"Oh, everything is peachy. Well, as long as I don't --."

"It's all right. You don't need to talk about it -- for now. Later the police will want to hear you tell them what happened," I said.

In almost a whisper, she said, "I can talk some now, can't I."

"I suppose so."

I looked around. The nurse had vanished and no one else was any-where nearby in the hallway.

"They told me they were going to hang me naked by my heels and skin me alive -- slowly."

"Who is 'they'?" I said.

"Roxana and her mother. Roxana even said she hoped I was still alive when they finished skinning me so I could watch her dance wear-ing my hide."

"That's awful," I said.

"Oh, it's worse. Roxanna said that, once I was dead, she was going to bury me in the big garden, bury me face down on top of Terry's body. That way Terry and I would be joined together as lovers until we rotted away to nothing."

I said nothing.

Wendy went on. "Roxana said her mother was going to let her skin me, because she'd already shown her how to do it. She said she'd practiced getting ready for me by skinning Terry -- with the help of her mother."

"Her mother is a wicked woman," I said.

"But I don't understand. Roxanna is my very best friend. Why did *she* want to hurt me?"

Jeezus! As the priests say*: Sancta Simplicitas*! Holy Simplicity! How fucking naive can this girl be? Or does she still believe all her lies? Now was not the time to goad her about screwing Terry Morowitz. Or trying to hang Ricky Claymore out to dry. No goading about anything. Let Sam Cuddleston and his detectives listen to her tale of innocence, then poke holes on it. Big holes.

Maybe being skinned alive would have been just punishment for Wendy. It was certainly more just than the couple of years she'll get for falsely accusing Ricky of rape. In fact, maybe she wouldn't even do any time. Her attorneys would portray her as a victim in all this mess, just another injured party tossed into the Galboni cauldron, distract jurors from her own culpability in having sex with Roxanna's boyfriend, then screaming "Rape!" and pointing her finger at Ricky Claymore. If the clichéd *Hanging's too good for her* applied, then maybe *being skinned alive* would be just right.

At the county jail I waited while the tedium of legal paperwork -- the law's delay, I believe Shakespeare called it -- unraveled toward setting Murky Murtrans free once again.

"Fletcher? Why are you here? What's going on?" he said when he finally emerged from the jigsaw-puzzle labyrinth of bars and saw me.

Of course, no one tells inmates anything, except to shut up and to behave. So I recapped as much as I was up to telling him.

Then I said, "You seem awfully calm for a man who has been wrongly imprisoned -- twice."

All the time while I spoke Murky massaged his arm muscles and joints. I imagined that sleeping on a jail cot didn't exactly suit him, especially as his age. Yet, he was in rare form.

"Yeah, I know. You'd think I'd be as goosed up as a nigger choir on Sunday, but I ain't. Still, oh, my achin' back. My traps are both stiffer 'n' a teenager's cock."

And then, to prove for certain he had not left his sense of humor behind on his lumpy cell cot, he asked me, "Fletcher, what did the pig say after he fell down the stairs?"

"Ouch?' I said, playing dumb.

"Nope. He screamed, 'Oh, my achin' bacon.'"

I smiled and then reminded him he should be glad Gianetta Galboni hadn't succeeded in frying his bacon.

"I know, I know. And to celebrate, let's go to Molly's Diner, where I can order me up six or eight side orders of her apple-smoked bacon."

On the drive to Molly's I continued explaining events he missed while he was in jail.

"All for a bunch of grape juice," was his first remark when I had finished.

I responded, "No, no. It goes deeper than merely a wine war. Revenge against the Claymores. That was Gianetta Galboni's motivation. Her daughter's motive was to get even with Wendy and Terry. Wendy's was to cover up for getting it on with Roxanna's young man."

Murky was quiet for a while, then said, "When I was in the ninth grade back in Hellfire a body turned up floatin' in Hellfire Lake. Turned out it was the nephew of my eighth-grade English teacher, Mrs. Pruitt. The dead kid's name was Wally Kingsley. Walter Francis Kingsley. Wimpy blond kid with a face full of freckles. Anyway, for a while the police thought Shandy Katz might have been the nasty prick who held Wally's head under water till he stopped breathin'. Shandy was the school bully. But then the cops decided a kid couldn't kill another kid. So Shandy skated free. Later authorities pinned the murder on some itinerant hobo who had passed through Hellfire. But I still think the real culprit was Shandy Katz."

"Did you hunt him down and punch him until he confessed?" I said.

'Naw. I didn't like Walter all that much. So I didn't really care who killed him. If I had been more in love with Wally, I might have cleaned ol' Shandy's clock."

I just shook my head.

"And CJ killed Cynthia, eh? No doubt with that bitch, Genesis, egging him on," Murky said.

I nodded.

"What's the world comin' to, Fletcher?"

"It's coming to about what it's always been."

"I'm tryin' hard to give a damn anymore, but it just ain't happenin'."

"Feeling old, Murk?"

"Yes, and maybe it's because I am old. You'd think I'd just sit back and get used to it. That funny fella Oscar Wilde once said, 'To get back to my youth I would do anything in the world, except take exercise, get up early, or be respectable.' To that I'd add: Or quit drinkin' bourbon."

I replied, "Wasn't it Wilde who also said 'I can resist anything but temptation'?"

Murky said "I believe it was. But I can tell you this, Fletcher, some temptations I can now fully resist. Wilde didn't live long enough. But right now the temptation I definitely cannot resist comes in the form of a bottle of Wild Turkey. Lead me to one, Fletcher. But first: Bacon!"

At Molly's Murky did indeed order six sides of bacon, then complained that his hash browns were not crisp enough.

"Speakin' of being crisp enough, Fletcher, I reckon authorities will now release Cynthia's body to me. Am I right about that? I need to arrange for her cremation."

"I hope the coroner will release her now."

He chuckled, then said, "At least I don't have to feel guilty now about not lettin' CJ mumble any dust-to-dust incantations over her or listen to that holier-than-thou Genesis wailin' out some wretched hymn over poor Cyn before I reduce her to ashes. Thank God for that!"

A broad smile and then a wink from him assured me that the Murky of old was back in form, full of jest, mockery, and cynicism -- a stage comic once again, full of life.

XLII

Murk held a celebration party at his ranch a week later. Attendance was far smaller than for his retirement party. Little CJ, of course was not present. Accused murderers don't get bail. Genesis wasn't there either, but not for want of trying. She pleaded innocent to being an accessory to her husband's act, claiming no one handed CJ the pool cue that came down on Cynthia's head. As for "egging him on", to use Murky's phrase, she practically denied even knowing who Cynthia was, let alone being angry with her. And after CJ murdered her? Same plea: Cynthia who?

Well, plenty of parishoners would testify they had seen Genesis not only present when Cynthia had visited their small church, but had, of late, heard Genesis and Cynthia argue violently on more than one occasion. Yet, by pleading not guilty she would give a glib-tongued lawyer an opportunity to persuade a jury such behavior was irrelevant to Genesis's being guilty of anything other than having a bad temper.

Lots of invited people failed to attend. Betty Sue sent regrets from La Jolla, sending a note saying she had a stage audition scheduled in Hollywood that conflicted with the date. Murky dryly noted that Betty Sue was too inept for her to be applying for a job as a stage-cleaning janitor after the final curtain came down on whatever stage then needed her charwoman talents.

When I asked if he was going to miss Betty Sue's presence, Murky assured me, "That woman is the one who drove me to drink like I do. It's the one and only thing I'm indebted to her for."

Murky was far too imperial to invite any of his hired help, except to ask them to serve as hired help on the grandiose buffet line he set up. Gustavo, Murky's chef, had outdone himself. Mirasol was in charge of maintaining the food displays. I noted that Ernie Stellhorn, the vine master, was not present. No doubt Murky didn't want the smell of compost to penetrate his dining room. Or to allow Quagmire any opportunities to steal ham and beef from the carving-table area. There was no piano player present either.

After finishing my plateful of fabulous food, I complimented Murky on both the quality and the quantity of his feast. He said that, when organizing the buffet with Gustavo, he kept in mind one of his long-ago Borsch-belt jokes.

He said, "A pair of elderly women were dining at a famous Catskill restaurant. I won't name it, because, well--. Anyway, the first lady remarks, 'I'm astonished. The food here is atrocious. Why, it's almost inedible.' And the second old lady chimes in, "Indeed it is disgusting! And such skimpy portions.'"

I could only nod and chuckle to myself.

Then Murky turned maudlin, if only briefly.

He said to me in a quieter voice than usual for him, "I find it hard to accept...no...hard to face...the fact that my first-born is a murderer. If only I had strangled him with his own umbilical cord. Oh, Cynthia, what I wouldn't give --."

But then he escaped from wherever that dark road was taking him.

"I need another drink," he said.

Peggy Ann and Nancy Lorgran were both at his party, dressed like the young and middle-aged trollops they were. Later I noticed that, the more Murky drank, the more fixated he became on Peggy Ann's ass. I guess there's nothing stopping old men from still imagining.

Neither Sheriff Cuddleston, Chief of Police Wallace Fry, or Judge Cole showed up, though all were invited, Murky said. So, too, were Murky's neighbors, Ben Rondle and his wife, but they also sent regrets.

I didn't really expect the banker from San Luis Obispo to come and he didn't.

Amanda Reynolds, however, showed up and immediately asked that I be in charge of pushing her wheelchair. She allowed that she had brought a pair of crutches and also a walker. But neither suited her, she claimed. I drove her chariot carefully and didn't even protest as she sniveled incessantly about her doctor's order forbidding her from partaking of alcohol.

At a late hour I took leave of being Amanda's chauffeur for a short while and went to speak with Peggy Ann.

"Did you enjoy the pop festival, Peggy Ann?"

"Damned right I did. It was groovy."

When I asked her what she liked best she took me by surprise.

"A young white gal named Janis Joplin sang the blues as well, maybe better, than any chocolate-colored blues chick I've ever listened to, and I've listened to a lot. I mean, I'm into Chippie Hill, Memphis Minnie, Big Mama Thornton, and, of course, Billy Holliday, in all her reincarnations. But this Janis chick was so cool, so hot. I mean, she was just it -- with a capital T."

It with a capital T? Okay. If I needed proof I was out of touch with people fifteen years my junior, that was it. I headed back to a member of my own age group -- Amanda.

Grumpy as she was at times, Amanda was the still the highlight of the party -- for a while at least. Then Ricky Claymore showed up, uninvited and certainly unexpected. Silence ensued as he stepped through the front door.

I thought back to what Murky had taught me. Ricky, as it turned out, was not a schlemiel, a perpetrator, but a schlimazel, a victim of bad luck, A victim of Wendy Simmon's calculated plotting.

Ricky took in the silence of the gathering, then he spoke.

"I've come to see Peggy Ann. My father and my grandfather have finally given me permission to see her."

More silence filled the room for what seemed like a minute, until Jocko Silverado broke the hush.

"Come on in, Ricky, and welcome back to the Murtrans's ranch. Let me introduce you to everyone you might not know."

When he came to me Ricky said, "I understand you are the one who finally figured out what was really going on. Thank you for saving me, for getting the charges dropped."

"You are welcome, but there were actually a lot of people involved in saving you from a grave injustice."

"No. It was you who figured out Wendy was a liar and Roxanna was a murderess, along with her depraved mother."

I saw no point in mentioning that his grandfather had tried to kill Giovanni Alba. No, actually he had succeeded in killing the hit man, I had just found out earlier that same day that Alba had lapsed back into a coma and then died. I was sure nothing would come of that. No crime, not even murder, stuck to El Condor. Or his son.

I also wondered what Ricky the Third knew about his father's being charged with raping and murdering Gianetta Galboni's sister that night in 1935 at Stanford. Despite that trial's having occurred a decade before Ricky was born, surely some mention of it had oozed through the seams of family conversations, had popped up as unwanted and as unexpectedly as Ricky's appearance today.

Or had it? Families, I was well aware, work exceedingly hard to suppress their darkest, ugliest secrets. My own had. Not until my parents were dead did I uncover the story of my Uncle Jack's misbehavior that had led a young woman to commit suicide rather than face the consequences of acknowledging Jack, married to another woman, as the father of her as-yet unborn child.

Anyway, I shook the young man's hand and expressed a wish that no permanent psychological damage would come of his being accused of raping Wendy.

"What will become of her?" Ricky asked.

I lied and told him that Wendy's fate was up to the courts. Actually it was up to the Santa Julietta County Prosecutor's Office, which, to use Aamanda Reynolds's phrase, was the "Guild of Chickenshits", meaning they only tried the safest, surest cases, ones they knew they could win for certain. Wendy's case was by no means a sure bet. *Terry made me lie.* And, of course, Terry Morowitz was no longer available to refute her claim.

After Jocko made all the necessary introductions, Ricky sat next to Peggy Ann on the back veranda while he feasted on Murky's buffet. Afterwards, with everyone gathered in the large family room, Murky said to Peggy Ann, "Now you and Ricky run along, Miss Peggy Ann. I can see that look in your eye. But I will not permit you to give young Mr. Claymore a blowjob right here in front of everybody, much as you might like to do just that. So git now. Git!"

As the two young ones reached the door, Murky added, "No using any of the guest cottages for any all-night ruttin'. Some of my other guests might surely want to stay over in order to avoid any potential Sam Cuddleston drunk-driver traps set up just outside my gates."

Peggy Ann said loudly, "Uncle Murky, you can be so rude, so undignified. Why, you totally lack respect for other people. You're a damnable scoundrel. That's what you are."

To which Murky replied, no doubt pulling up a piece of his vaudeville patter, "I don't know what a scoundrel is like, but I do know what a respectable man is like, and it's enough to make my flesh crawl. Politicians, ugly buildings, and whores like you, Peggy Ann, each eventually gets to be respectable, if you last long enough. If you don't believe me, look at your mother. She's nearly old enough now to be almost respectable. Still a bit tarty around her edges. But me? I want no part of that. I am what I am."

Cadaver dogs did find Paolo Galboni, where I said they would. Thus, in a matter of days the murder count was now up to six -- seven if I counted Tony Bardello, which I didn't. Before taking my leave of his party, I poured Murky and myself another round of whiskey, then those still left standing all raised their glasses and toasted everyone's continued good health.

Afterwards I carefully drove home to Santa Maria. When I woke up the next morning my calendar read: July 1st. So the story I've told you pretty much filled my June of 1967, which, as it turned out, journalists at Haight-Asbury's hippie newspaper, *The San Francisco Oracle*, were calling The Summer of Love. My, oh, my. Surely I missed something there.